THE
BITTER ROAD TO
DACHAU

THE
BITTER ROAD TO
DACHAU

ROBERT L. WISE

BROADMAN
&HOLMAN
PUBLISHERS

NASHVILLE, TENNESSEE

© 2005 by Robert L. Wise
All rights reserved
Printed in the United States of America

13-digit ISBN: 978-0-8054-3073-8
10-digit ISBN: 0-8054-3073-3

Published by Broadman & Holman Publishers,
Nashville, Tennessee

Dewey Decimal Classification: F
Subject Headings: ESCAPES—FICTION
WORLD WAR, 1939–45—CAUSES—FICTION
HOLOCAUST, 1933–45—FICTION

1 2 3 4 5 6 7 8 9 10 09 08 07 06 05

for
the Confessing Church Believer
who did not turn back

CONTENTS

Preface / ix

Acknowledgments / xiii

Chapter One: **The Beast Yet Alive—1946** / *Page 1*

Chapter Two: **Descent into Hell—1940** / *Page 10*

Chapter Three: **The Devil's Work—1940** / *Page 33*

Chapter Four: **The Grind Goes On** / *Page 55*

Chapter Five: **To Survive—1940–41** / *Page 68*

Chapter Six: **A Light in the Darkness—1942** / *Page 85*

Chapter Seven: **The End of Summer—1942** / *Page 109*

Chapter Eight: **The Roll Call—1942** / *Page 121*

Chapter Nine: **Prey for the Beast—1942** / *Page 136*

Chapter Ten: **The Dragon Attacks** / *Page 155*

Chapter Eleven: **Shadows of Death—1943** / *Page 169*

Contents

Chapter Twelve: **The Hospital of Death** / *Page 188*

Chapter Thirteen: **Bent but Unbroken—1943** / *Page 202*

Chapter Fourteen: **The Final Cauldron of Pain—1944**
Page 223

Chapter Fifteen: **The Unexpected Monster** / *Page 242*

Chapter Sixteen: **Babylon Is Fallen—1945** / *Page 254*

Chapter Seventeen: **A World Come to Its End—1945–46**
Page 274

Chapter Eighteen: **The Pestilence Returns—1946**
Page 293

Epilogue: **... And They Did Not Turn Back** / *Page 300*

PREFACE

I first met Christian Reger in 1978 at Dachau Concentration Camp where he had become chaplain of the memorial. Day after day he shared the story of struggle, subjugation, and survival. By 1978, the camp had become a respectable, sterilized commemorative site as well as a remembrance of its own macabre statistics, reminding the world that the Nazis had caused the deaths of at least twenty-five million Russians, twelve million Germans, and six million Jews, not counting the deaths of the Allied Forces. Christian Reger's story was a reminder that the vast majority of the citizens of the Third Reich had quietly acquiesced to Adolf Hitler's reign of terror without any idea what the Reich was doing. Reger, and the few protesters and resisters of National Socialism, were sent to Dachau.

There are no complete records of how many people died at Dachau as political prisoners because the Nazis purposefully obscured such details. We now know that at least 10 percent of Dachau inmates were clergy, housed in the area where

Christian Reger lived. These good men had been caught in the crossfire of treacherous times, trying to live decently in the midst of deceit, fear, and violence. Following their convictions, they descended into one of the fiercest maelstroms of the twentieth century.

Standing before the foundations of the Pastors' Barracks where Reger had lived, I wondered why the dissenters had said no to National Socialism while the rest of Germany looked the other way. From whence came their courage when others showed only cowardice? What secrets of strength might their spirits share with the world? My quest for answers led to an enduring friendship with Christian Reger.

I found in his story the recurrent theme of the confrontation between good and evil that ebbs and flows through every generation. The deeds of the Nazis mirrored the predictions of the book of Revelation that many times throughout history an eternal clash would break through the boundaries of time and take on an ultimate dimension of Tribulation. During these hours of torture, the beast himself would descend on the saints. When the Third Reich arose from the pit, it came with such objectives. Christian Reger and his friends lived through this assault.

Christian Reger's story may have meaning of crucial importance in a distant day of decision. Possibly truth will again be on the scaffold, and believers will be called to stand again for the right. We do well to recall his tenacity.

The last time I saw Christian Reger was in Amsterdam. We talked about the people in this story and what had become of them. He assured me that none of the faithful had shrunk back. As I studied his unpretentious manner and listened to his honest, direct speech, I was reminded of how deceptive ordinariness can be. I tried to etch his face into my mind so that in a moment of crisis I might recall that worn but steady countenance again. Shortly after that visit Christian passed away, but he will always remain for me a portrait in courage.

Robert L. Wise
Oklahoma City, Oklahoma

ACKNOWLEDGMENTS

A special thank you to Rhonda Whittacre for her secretarial assistance in preparing the manuscript, and to Betty Beck for her thorough and helpful reading of the text. The book of Ecclesiasticus says, "a faithful friend is a strong defense; and he who has found such a one has found a treasure." Absolutely true.

CHAPTER ONE

THE BEAST YET ALIVE—1946

*E*ven the colors of the matchbox were the same as the one that had been slipped into his hand in prison. The red and green cover in the bishop's hand had a hypnotic effect on Christian Reger when he first noticed the small box. Like a mystical reappearance of an old token of hope, he felt captured by it.

"We believe this is an hour of unprecedented importance," Bishop Dibeilius emphasized, tapping the box forcefully against the large oak desk. The movement of red and green caused Christian's attention to drift away. After all, his life had been sustained by such a matchbox.

"Few people have seen, much less lived through, what has been your daily experience for the last five years." The bishop's voice betrayed a slight irritation because he sensed he was not receiving the full attention he wanted. "Great strength and courage were required to resist and endure as you did."

Christian got out of his chair and limped to the window. *Perhaps if I look in some other direction,* he thought, *I will not be as distracted.* From the window, skeletons of steel and stone stood as ravaged monuments to the past glory of Berlin.

"Reger, you have been the recipient of enormous gifts of grace," the bishop added, rising from behind his desk.

"Well," Christian finally answered, "grace sometimes comes to us in small things."

Thoughts of the matchbox gripped him. When he was first arrested, the terror had been almost unbearable. Later, as imprisonment ate away his self-confidence, an unshakable depression settled into his soul. It was in the darkest moment of despair that the matchbox had been slipped into his hand.

When he opened it and found the piece of paper with the special message, his sanity had been restored. Such a small object—and yet it meant so much!

"Christian," Bishop Dibeilius continued, bearing down hard now, "there is no question that you are the man for this position." The bishop paused as he studied the face of the pastor who seemed so unmoved by his status. Reger's sunken brown eyes were underlined by dark circles. Much of his dark brown hair had grown back, but its straight-back style seemed to belong to a man who didn't worry about making an impression. There was no sign of retreat or hesitance in his face, but a deep tiredness was etched on his mouth and forehead. Reger still had the muscular look of an athlete, but now his clothes hung limply on his thin frame.

"We believe you can go into the new Russian sector of Berlin and be most effective."

"Thank you, Bishop." Christian smiled politely. "I am honored by your confidence in me." Now he studied the man before him with his well-combed gray hair and carefully trimmed mustache. Although the bishop's coat was several years old, it still had a flair that set him apart as one of the upper class. Even in this room stripped of every luxury, the bishop remained a striking reflection of the days of the kaisers.

"But," Reger continued, "I am not sure that any German will be acceptable to the Communists. We are living in a new world, and the old order is gone forever."

"Oh, but that is exactly my point! Because you were imprisoned and the German courts declared you to be an enemy of the Nazis, you are a man for this new day."

Once more the bishop took measure of the man. There was nothing pretentious about Christian Reger. Yet his penetrating look left no doubt about his intelligence. Simple rimless glasses added to an impression of studiousness; the strong set of his jaw with its cleft chin conveyed determination; and his prominent nose completed the appearance of a person who had the ability to set his will and not be moved.

"The Communists would let a man like yourself work when other men would be harassed or arrested," the bishop concluded.

Slowly Reger sat down again as if he were bargaining for time to avoid the inevitable. "Bishop, I have been through so much during these last years that I am not sure I have the strength left in me. Perhaps I will never be completely free of my physical problems."

The bishop sighed heavily, no longer able to find the right words for his arguments. He remembered how he had refused to believe the stories about the concentration camps. He recalled conversations in which bishops assured one another of the great promise that National Socialism held for the church. He thought of how long he had waited before taking any public stand. Yet he could let his mind drift only so far. Then like a steel curtain abruptly falling, those thoughts were sealed away. Yet as much as he tried to dismiss those memories, a vague embarrassment remained.

"I'm sure I cannot appreciate what your condition has been or what your wife Mina has lived through." He sat down behind the desk again. "I asked her to wait outside because I didn't want to say anything that might disturb her. Of course, I have received reports of her exemplary leadership in the parish. I am truly sorry for what she has . . ." For the first time the bishop's voice lost its self-assurance and started to fade. "I understand that Mina . . . that she has suffered greatly.

"The example of both of you is what we need right now!" The bishop had found his official voice again. "You are an ideal whom people can follow."

"I am no example!" Christian snapped, and then stopped as his eyes became moist. "I have just survived. I have done only what had to be done. Many others did much more, and they are gone. We have survived, and that is all."

"No, Christian," the bishop said softly but firmly. "I cannot agree. Few people have stood where you have walked. I know of your deeds in the camp, and they speak for themselves. Your life's work is the essence of what we profess."

Christian shifted his weight in the chair and looked at the floor. As long as the conversation seemed austere, he could resist the pressure; but when the praise was honest and personal, he felt awkward and unsure of what to say.

"I know I have no right to ask you to go," the bishop went on, "yet I have no one else of your stature to send. Truly, you have wrestled with the dragon and have survived. Such a credential is earned only through fire. I cannot ignore the possibilities that your background offers. Now that the beast has arisen again among us, we must send only our best warriors to the battle."

As Christian rubbed his hands together and felt how leathery they still were, his eyes fell again on the matchbox now resting in the middle of the desk.

"I am a simple parish pastor," he protested. "I came to Stieglitz in 1931 after I had been out of seminary only a year and served there until I was arrested in 1940. I have not been in many places."

"Berliners under the heavy hand of the beast will not need a great theologian to answer profound questions. In their world they will not need some great orator to impress the congregation with flowery speech. They must have a man who knows the truth and who will not compromise in his obedience.

"Before the war I studied the lives of the saints and martyrs. I suppose it was sort of a hobby," the bishop reminisced. "I was intrigued by the people who said yes under terrible circumstances. I wondered what made them stand firm when all the others were giving in. Of course, their courage was what made these ordinary people extraordinary. However, I found I could never quite grasp their secret." His voice trailed off in reflection and then came back with painful honesty. "I was too sophisticated, too complicated, too calculating. I knew I could always find good reasons to say no."

"It was very hard for any of us to decide the right thing to do," Christian replied, trying to minimize the bishop's self-deprecation. "None of us could know how complex matters were. We were all deceived in many ways."

"It took great strength to say yes." The bishop ignored the consolation and excuses that Christian was offering him. "Sometimes the yes comes about by simply saying no to evil. Such answers are not really so difficult."

"Was it really that simple?" The bishop motioned with his hand to keep Christian from speaking. He was clearly not going to take no for an answer. He needed someone to go to East Berlin, and he knew he was looking at the right man.

"Oh, yes, we have all lived through hard days during these last years of the war," the bishop continued. "Many people have had little or no food. Certainly every family has lost someone or perhaps everything. But those of you who survived the concentration camps have survived hell itself. You were not there because you deserved punishment, but because you stood for the truth, and that is a profound difference."

"I will not minimize what happened to those of us who were there," Christian said. "The memory of our fallen comrades would be poorly served if I did."

"I can honestly tell you that most of us had no idea that the conditions in the camps were so horrible."

"Oh?" Hidden within the inflections of Christian's voice was a sound that interrogated. His eyes narrowed, and his gaze became intense.

"Well, I mean—" the bishop fumbled for words, "I mean, we, or at least *I*, didn't know. People, ah, er, people didn't talk of such things."

"Oh?" Reger's response continued to question.

"Of course, there were rumors, but confirmation was not possible." The bishop suddenly gestured forcefully as a preacher might when trying to camouflage a weak point. "And what could I have done anyway?"

"Of course." Reger seemed to confirm his excuses.

"Surviving was the point, wasn't it?" the bishop pleaded. "We all had to do what was necessary to live, didn't we? What good would have been accomplished if we had all been swept away? Compromise is an essential and unavoidable part of life. Courage is very difficult to define."

"I make no claims on courage," Christian responded. "I'm not sure that I even understand what it is."

"Oh, but you do!" the bishop insisted. "You do! You must. You survived because of your courage."

"Survival is always a gift of grace." Christian's smile exposed spaces where teeth had once been. "Compromise and courage have nothing to do with whether the heart continues to beat. Cowards have lived when better men were being lowered into their graves. *Whether* we live or die is God's business. *How* we stay alive is our business."

"See! See? You understand the matters that Berliners must now live with every hour of their lives. People will respect you. You have earned the right to speak of such questions. Your whole life has been a preparation for these days."

Instantly a myriad of thoughts crowded Christian's mind. During the *vez sacrum*, the holy spring of spiritual renewal in the days of his youth, the message had come of Herman Schmidt's death in the World War. The boyish face of the young man he had so greatly admired came into sharp focus as Christian felt again the experience of Herman's death. He remembered how he had begun to think of becoming a pastor so he could also comfort people. He remembered his mother crying because their bread was gone when ravishing inflation had destroyed the value of their money. He felt the fear that had surged through their village when talk of a Communist uprising was feverish.

From yet another decade, the sounds of shouting filled his inner ears. Once more he saw doors flying open and SS troops rushing into the church's secret assemblies. Then another collage of faces assembled before him as Karl Leisner, Werner Sylten, Wilhelm Dittner, Heinrich Gruber, Helmut Hesse, and a multitude of comrades from the camp at Dachau marched on review across his mind. As they passed it seemed as if their searching eyes probed his integrity.

"I said," the bishop repeated himself, "your whole life has been a preparation for this assignment."

"I suppose it has," Christian said slowly, sounding more and more convinced. "You are right, Bishop. Evil has cast a long shadow over my entire life."

"I am sorry that the beast is not dead, Christian. The battle is not over. Regardless of what we have done right or wrong, we must all go on from here. Whether the price we paid is great or small does not change the issues at hand." Sensing that he had almost persuaded his man, the bishop nervously reached over and picked up the matchbox again. "Now will you say yes?"

Reger's eyes moved from the red and green box to the massive wooden door that led out of the room. As he looked at the door, another image floated before his eyes—a door that had opened in 1940 to plunge him into a world of terror and chaos.

CHAPTER TWO

DESCENT INTO HELL—1940

One

The huge wooden door slid open to a thudding halt, rocking the entire boxcar. Days and days of riding with only slits of light coming through the cracks had caused the men's eyes to adjust to near total darkness. Suddenly daylight flooded into the car with such brilliance that no one could tolerate the light. Christian felt stabbing pain in both eyes. He shielded his head, only to be confronted by the stench that rose from the floor.

The hay had become foul during their first week of transportation. In the summer heat each passing day only made the smell worse. The odors of hot, sweaty bodies and unemptied urinal buckets mingled together to become an almost visible blanket of suffocation. When the door opened at last, Christian gulped down the breeze in relief.

Beyond the boxcar doorway, chaos prevailed. Dogs were barking, men were shouting, and hordes of prisoners were tramping off somewhere. Like some great whirlpool sucking life down into its depths, the whole process seemed to be pulling the prisoners closer and closer to the point of no return.

"Hurry up, you swine! Everybody out!" The ear-shattering screech of a police whistle punctuated the commands. "Quickly, you fools. Out!"

Immediately, the prisoners in the front of the boxcar began piling out on to the sidewalks. The surge of pushing and shoving carried Christian forward. As the fresh air hit his face, he tried to purge his lungs. For the first time he glimpsed the concrete docks and the barbed wire-lined corridors in front of him. Dismay, disorientation, and apprehension swept through his mind.

"No waiting! Move!" The SS officers strutted back and forth, barking orders and kicking at the men as they passed. "Faster! Now! Quickly!" Shouts accompanied the constant snarling and barking of ferocious guard dogs, whose taut leashes were relaxed whenever a slashing bite might serve to quicken the pace. Men stumbled and stepped on one another while the press of the crowd pushed them onward.

A small Jew, whose acquaintance Reger had made during the long weeks on the train, suddenly lost his footing and fell from the boxcar, sprawling on the tracks. As Christian started to jump from the car to help the man, a hand grabbed his arm and held him back.

Immediately, an SS guard jumped down from the concrete dock and smashed his large rubber club across the Jew's back, flattening the prisoner against the ground.

"Welcome! Welcome to Dachau!" the guard screamed at all of them and hit the Jew again.

"Those who have trouble moving, I help!" He dug the toe of his black leather boot into the man's ribs. "Those who don't try to conform, I teach to adjust!" He grabbed the back of the Jew's collar and threw him into the curbing. The man's body slid along the side of the wall, scraping the top of his head on the cement.

Christian strained forward again as his whole being wrenched in violent protest against the brutality. Though he had been in custody for several months, he still could not think of himself as a prisoner. His arms ached to stop the clubbing and kicking, but the hidden hand restrained him. He turned to see Wilhelm Dittner holding tightly to his coat sleeve.

"Try something and they will beat you to death," Wilhelm growled. "I know what I'm talking about."

Christian searched the dirty, tired face of this strange man who had become his friend as the train rumbled across Germany. The stubble of his unshaven beard had long since transformed the handsome appearance of this fellow clergyman into that of an exiled drifter. Dittner's cold, hard eyes spelled out the truth. He had been a prisoner much longer and seen cruelty worse than Christian could conceive. Christian's tense muscles went slack, and he tried to look the other way.

The carload of men had stopped in place during the beating, but the pause was only momentary. The press of emptying the car swept Reger past the Jew lying on the ground.

"Faster! Faster! Faster!" echoed from all sides. The guards had a mania for speeding up the process. As best Reger could tell, they were being pushed into a converging narrow walkway that pressed the prisoners tightly together.

He stumbled twice and could feel a sharp sting in his knee. Yet he dared not look, but kept trotting through the entranceway. The route turned and opened before a huge metal gate. The flow of men stopped as they spread out again in the open area before the gate.

The image of the little Jew lying face down on the ground haunted Reger. He could see the man trying to cover his head from the blows while his legs thrashed up and down from the pain. The many conversations they had engaged in on the train echoed in Christian's ears.

"You can live through this," the Jew had assured Christian. "My people have lived through such for centuries. The secret is to have a strong enough reason to live."

"Is survival so simple?" Christian had asked.

"Certainly it is hard, but it is possible," the Jew had insisted. "Nietzsche said, 'He who has a *why* to live can bear almost any *how* he must endure.' If you believe enough you can survive."

Bewilderment swept away Christian's memories. Never in his life had he experienced or even imagined the possibility of what had happened to him during the last several weeks and especially in the past few minutes. Anger and confusion blended together into an emotional muddle that left him immobilized.

Yet the crowd crawled forward. Like an hourglass con-
strictor slowing down the sand, the gateway was delaying
their march. Christian looked up and saw huge letters above
the wrought-iron gate: *Arbeit Macht Frei.* "Work Makes You
Free?" A coarse voice whispered in his ear. "I bet it will also
make you dead."

Reger turned to find Dittner directly behind him. His
six-foot frame made him tower over Christian even though
he didn't seem that much heavier or more muscular. His
thick black hair and deep blue eyes gave him a striking
appearance. Christian had learned that his fellow prisoner
and pastor friend often spoke with irony to conceal a deep
bitterness that lurked just below the surface.

"They might better have written, 'Welcome to the
Dragon's Lair,'" Dittner snarled.

"Shut up, you vermin!" a guard screamed from somewhere. "Stop that talking and get this line moving!"

Squeezing past the iron gate, Christian found himself
inside a courtyard that ended in front of the Jourhaus, the
administrative building. Another voice muttered, "Maybe the
sign should read, 'Give up hope, you who enter here.'"

"You are being processed in the Jourhaus!" a loudspeaker
boomed overhead. "Move quickly; we have no time for
delays!" Once again an invisible whirlpool began to suck the
men into another entryway, pulling Christian along with it.
But as he stepped through the doorway, a fist suddenly
smashed against the side of his face, smacking him against
the doorframe. "Swine! You are not here for a vacation!" a

faceless voice yelled. "Take off your hat and stop delaying the line."

Stunned and terrified, Christian shuffled ahead until the line halted. As he felt the welt swelling on the side of his head, he thought of another attack en route to the camp. In Mannheim, as the manacled prisoners were being moved to a different cattle car, a man bolted across the train platform and struck the prisoner in front of Christian. As the prisoner fell, the villager turned his fury on Christian.

"Traitors!" he screamed in Reger's face. "How dare you oppose our Fuhrer!" With his umbrella, the businessman began swinging in every direction. The guards watched and did nothing. "You should be castrated for this!" he screeched at the man behind Christian. "Your disrespect for Adolf Hitler is vile!" Having spent his anger, the businessman walked back into the watching crowd. The guard tipped his hat to the man, nodding his appreciation for a service well rendered.

Christian's mind snapped back to the present. In a few minutes he walked past information tables and questioners. Jerked in front of a camera, he was hit again and pushed on to another part of the administration building and then to the dressing room. His clothes were removed and piled into the heaps strewn along the walls. Left with only his belt, he stood naked in another line.

"In here! Step up quickly," a prisoner insisted. In front of Christian were a number of men in prison garb standing ready with razors, scissors, and clippers. They seized the new prisoners and began shaving their heads. In a matter of minutes each man had his hair peeled. Christian discovered that the endless flow of men had dulled the razors and scissors so that he felt as if half his hair had been pulled out.

At the far end of the "barber shop" were showers. On the other side were the striped prison uniforms and wooden clogs each man was ordered to wear. Stripped of his possessions, his head and body aching and bald, Christian realized that the uniform did little to keep him from feeling exposed and naked.

His eyes searched about the dressing room for a familiar face. He was surrounded by other white-skulled, degraded men. He did not recognize a single person.

Perhaps, he thought, *I have had many conversations with some of these men during the trip here, yet I don't know them. Every sign of individuality is gone.* Reger groaned. He had also taken on an anonymous appearance. He felt if he were being swallowed up by his surroundings.

"They are trying to make us into animals," he confided to a blank face before him. "We are being stripped of all dignity." But the nameless face only stared back.

Once again the mass of men turned into a line, and Christian was moved on before another interrogator. "Name!" the guard barked. "Your name!"

"Reger," he answered haltingly. "Christian Reger."

"No longer!" the guard snapped back without even looking up from his clipboard. "You are now No. 26 661. You are not worthy of a name. Only when you are proven ready to reenter German society will your name be given back."

"But . . ." Christian tried to protest.

"Move on, 26 661!"

"Your crime?" the next guard demanded.

"Political, I suppose," Christian mumbled.

"Wear this on your shirt." The guard handed him a red triangular patch. "And what is your occupation?"

"I am a clergyman, a church pastor from Stieglitz in the province of Pomerania."

"All of you fanatics are in No. 26!"

"26?"

"Yes, you fool, 26! That's the number of your barracks." With a twisted smile he added sarcastically, "Those are our special religious accommodations. We call it the Pastors' Barracks. Now, get out!"

When Christian stepped through the last door, he found that for the first time in weeks he was not in the midst of a herd of humanity. He felt almost as if he were by himself. Yet before him stretched rows and rows of wooden buildings with men walking in every direction. Wide, straight streets ran through the rows of buildings, then abruptly ended before rolls of barbed wire. Next came a wide moat filled with water. On the outer perimeter of the camp were either concrete walls or electrified fences of razor-sharp wire. Each corner was punctuated with a guard tower, and mounted machine guns were everywhere.

After taking a few steps, Reger stopped to savor the illusion that he was alone. No hand was chained to his wrist or pushing from behind. Everything felt unreal and dream-like.

Possibly none of these indignities had really happened to him. Yet as his hand rubbed across his sore, bare head, the rough stubble sent a sensation through his body that left no doubt about reality.

He took several more steps before realizing that he had no idea about where to go or what to do. Seeing a prisoner with a uniform much dirtier than his own, he asked, "Which way is Barracks No. 26?"

"Up the bunker," the man said, pointing to the north end. Noticing the clean uniform, he added, "The bunker's what we call Main Street. Just keep going down the middle and you'll see 26."

A peculiar, foul odor filled the air. It seemed to come and go as if it were blowing in from somewhere. The scent was unlike the rotten floor of the train. "Perhaps I am smelling the dragon's breath today," Christian said aloud as he walked. A passing prisoner stopped as he spoke and stared at him in consternation. Christian continued on his search for No. 26, the Pastors' Barracks.

Two

All the barracks were exactly the same: wooden, oblong, cracker boxes constructed to be stuffed full of nameless creatures. Inside, the walls were lined with two-decked tiers of crate-like boxes that served as mass beds made to hold 180 people. No. 26 was already filled with 250 men. Clearly, many more would be coming.

When Christian walked down the center aisle of No. 26,

he was astonished to discover the many nationalities of the prisoners.

"You are a minister?" he asked doubtfully.

"Oui," a Frenchman answered.

"And you?" he said, turning to another prisoner.

"Ja," a Dutchman answered.

As he looked around, he saw men who appeared to be Czechs, Poles, Italians, Belgians, perhaps even a few Yugoslavs. It was as if he were attending some sort of bizarre European convention of poverty stricken clergymen.

"You are Protestants?" he asked a small, huddled group. "Are all of these men from the Confessing Church?"

"No," a tall, thin man answered. "Many of us are Catholic priests, and a few are Greek Orthodox."

"I see," Christian said, raising his eyebrows. "I have just arrived and do not understand."

"Few people would," a smaller man added. "The SS has done a good job of concealing our existence."

"Let me introduce myself," the tall, thin man said. "I am Leonard Steinwender." He had a noble bearing that conveyed good breeding and education. The strong, proud face with intelligent eyes seemed a strange contrast to the dingy, dirty uniform. But the strength in his voice was reassuring evidence that the past months had not broken his spirit. "I came here from Buchenwald prison and have been here six months."

"I see," Christian said. He had never been around many Catholics, and they made him feel ill at ease.

"We no longer make distinctions about our different doctrines," Steinwender said. "Here we have found that we must all stand together in order to survive."

"I see," Christian said again, sensing he sounded distant and professional.

"My name is Werner Sylten," said the smaller man, extending his hand. "I am a Lutheran pastor and have been here nearly a year." His cheeks were unnaturally shrunken, and the grayness in his hair seemed to run into his colorless face. Though his handshake attempted to be firm and hearty, Christian felt a feebleness in the grip. Obviously, the man was not well.

Christian noticed that he could gauge a man's imprisonment by the length of his hair. To the left was a man whose hair was short.

"And I am August Schmidt, a Catholic priest." The twinkle in his eye seemed out of place. In fact, his whole face conveyed a warmth that was inviting and comforting. The missing tooth on the left side almost added a touch of comedy. Instantly, Christian knew he would like this man.

"I am glad to meet you all." Christian felt himself beginning to relax.

"Let us give you your first lesson in life at Dachau," Schmidt began. "In the Pastors' Barracks you are among brothers, but outside you must trust no one."

"We are in a time when deception reigns supreme," Leonard added.

"Indeed!" Sylten's voice became flat and hard. "Betrayal sent me here. When I was first imprisoned at Frankfurt, I managed to escape. On my way home I decided to stop at a fellow pastor's house. I was hungry and thought he might help me. When I told him of my predicament, he invited me in for coffee."

Reger noticed the man's hand began to curl in a fist. Although his voice was without emotion, the whiteness of his knuckles spoke clearly.

"While I waited for the coffee, this 'servant of God' went into the back room and called the police. He kept me talking while the SS came and surrounded the house."

"Many of us are political prisoners," Leonard said, "but there are also gypsies, criminals, and a number of Jews. You must remember that there are many collaborators who will do anything to save their hides. There are some good *capos*, but not many."

"*Capos?*" Christian mused. "What are *capos?*"

"*Capos* are prisoners who have been selected for the job of overseeing their fellow prisoners," August explained. "The Nazis use this quaint method to try to divide us. Some *capos* just try to survive, and others tend to be a mite brutal. They will test your sense of humor!"

"You must never be late for roll call," Leonard interjected. He drew himself up to his full height with Prussian stiffness, his iron jaw jutting. "Twice a day we line up in Roll Call Square. Everyone must stand at absolute attention regardless of his health or circumstances until every prisoner is accounted for. No matter what the weather, you must stand with your cap off."

"Any error can subject you to a severe beating," Sylten said, pointing his finger in Christian's direction, "and you must not cause suffering for the rest of the group by keeping them standing outside when the winter has set in."

Christian nodded his head vigorously. As a good German Protestant, he had learned that magistrates were God's left hand, using force to keep order in the streets. Their commands were to be obeyed. For a brief moment the irony of his situation struck him forcefully. He and the men who surrounded him were devoted to obeying the law absolutely as a matter of Christian principle. Yet here they were discussing survival in a prison more severe and cruel than any Christian could ever have imagined.

Schmidt lowered his voice and leaned into the group. "There is a rumor that a Catholic bishop from Munich has been put in the special detention cells in the camp jail. They say that the Gestapo arrested Bishop Neuhausler to 'cool him,' as the SS calls it. Also, I heard that Martin Niemoller has been sent here."

"Niemoller!" Reger exclaimed. "I know him. He is one of us—a leader in the Confessing Church!"

"I believe they are concentrating all of us in one place," Sylten warned. "It is a bad sign and may mean worse things are ahead."

"Worse?" Christian asked incredulously. "What could be worse than this?"

"The answer is blowing through the trees," Steinwender said cynically. "It is in the air."

The entire group laughed nervously.

"What do you mean?" Reger asked. "You speak in riddles."

"Didn't you smell it?" Sylten sounded harsh. "Surely you noticed when you came in. The smoke blows through constantly."

"Yes, it did bother me, but I have never smelled anything like that."

"It's from the crematoriums," Steinwender whispered. "The wind blows the smoke from the crematoriums through the camp. The ovens are located next to the far wall."

"What are you saying?" Reger asked.

"My new friend," Sylten said with intensity, "prisoners are being burned up every day of the week in this place. People who die go up the chimneys!"

"They are killing people here?" Christian could barely mouth the words. "People are dying in this place?"

"You have come to the place . . ." Father Schmidt stopped, his smile vanishing and his eyes narrowing. Slowly and carefully he chose his words. ". . . from which most of us will probably never return."

"This cannot be!" Christian protested. "We all know what the Nazis are, but this is Germany. We are citizens of a civilized nation!"

A coldness fell over the group that left each man feeling isolated, lonely, and silent. Christian searched their faces for a denial. Instead, he found a stony affirmation in each man's eyes.

"Warn him about the infirmary," Sylten said. "Karl Leisner can tell you best because he has been there. Karl, tell our new prisoner about the hospital."

A frail, worn-looking young man with sunken cheeks crawled from the back of the wooden crates. He wore small, round glasses so thick that his deep-set eyes looked like beady, black dots. "Karl is a deacon and hopes to be ordained to the priesthood," Sylten explained. "His health is not the best."

"If you must go to the infirmary," Karl said, sitting up, "make sure you get out as quickly as possible but under no circumstances let them certify you for the invalid transports. They will try to tell you that they will take you to another camp where the work is easier."

"And then you will disappear off the face of the earth," Sylten concluded.

"It took us some time to piece the whole story together," Karl continued. "At first shoes, glasses, clothes, and even artificial legs of sick prisoners began to reappear in the camp. One of the *capos* noticed that those who left on transports were forced to exchange whatever they had for even more inferior shoes or clothes. All items of value were taken away."

"One of the prisoners who worked in the administration office found that the transportation orders were for Hartheim Castle near Linz," another inmate chimed in. "Before the war, the castle had been used as an asylum for the insane."

"Finally the rest of the story was smuggled back to us," Karl said. "The sick are being gassed to death in that old castle." Pathos and compassion seemed lined in his face as he continued nodding and shook a bony finger at the bewildered Reger.

"They will assign you a work detail in the fields, and you will be worked to exhaustion," Sylten picked up the theme again, "but do not use the infirmary as an excuse not to work."

"Thank you." Christian nodded to each member of the group. "Thank you for your instruction."

Reger turned around, noticing that Wilhelm Dittner had also arrived in the barracks. Perhaps someone would start explaining things to him. As Christian peered into the darkness, he could hear the heavy breathing that surrounded him. The heat of the summer day was still radiating from the men and the walls. Fortunately, he had discovered an open knothole in the wall. By placing his face to the opening he could inhale a cooling breeze from outside.

He tried to find some comfort, but lying against uneven pine boards offered no hope of that. For a while he wondered if he could ever learn to sleep with such constant distraction, but then he remembered how even that had become possible while being forced to sit up in the boxcar.

How did I get here? he questioned himself. *How did I ever get here?*

Scenes of home, church meetings, and friends began floating through his mind. And at each change of scenery, he wondered if he were a fool.

The guardhouse lights flashing outside the barracks reminded him of the first night the Brownshirts had attacked his home eight years ago. The lights of the trucks had beamed into the bedroom windows first. He remembered the sounds of men leaping from their trucks and shouting. Suddenly, shock waves vibrated through the small parsonage as the mob began beating violently on the sides of the trucks and screaming at the top of their lungs.

"Christian, what are they doing?" his wife Mina had asked, clutching at his arm and the bed sheets and trying to hide beneath both.

"I don't know." He tried to lie still and listen. "I can't make out what they are saying."

Then a single cry began to emerge above the babble: "Traitors of Germany! Traitors of Germany! Traitors of Germany!"

Huddling together beneath the covers, Christian and Mina clung together as the roar and the truck lights continued to pierce through their windows.

"Oh, no!" Mina whispered in his ear. "We are being attacked just as they warned us they would do. Maybe we can escape through the back door."

Christian had already begun inching toward the edge of the bed. Carefully they approached the windows to peer out through the curtains. Against the lights of the trucks they saw the silhouettes of party uniforms. Faces were not visible in the darkness, but the men looked young and were clearly holding sticks and clubs.

From atop one of the trucks a lone voice began growling,

"Clerics and their followers are traitors of our country. Those who don't follow us, we take you out!"

Then the chant began again like a litany of death: "*Wir schiagen sie zusammen?* We take you out! We take you out!" Finally the chorus ended, and the men began piling back into the trucks.

One last voice shouted, "You have been warned. You will come into line, or worse will happen!"

After the sun set, Christian lay cramped between the hot bodies in the wooden bunks. He remembered how he and Mina had lain in bed until late in the night wrestling with what might follow. Should they stop holding their meetings of the Confessing Church? Should they stop organizing other groups? Perhaps it would be wiser to give in to this new fanatical patriotism.

In the end, Mina had put her arm across his chest and said, "I am not afraid of anything but losing you. Do not retreat an inch on my account." With that, Christian's fear had turned into anger and indignation.

Perhaps that's when I should have stopped, he thought, *but I would have violated everything I ever stood for. And I had to correct the first impression I left in the church. I couldn't let the people think that I agreed with the National Socialists.*

He was embarrassed to remember how he had once worn the Brownshirt uniform when Hitler first came to power. But then everyone was doing the same thing to demonstrate patriotism and his hopes for the future. While Christian had not been enthusiastic about Hitler, he did appear as the only alternative to the Bolsheviks and to the rampant depression devouring the country.

Another face intruded into his reverie. Grell, the provost, and his band of racists appeared. Christian remembered when these "German Christians" had come to a minister's meeting to persuade the group to endorse their stand on Aryan superiority as reflecting God's intentions. He recalled their strange manipulation of words that said one thing and meant another.

"My fellow pastors," Grell began that fall afternoon, "there is some confusion among us about how to relate to this new marvelous opportunity that God has given us in National Socialism and Adolf Hitler. We have come to discuss this matter as we are promoting the wonderful ideas that can bring spiritual revival to our nation."

Christian remembered how appealing the words had been. Each promise had touched a yearning in every person there.

"German Christians recognize that there must be an Aryan solidarity on the issues of faith and politics." Grell's voice became more emphatic. "We must not have a divided house or our enemies will triumph! We are only advocating that love of country is part of our faith. In this great hour of hope, we must band together to eliminate all enemies to our progress."

The word *eliminate* sent the meeting into a wild debate.

Rzadki, a fellow pastor, attacked the German Christian plat-form. He accused Grell of being an antichrist. "Your words are one heresy hunting another!" he shouted at him.

Grell became livid. Many of the pastors were uncertain. And the meeting ended in confusion.

During the ensuing year, a rumor circulated that Rzadki had been taken to a concentration camp at Sachsenhausen, interrogated mercilessly, forced from his church, and banished to East Prussia. Christian remembered how hard it had been for him to believe such reports. *Exaggeration, overreaction,* he had thought to himself when the details were whispered. Even now, lying in the midst of a crowded loneliness, he found it hard to comprehend that people who called themselves Christians had contributed to persecution and imprisonment of fellow churchmen and, of course, himself.

Finally, as was always the case, Mina's face was the last to return. He had found that his mind could become a motion picture projector that would play her face over and over again in his memory. He tried to bring back their times together as if replaying them might let him crawl back into the scene again.

She was lovely. Oh, yes, she was more than lovely. Her face was softly rounded, and her light blue eyes seemed always to comprehend more than was being said. Mina had a gift of sensitivity.

Blonde hair framed her face with just the right touch of femininity. That special womanly quality extended to the taper of her graceful fingers that were so adept at the keyboard. Indeed, the melodies that poured from her piano had always fulfilled Christian's own love for music. They had spent hours together as he played the violin or sang while she accompanied him.

Always proper, she had never been a person given to special allurements. Yet even with high-necked dresses and hair pulled back in a tight bun, Mina radiated a unique beauty filled with goodness and kindness.

One of their little songs seemed to be almost audible now. In his memory, Christian could see her fingers run up and down the piano keys. With the introductory notes finished, she would nod her head and he would begin in his tenor voice. A sound almost escaped from his lips, and he had to keep himself from humming.

Mina Rothenhofer had been the only woman in his life. His family's meager income and his own resources had been strained to the limits completing his education. There had been no time or money for a social life. In fact, if she had not been a parishioner in his first church, they would probably have always remained at a distance from each other.

Again he almost chuckled aloud as he remembered how he had used every excuse a pastor could have for visiting her house. In the Protestant parish of Hockenheim, a schoolteacher was always an excellent prospect for volunteer service. How he had worked that opportunity!

Formality and propriety had been essential. Custom dictated a distance that placed the vicar on a lofty pedestal. Yet their companionship had satisfied a hunger that Christian had not even realized he had.

Hockenheim had been inundated with the same economic disaster that had befallen all of Germany. Each day, unemployed people clamored after bread and talked of radical political solutions. In that cold winter of uncertainty, she had become a springtime of warmth, grace, and abundance for him.

"Mina, I want to marry you." He remembered how the words had come out so suddenly, so bluntly, so clumsily. He had no idea how to say such things.

"Oh, Christian!" Her voice had been so warm, yet pained. "This cannot be. The villagers will talk. They will gossip that I am much too old for you. I am expected to become the spinster schoolteacher of the village. I can only bring you trouble."

"I don't care!" he replied, surprised at his growing forcefulness and sense of control. "I don't care, Mina. I only want you."

"Christian, I do love you." Her sensitive eyes had probed his face for any hint of reservation he might have. Then she had answered, "I would be honored to be your wife."

With the simplicity of those words, their lives began blending together. On that night they had embraced for the first time.

As Mina had predicted, a storm of gossip surrounded their quiet, simple wedding. The Hockenheim parish was a small place in a world in which unusual events seldom happened. People who have little to do are easily preoccupied with little things. Their romance was quickly blown out of proportion by village busybodies.

Consequently, in a few months they were on their way to Pomerania and the village of Stieglitz. They could never have realized that the uproar in Hockenheim would be nothing compared to the turmoil they would find in their new parish. But in those following years she stood in the midst of all the threats like a tower of steel. Mina had always been his source of consolation.

Once more the matchbox came to mind. Even in that special intervention of God, Mina's words had strengthened, encouraged, and sustained him. The message of faith he had found inside the box again insisted he could live through this time of extreme testing.

Then August Schmidt's words of the afternoon began doing their haunting work. *Most of us will probably never return.* As the afternoon unfolded, Christian had to fight back a creeping fear that now seemed even closer in the darkness of the barracks. Every resource of memory, love, and faith would be required to endure. At last his thoughts fused into a prayer that merged with drowsiness and then restless sleep.

He had finished his first day at Dachau.

CHAPTER THREE

THE DEVIL'S WORK—1940

One

"Psst, how long have you been here?" the short man next to him whispered.

Carefully holding his place in the roll call line, prisoner No. 26 661 turned to the white-skulled prisoner in a clean uniform. Almost instinctively he ran his hand through his own chopped, brown hair and was amazed at how long it had become. *No. 26 661?* For a moment he stumbled over his own name and realized that somewhere in the past weeks he had lost a piece of his humanity.

"A long time," Christian finally answered, trying to sound disinterested. But to his surprise, he could not recall how many weeks or days it had been. He puzzled over the answer for a moment before the panic finally gripped him. He had lost track of the weeks! Time had run together, and days had lost any distinctiveness. All he could remember was the endless work from dawn to dusk, and now the sun was about to come up again.

"Attention! Caps off!" echoed down the rows behind him. Instantly his body became erect as he snatched the cap from his head.

When he had first arrived, the heat of summer was almost unbearable. Now it was much cooler, and the mornings were almost crisp. *Surely it has to be September*, he calculated.

"Keep the rows straight, or you will be here until the snow blows." Somebody somewhere was in trouble. He stiffened. No. 26 661 knew well how severe the consequences could be if the roll call was not met with absolute punctuality and precision. Regardless of health or circumstances, each man had better stand motionless and straight until every prisoner was accounted for or else face severe punishment.

The count seemed to wear on endlessly as threats and accusations rang through the morning chill. Christian tried to focus his thoughts as he pondered his lapse of memory. As usual, he had been up since 4:00 a.m. The 6:00 a.m. roll call was only a pause before the day of grueling work that would continue until 8:30 that night. Nothing made this day any different from any other. Still, he agonized, *I must remember exactly how long I have been here.*

"Some have not yet learned the lessons of Dachau," the voice boomed over the loudspeaker. "We remind you of the penalty to be paid by those who will not cooperate."

From behind the rows of prisoners a group of naked men, cowering between guards with clubs and sticks, was marched to the front of the assembly. The soldiers whipped and swatted at the men as the procession took center stage. The result was a bizarre, comic dance—a performance that the guards obviously enjoyed.

As the prisoners stood trying to cover themselves, the loudspeaker listed charges of "slacking in the fields," "trying to escape work," and "unconstructive attitudes," as the guards struck the men until, one by one, each was prostrate on the ground. The first time No. 26 661 had witnessed one of these spectacles, he felt as if he would bolt from the line. Now he maintained a stony stare, fastening his vision on a tree-lined ridge far beyond the fence. But there was no way he could erase the memory of that first horror show when he had seen two men beaten to death for trying to escape.

"To show our mercy," the loudspeaker explained, "these examples will now be taken by invalid transports to other camps for new assignments."

Shuddering at the thought, No. 26 661 took one last look at the men on the ground to see if he might identify any of them. Although none was familiar, he was not surprised to see that they looked distinctly Jewish.

"Assemble now for your work details," the loudspeaker instructed. "Remember, work makes you free!"

The lines of prisoners relaxed, and the men began to shuffle in various directions. To his left, Christian recognized one of the pastors from the Confessing Church. He turned and walked casually toward the fellow prisoner.

"Niemoller?" he queried inconspicuously. "Have you seen or heard of Martin Niemoller?"

The man seemed not to hear. Though he paused, his eyes looked straight ahead. Then he spoke in a stage whisper. "Ya, Niemoller is here. They are keeping him in a special cell near the Jourhaus."

The two men then shuffled on in opposite directions.

It would be impossible for me to ever see him, No. 26 661 thought to himself. Certainly it would be foolish to try.

Reger had almost dismissed the thought when it occurred to him how quickly his mind had dropped the idea. Though he was by nature concerned with the welfare of other people, that sensitivity seemed to be slipping away. Earlier he hadn't even cared to answer the new prisoner in line next to him. In fact, taking care of himself had become his main interest.

As he walked into the midst of his work company, he looked around at fellow clergymen and wondered if they had the same feelings.

Men nodded to one another as they formed the lines in which they would march out to the fields. Each was quietly steeling himself for the day ahead. No. 26 661 found his usual place and stared aimlessly into space.

"We must not lose ourselves," an elderly man said to him. "Reger, we must continue to care." Hearing his name immediately felt reassuring and humanizing.

"Ya," he replied, "that is most certainly true."

Fritz Seitz had been the first German Catholic priest to be sentenced to Dachau. Each day they marched out together. His unexpected admonition surprised Christian, but it also gave him encouragement.

"Begin!" the captain shouted to the group. "A rousing song should prepare us. Let us go forth to our glorious work singing the songs of our nation." The captain clicked his heels and roared the *"Seig Heil!"* Nazi salute.

The guards' patriotic chorus started the group marching in place, and the men picked up the tune and the tempo as they tramped out under the gate and toward the fields. Each morning and night they were greeted with the same lie: *Arbeit Macht Frei*—Work Makes You Free.

The "glorious work" shared by No. 26 661 and his comrades was the maintenance of the herb fields. The SS kept an enormous plantation of medicinal and spice plants just beyond the camp's barbed-wire fences. The impressive, meticulously kept rows were cultivated at a high cost to the prisoners. Regardless of the fierceness of the south Bavarian winds and weather, these fields were worked seven days a week.

When the men came to the edge of the fields, the threats and harassment began again. "We have no time to waste," echoed even from the *capos*. "Come on, you pigs, into the trenches. Faster! Hurry!"

No. 26 661 inhaled deeply, knowing there would be no relaxation time until evening. The rules of the field did not allow breaks.

"I will try not to lose myself today," Fritz said, smiling at him.

"But let us not disappear either," No. 26 661 warned, motioning toward the chimneys.

"Now that it is cooler, the midday will be more bearable."

"For you, it will be," No. 26 661 answered, "but the weather makes little difference when I am carrying the buckets."

"Begin!" echoed across the field. The two men nodded to each other and went their separate ways.

That morning seemed to move quickly. For some reason Christian didn't feel as physically tired as usual. But as the sun rose higher, he felt the dread rising in him. Noon was the worst time of all.

"All right, No. 26 661, start getting the buckets out." The *capo* dipped his ladle into the boiling pot and poured the steaming mush into the buckets at Reger's feet. "And if you spill any, you know what the rest of the prisoners will do!"

The metal handles always cut into Christian's hands, increasing his fear that he would stumble and drop the buckets. If he did, many prisoners would be left without even the meager gruel. Such a mistake might even cost him his life.

With the huge buckets in each hand, he strained forward, stepping carefully between the rows and trying to see any holes in the ground. The steam seemed to crawl up his arms, and he felt his own sweat making the handles even more slippery. His only pause would come as the men cleaned out the buckets. Their hunger was such that the pails seemed to drain in a matter of seconds.

"Hurry up!" the *capo* snarled. "Other men are waiting. Your slowness is costing us rest time."

No. 26 661 snatched the buckets and started back to the black pot. Back and forth he went across the field until every prisoner had received the tasteless meal. More palatable to pigs, it was still their only food, so it was always eagerly devoured.

Two

When noontime passed, No. 26 661 was sent to another task. Today the men were moving dirt back and forth across the field.

"Let the lunchman push the wheelbarrow now," one of the guards ordered, sneering at the crew. "He's had a nice rest. Let him take it a couple of turns."

Christian's back muscles strained and wrenched as he started to push the cart forward. At least the weight didn't seem to cut into the palms of his hands. Up and down he traveled once, then a second time.

"Here! Stop this slack," a guard demanded of one of the prisoners holding a shovel. "Don't waste time! Fill it up!"

Immediately, more dirt was piled on top of the already full wheelbarrow. Christian wasn't sure he could push it, but somehow the wheel began to turn and he struggled off to the opposite corner of the field to dump it. Immediately, he went back for the next load.

Back and forth he went. The wheelbarrow cut through the furrows and wound down the path. Sometimes he got away with a small load, but most of the time the cart was filled to overflowing. Even when the sun had begun to set, the pace did not slacken.

Back and forth. Back and forth. Back and forth.

If it had not been for his unusual athletic build, Christian probably would have cracked that day. The years he had spent as a youth working out in the school gymnasium were his salvation. The parallel bars, the Roman rings, the exercises had built an endurance into his back and shoulders that was the envy of his schoolmates. The residue of that strength was all that held him together.

Near the end of the afternoon, he tried to distract himself and make his mind forget about his body. Only then did he reflect on the assignment. Dirt from one place was being taken to another. There was no purpose and no meaning to the task. The endless trips with the wheelbarrow were an exercise in futility.

"Tomorrow you can move the dirt back to where we began," the guard announced to the group.

No. 26 661 put down the empty wheelbarrow and straightened up. His back felt as though another move would break him in two. "These exercises will help you learn the value of obedience. Eventually you will get your priorities straight," the guard declared, his voice full of condescension.

No. 26 661 glanced at the other men. The degradation of their situation no longer seemed to register with them. Perhaps they lacked the strength to care. With exhaustion and anticipation, each eyed the end of the field where the sun was falling.

When the whistle blew, the prisoners mechanically shuffled together into a unit for their return. The pace even picked up as they tramped down the road. The wind had increased somewhat, and the smoke drifted out to meet them as they approached the gate.

The aroma of death is still everywhere, Christian thought to himself. *It is in what we do, how we do it, and what is done to us. Smoke seems to cloud what we think, believe, and hope.* Then he lost his train of thought.

Once again, an all-pervasive loneliness engulfed him as he marched along in the cluster of men that blended into the assembly on Roll Call Square. The 8:30 head count harangue was about to begin.

Standing in line did not expend much energy, yet there was no relief either. Another typical day had slipped by. Defeat and despair were its only profit. The pollution from the skies seemed to have seeped through his nostrils and into his soul.

From somewhere within, a new and unexpected thought arose. Maybe today there would be a letter for him. While it was a remote possibility, the thought alone offered solace. Might it be? Yet he knew he must sit down or stretch out on the ground to recover any vestige of energy that might be scavenged for the rest of the day.

When the dismissal was sounded, he sank in a heap. The other prisoners escaped into sleep, but he fought back drowsiness for fear that he would lose a grip on time and sleep through the supper hour.

His muscles were already getting stiff, and he knew how important it was to keep moving. With more resolution than reserve, he started toward the mail office.

At the edge of the bunker, a small crowd was standing in front of the infirmary. Two guards came out the door carrying the limp body of a prisoner. Though he was obviously dead, his clothes were soaked. As the men shuffled past with the body, the SS guard in charge pronounced indifferently, "Heart attack."

"He was a Jew," Auboiroux, the Communist, whispered to Christian as they disappeared around the corner. Responsible for brushing door latches throughout the camp with disinfectant, Auboiroux was recognized by everyone as a good source of information.

"A Jew?" Reger asked in consternation. Ignoring his question, the Communist added, "The man did not die of heart problems. They killed him."

"Killed him?"

"Of course! The block leader had them take him into the washroom." The Communist lowered his voice even more. "They held him against the wall and sprayed cold water around his heart until it failed. That's why he is so wet."

"My God!" No. 26 661 exhaled.

"There is no God." The Communist walked back into the infirmary.

The scene dissolved before Christian's eyes like a grotesque dream. Had he really seen two guards and a dead Jew? Was his tired mind deceiving him? Yet he did know Auboiroux, the French Communist. He trudged on to the mail office.

To his astonishment, a letter *was* waiting! The whole group crowded around to savor any morsel of contact from the outside world. Dittner was always busy about the mail office, and he elbowed his way to Christian's side.

"Who is it from?" Dittner asked feverishly.

"Just a minute." No. 26 661 motioned the crowd back. "Give me some breathing room."

"Every bit of news can be vital," Dittner insisted.

"It is from my wife," Christian said. "I'm sure it is." Ripping open the envelope, he found his dreams confirmed.

"Is there word about how the war is going?" a voice implored.

"Has she been harassed?" someone else asked.

"Please, please!" Christian begged, waving the letter in frustration. "I can't even read with all your questions. You know that anything of any real significance has been censored. Please give me a moment."

The group became quiet as he devoured every sentence, every phrase, every word. Finally he sighed. "My wife writes that since they have stopped my salary she must find some other source of income."

"What will she do?" A man grasped at his sleeve. "How will she survive?"

No. 26 661 studied the man's face for a second. The question was really about the other prisoner's wife. How would any of their wives live?

"She writes that she thinks she has found a job as an organist. She says it is not much, but she believes it will carry her through. My wife is a very talented person."

"Good!"

"Excellent!"

"Also she writes she is doing her best to keep our church together during my absence. Many of the people have forsaken us for fear of reprisal, but a faithful core still remains."

"That is an encouragement!" said one of the men, nodding and smiling.

Someone else received a letter, and immediately the group turned its attention to the next piece of mail. Again they clamored like hungry children at mealtime. All moved on except Dittner, who pulled away from the mail office and followed Christian.

"I have an important message for you," Dittner said, looking in all directions to make sure no guard was around. "Contact has been made with the outside."

"How can that be?"

"A few prisoners who have been released have helped establish this link," he explained as they strolled back down the bunker. "They were threatened with immediate arrest and return if they spoke of what they saw here. Of course, return would mean a quick death."

No. 26 661 nodded, remembering the special patches given to returnees. He had seen the work details they received.

"Nevertheless," Dittner continued, "they are helping the best way they know. They have helped smuggle a few radio receivers into the camp. We will be able to know about the outside."

"Wonderful!" Christian exploded, then grabbed his mouth for fear the outburst would be heard.

"Perhaps your letters will help get a bit of information through some day."

"Of course, of course."

"I will let you know, but tell no one."

"I will see you at the barracks," Christian said, walking off in the opposite direction to appear as if the contact had no significance.

He would not tell Dittner, but he questioned whether he should involve Mina in any schemes to convey clandestine information. Now that he understood the consequences, he would do nothing that might send her to a place like Dachau. *Surely there is a limit to what one can do,* Christian thought to himself. *There must be a line somewhere that one does not cross.*

The whole issue confused him. Obviously, Mina had intended to be a part of this stand against evil, and they had stood together. Yet would they have done all of those things if they had known the consequences? He couldn't decide what they would have done if they had realized how diabolical the Nazis were. His motivations seemed unclear, undefined, and confused. Naïveté, courage, and prudence melted together into a mental blur.

Three

"Come in, my friend!" Fritz called, as Christian approached the doorway of No. 26. "Come in and be a human being again."

"Christian is back," Leonard Steinwender echoed through the crowded barracks. "He is all right."

"We missed you at the service," Werner greeted him, "and were concerned something might have happened. The worship was inspiring. We were lifted by it."

Christian smiled for the first time that day. "I was delayed. I had a letter from my wife and read it very slowly."

"Oh, of course."

"How wonderful."

"An answered prayer!"

The little group sat down together to assess their day. The few moments of reflection each evening sustained them emotionally. Each man leaned forward with eagerness. Leonard and Fritz sat on the edge of the wooden beds, and Christian and Werner sat on the floor. Heinrich Gruber walked over and leaned against the crates. Gruber had only recently joined the inner circle of Christian's friends. Though his plain, round face looked peasant-like, Heinrich had a sharp mind. When he began to speak, he stood out in any group. Such ability had earned him a free trip to Dachau.

"We have survived another day," August Schmidt declared, poking his head over the top of the wooden rack. "Another glorious, typical day is done." His impish grin and ironic jokes were always reassuring.

"I'm not sure of the month." Christian frowned.

"It is October," Dittner answered as he emerged from a cluster of men in front of them. "Today is October 24. Another month, and the snow will start to pile up."

"Why do you think they have allowed us to build the little chapel area in front of our barracks?" Heinrich asked. "In the midst of all the persecution, this seems like a strange privilege."

"I overheard the SS say it was a concession to the priests," Dittner replied, squatting down. "They said it was the result of official pressure."

"I'm sure the Vatican pressured them," Leonard added. "They know what's happening to us priests."

"We are surrounded by ironies." Dittner chuckled cynically. "On the other hand, you Catholics have suffered ten times what we Protestants have at the hands of National Socialism."

"Oh, there has been plenty for all of us," Leonard countered. "I was imprisoned first at Buchenwald where I saw a Protestant die a tragic death. His name was Paul Schneider."

"You knew Paul?" Christian became animated. "He has been one of the key leaders of the Confessing Church!"

"His courage was unbelievable!" Leonard stared at the group. "In the camp he would not salute the swastika flag, so they put him in a special torture cell that overlooked the assembly area. When the prisoners lined up for roll call, he would shout out the window, 'Jesus says, "I am the resurrection and the life."' Immediately, the guards would descend on him and beat him into silence. We could hear the blows clear out in the yard."

Christian inched forward, his face unable to mask his shock. "How did he endure?"

"On occasions when the SS camp leader was reviewing the prisoners, Paul would shout, 'You are a murderer! I accuse you publicly before God's tribunal of massacre.' Then he would start to name prisoners who had recently died. The beatings that followed were inhuman."

"How long did he last?" Fritz asked.

"For thirteen months he kept at it. Then one morning in the spring, after the guards left, no sound ever came from the cell again. As I said," Leonard concluded, "we have all paid our price, but he was a true saint."

"What is it we are fighting for?" Christian shouted angrily. "What are we fighting? Sometimes I'm not sure. Are we battling over politics? Are we fighting for truth? Is it all worth the death of one man like Paul Schneider?"

"Have you forgotten our motto?" Dittner snapped back. "What has been the battle cry that the Confessing Church has sounded?"

"You mean the quotation you use from the book of Hebrews?" a priest asked. "Isn't it something like, 'We are not among those who shrink back and are lost; we have the faith to make life our own'?"

"Exactly!" Dittner sounded bitter and hard. "We are in a spiritual battle that cuts across every line—political, national, religious, and personal. These are external issues!"

The group was silent, but they listened intensely as Gruber stood up like a preacher mounting his pulpit. His blue eyes flashed.

"In 1932, when I was studying the book of Revelation, I

saw the truth. There is a trinity of evil that is loose in this world, and no one avoids the conflict. The embodiment and source of all that is diabolical, corrupting, and painful is the ancient dragon that seeks to work his will by riding into our midst on the back of the great beast. The beast is the biblical symbol for corrupted governments that yield to his will. When I understood that, I knew Hitler, National Socialism, the SS, the Brownshirts—all of these were manifestations of that beast!

"And the third part of that trinity is counterfeit religion," Heinrich Gruber continued. "Nazism is a religion—a vicious, devouring religion! That's why they attack the Jews, us, everything that is holy!"

"Isn't it strange," Christian pondered, "how none of us saw this in the beginning?"

"That's true!" Leonard gestured vigorously. "Remember how we talked of Nazism and National Socialism as being a 'German sunrise'? I remember many theologians at the university speaking of a great spiritual revival that Hitler would bring to the country."

"Although it's very painful to admit," Christian confessed, "I even bought a Brownshirt uniform in '32. The parishioners applauded it, and I even wore it in the pulpit."

"Certainly!" another Protestant chimed in. "Many of us felt that wearing the uniform was the patriotic thing to do."

"I mean nothing personal," Gruber interrupted, patting Christian's arm, "but you Protestants lost your direction much earlier than '32. You became man-centered instead of

God-centered. Many of your leaders could not see the religious implications of what Hitler proclaimed."

"And that is why you opened your office to protect Jews in Berlin!" Insight exploded in Christian's mind. "That is why you started your work to help persecuted Jews!"

"My concern was humanitarian," Heinrich added, "but the issues were also religious, and that is why I felt no regret when the SS arrested me."

"Oh, you are so right!" Christian was becoming more excited. "My wife and I finally saw this religious side of Nazism in 1933. We happened on to a group of Brownshirts out in the woods near our church. They had spread a swastika flag over a tree stump to make an altar. A young father held up his baby and recited a pledge to die for Germany. He said, 'I believe in the deaths of those who die for the people because my god is my people.' Then they baptized the baby 'in the name of the Fatherland and to the glory of Germany.' After that experience, I knew there would be no sunrise."

"Remember what they did to Fritz?" August continued. "He was the first German Catholic priest to be sent here. Tell them why they sentenced you."

"You won't believe this," Seitz explained. "I am at Dachau merely for hearing the confession of a Polish citizen. Can you imagine?

"But nothing compares with my humiliation on that first day here. When I came through the gates, an SS guard pulled my rosary from my pocket and hung it around my head so that the crucifix dangled on my forehead. He drove me around the assembly ground screaming, 'The first pig from the Old Reich has arrived!' When I fell down, he kept screaming that after the war all priests would be locked up and the Catholic swindle would be over."

"That is not the worst part." August prompted him.

"When they found my picture of the virgin Mary, they told jokes about her virginity so vulgar that I can't even repeat them."

"These devils must be annihilated!" Dittner shouted. Then he lowered his voice lest a *capo* hear him. "This is a battle to the death. The cross is the great sword by which we must smite this enemy. We must strike them in God's name!"

"No! No!" Leonard corrected him. "That was not the way Paul Schneider fought. And we will remember him long after we have forgotten the warriors who spilled blood with the sword."

"And he is dead." Dittner's voice was angry and hard.

"But his courage is an example that cannot be killed," Fritz insisted. "In the end, his witness and his faith will be the ultimate victory."

"In our battle we must be different from them," Heinrich lectured Dittner. "If we fight evil in the same way, have we not actually joined the other side?"

"Do you know why I am here?" Werner Sylten asked. "I am a Protestant pastor, but my mother had a Jewish grandmother. Can you imagine? Because of some distant ancestor, I am a candidate for death. If I am to die, I want to stand for something more than just hating."

"There are Communists here who are brave men." Christian's voice was uncertain and seemed to be searching to find the way. "And there are Nazis who are more than willing to die for their cause. Surely we are in some way different from them."

"If courage is only putting convictions ahead of survival," Leonard commented, "then we are all the same. Dittner, you suggest nothing more than another alternative in a world of passionate ideas. Does that really make us any better?"

"But we must be responsible." Dittner seemed unmoved by what he had heard. "There is no integrity unless we uphold our sacred obligations."

"Therefore the Communist believes in his obligations to the workers, and the Nazi believes that Aryan purity is sacred," Christian concluded, "and you want us to kill for Jesus' sake."

"Paul Schneider was different from you," Leonard said quietly. Because he was taller than Dittner, he needed only to look down on him for the intensity to be felt. "Surely he believed in the truth, but his faithfulness was much larger than doing his duty. His ultimate commitment was to the love he found revealed in Jesus Christ. In the name of that love, he gave life rather than taking it."

"It is not enough to passionately believe in some ideology!" Werner hammered away at them. "The world is sick from doctrines and creeds. Nobody's completely right! We're all egotists. If we don't have a love that is greater than ourselves, it all turns sour and putrid."

"The Nazis have taught me something important." Heinrich got to his feet. His face was flushed, his bulbous nose fiery red. "I have learned that they believe they are totally right. There is no place for any doubt in their minds. You know why? They must be absolutely correct to justify what they do. Every fanatic takes his little piece of the truth and tries to make it the whole for the rest of the world." He paused and pointed harshly at Dittner for a moment. "We must be humble even about the things for which we are willing to die."

"I think," Christian said, trying to sound reconciliatory, "true courage is larger than just obedience to the truth. I think it is also expressed in those times when we venture beyond ourselves without any certainty that we are truly right."

"I don't know very much about courage," Heinrich grunted. "I only know that I must trust God to help me live in the best way I can. I do not worry much about dying. Living honestly seems to occupy most of my attention."

Suddenly the lights went out, and men began to scramble in all directions. In the darkness, the discussion group was over as men groped to find places to sleep. To his surprise, Christian found he had ended up next to Dittner.

"Let the theologians think what they will," he complained to Christian. "I am going to fight my way out of this place. I will survive, and there will be a day of reckoning."

Christian said nothing; he only stared into the blackness. At least he now knew how long he had been in the camp. Paul Schneider's face came back to him. He tried to picture

Paul yelling from the cell window and not retreating in the face of his awful beatings. He wondered what it all had meant, what difference Paul had made. Could any man fight the dragon and survive? Or was that even the issue?

Christian's fatigue overwhelmed the soreness in his shoulders and back. Almost immediately, he stopped feeling the hardness of the boards and drifted off to sleep.

CHAPTER FOUR

THE GRIND GOES ON

One

Christian Reger had always been a modest man. Gentle by nature, he went about his parish business with diligence and an unassuming air. A strong pastor, he worked in Stieglitz with a sense of urgency that kept him on the move. Behind the faithful pastor's loyalty was a stern ethical sense of rightness, appropriateness, and the priorities that made a nation endure. His early support of National Socialism deteriorated steadily because Christian observed the Third Reich violating the protocols of a decent society. In a short time he became alarmed at the violence the state propagated, and that led to trouble. Reger would not count the cost when the issues involved standing up for propriety.

In the same way, his sense of decency was violated by everything in the Dachau Concentration Camp. Nothing fit with what church people expected from their government. While Reger recognized what the Nazis were capable of, his own values had been kicked around the prison camp like a worthless tin can. No matter how he tried to push the problems to the back of his mind, he couldn't stop worrying and fretting over what occurred day after day. How could human beings treat one another with such callous indifference? He could make no sense out of this upside-down world that the Nazis forced on him.

One evening Christian noticed three men talking together between two of the barracks. Giving the appearance of being an intelligent, educated group, the three prisoners stood close, talking softly. Christian looked around to make sure no guards were watching before slipping up on the group.

"You will remember that Dante wrote in his *Divine Comedy* that above the entrance to hell stands the motto, 'Give up all hope, you who enter here!'" The heavy-set man pointed his finger fiercely at the other two. "Could there be a better slogan for this place?"

"Excuse me," Christian edged in. "I am a German Protestant pastor, No. 26 661. The name's Reger. Might I join your group?"

"All courageous men are welcome among us," the speaker said. "No one gets in this group without having paid a personal price."

The other two men welcomed Christian, but they didn't give their names.

"Yes. Yes." The man to Reger's right continued. "The Nazis are out to destroy all sense of hope and purpose. If they can do so, then we will be defeated."

"Have you seen anything of the interrogation officer?" a thin man asked Reger, casting a sharp scrutiny of Christian's face. "You know what I'm talking about?"

"Sorry," Christian said. "I don't."

"This creep's an SS officer with the job of keeping an eye on everything in the camp while harboring a particular interest in passing out death sentences to violators." The thin man kept looking straight at Christian. "This dog operates by spying."

Christian took a quick look around to make sure no one was watching. "Listen," he said in a low voice, "I've only been here a short time, but I've never heard of such a secret agent. Tell me more so I'll have some idea who to watch out for."

"It takes a long time to learn all the ins and outs of this camp," the thin man answered. "The Nazis purposely tell you nothing to keep you in the dark. You find out by trial and error, which means you are likely to end up paying a high price for what you need to learn." He seemed to retreat slightly from his attentive scrutiny of Christian.

"Yeah," the first man agreed. "The whole point of this hell-hole is to scare us to death so we'll keep our mouths shut when we leave. The interrogation officer is an effective part of this system."

"How?" Christian asked.

"They use the prisoners," the thin man said. "The guards call these stool pigeons 'confidential prisoners' because they slink around the dormitories spying on their fellow prisoners and then reporting infractions back to this headman. You've got to watch out for these guys because they can be deadly. You never know when one will turn up."

"But how could such traitors exist among us when we have been arrested for being people of principle?" Christian protested.

"Prisoners want to survive," the heavy-set man answered. "And more than a few want to avoid the pain the guards dole out."

"Don't forget that prisoners have been arrested for a wide range of offenses," the thin man added. "We've got Jews and gypsies in here who only had a mother with the wrong nationality. Do you read me?"

Christian nodded. "Perhaps I am peculiar, but I can't seem to answer a question that haunts me. No one appears to understand all that is going on around here. The SS guards certainly don't tell us." He pointed beyond the wire fence. "Every aspect of camp life is shrouded in a cloud of darkness. They say the local citizens of Dachau don't understand what happens in this camp, either. I can't make any sense out of this bizarre atmosphere of secrecy."

"You are a sensitive man." The third man spoke for the first time. "I appreciate your concern. My name is Emil Muhler, and I was brought here from just over the hill where I was a priest in Munich."

Christian stared. "You're *Doctor* Muhler? The city pastor of Munich?"

"We try to conceal our identity so we don't end up in

trouble with the interrogation officer," Muhler said. "Let's keep the conversation confidential."

"Certainly," Christian said.

"In this prison the root of evil is the great secrecy with which all persecution is done," Muhler continued. "No one knows exactly how many prisoners are being shipped in here, though I'm sure the count is in the thousands. The Gestapo keeps every detail under cover so no one can figure it out. Their nasty work flourishes in the darkness. Consequently these perpetrators of malice are all the more able to inflict over and over again the wounds that we bear."

"I am Father Franz Goldschmitt," the heavy-set man said. "Never forget that evil loves the darkness and hates the light. Many times you will see SS officers lash out in secret with a viciousness they would never use in front of people on the outside. That's their style—absolute blackness used to hide all expressions of truth!"

"You cannot make sense out of this site," Muhler added, "because everything is hidden from us and the view of the outside. Oh, yes, some people in your town or village knew you were arrested, but they quickly received threats that they would also be locked up if they made noise about your plight." Muhler's eyes narrowed. "You'd be surprised how few German citizens want to argue when they figure out that winning their disagreements only gives them a free trip to this death camp."

"We now live in a world that contradicts all normal human emotions," Goldschmitt added. "I am making notes that I keep carefully hidden. My hope is that some day I will be able to publish this secret diary. It's the only way the truth will ever come out."

"Of course we must survive," the thin man said, still not revealing his name, "and don't underestimate how difficult that strain may be. I can't believe that the Nazis can win this war, but I don't see much hope that Hitler will fall. Remember that if the *wehrmacht* should fall, you can bet the Gestapo will burn the records about this camp. That's another reason why Goldschmitt's diaries may be so important."

"I don't want people ever to forget what sort of situation existed here," Father Goldschmitt added. "Once this war is over you'll find citizens saying, 'Let the grass grow,' or 'Don't make such a fuss about it all'." He pounded his fist in his hand. "Not me! I know Jesus taught prisoners to forgive, but the world must never forget."

"You probably haven't seen any of the children in here yet," the thin man added. "But the Nazis have run kids through this camp. I've seen adolescent boys come in as well as a few who looked like they were as young as seven years old. Of course, these boys quickly disappeared." He stiffened. "Little people vanish easily in the darkness."

"Far too many Germans encouraged the extermination of the Jews from their communities because the Nazis continually cultivated hatred," Muhler said. "Don't worry! The Jews were the first to evaporate in Dachau."

"I can't put all of this together," Christian concluded.

"Nothing in my life prepared me to face what we can't escape here." Shaking his head, he started to turn away.

"You are a good man," Goldschmitt said. "But goodness cannot help you understand such evil. All of us have walked into a world of darkness and must keep struggling to find our way back into the light."

"I guess so," Christian said, and walked off.

Two

Two days later Dittner grabbed Christian by the arm while he was walking down the major boulevard between the two divisions of barracks. "Pay careful attention today. I'm not sure what is going on, but something important is happening."

"What do you mean?" Christian stopped and looked around quickly.

"The word is out that the Nazis are moving a special prisoner in here from Sachsenhausen. I haven't gotten any word on who he is yet."

"Where will they put him?"

"I suspect down there in the special cells by the Jourhaus where they keep their eyes on the big-name naughty boys. When we know who this prisoner is, we'll have a better idea of what's going on."

"What are you telling me?" Christian asked. "You got something in mind you want me to do?"

"Yeah," Dittner said. "I need your help in figuring this one out because it might turn out to be an important arrest.

Could you wander around with me down there where this new prisoner is supposed to be coming through? See what you can find out. You take the west side of Roll Call Square, and I'll stand on the east."

"That's presuming a lot," Christian said slowly. "What excuse could I offer for walking around if a guard jumps me?"

"Tell him you heard that mail was coming in, and you are expecting a letter. That ought to do the trick."

"I don't know," Christian said hesitantly. "Sounds a little shaky. We have to pay careful attention about what's said. A guard could crack me over the head for nothing."

"Then keep your head down," Dittner said cynically. "Let's go."

Reger fell in alongside Dittner, but he didn't like the scene. Too many inmates had already been worked over for some minor infraction of the rules, and he didn't want to get his head busted for nothing more than standing in the wrong place.

An ominous quiet hung over everything around the prisoners. No one spoke to the two men when they walked past the other barracks. Possibly other inmates had gotten wind that something important was going on. Obviously the SS guards had terrified everyone into strict obedience, or so it appeared. The two men kept walking.

Near the end of the camp's main street, the large Roll Call Square opened before them in a large rectangular shape. Day after day the dreaded morning and evening roll calls occurred on the large flat surface. Even worse, when prisoners were caught breaking the rules or attempting to escape, corporal punishment was applied on this square. Loudspeakers were hooked up along the sides of the area. Often when inmates were forced to stand in punishment, the SS guards maintained a constant barrage of messages proclaiming the endless victories of Hitler. Nothing about the roll call plaza endeared the scene to Reger or Dittner.

Christian could see a group of prisoners working furiously near the entrance to the special cell area. They appeared to be carrying pieces of wood and metal in and out of the building while several men worked outside. Reger made a quick survey of the entire area and discovered no guard watching him. With a sauntering gait, he moved closer to the men. He spied one of the workers standing over a long wooden vat, stirring wet cement with a hoe.

"What's going on in there?" Christian stood next to the inmate as if he were part of the work detail.

"Big dog's being sent down from Sachsenhausen," the workman said quietly. "We've had to enlarge the room for him."

"Enlarge?" Christian said far too loud, and then quickly bent over to speak more quietly. "Why would the SS go to such trouble for a prisoner?"

"I've heard this guy is Georg Elser. They say he made an attempt on *der Fuhrer's* life in 1939." The man kept pushing the hoe back and forth to keep the cement moving.

Christian stood up and scratched his head. "Never heard of it."

"Yeah. The Nazis call the attack the 'Burgerbrau outrage.' I gather that they are holding Elser in complete concealment until after the war when they'll put on a big showcase trial before executing him in a public display. I guess they're taking good care of him before the slaughter starts." He kept pushing the hoe.

Christian nodded and started backing away. The episode sounded as crazy as everything else in Dachau.

Fortunately no guards had noticed him, so he could back away from this special section of the camp. Christian walked slowly away, trying to give the impression he was going somewhere while doing nothing. Out of the corner of his eye he saw Dittner walking toward him from the opposite side. He slowed down.

Marching up with his usual confident stride, Dittner slowed. "Learn anything?"

"Yes. A man named Georg Elser's being shipped in."

"Ah! That's it!" Dittner shook his head. "The men on the other side called him Eller. Of course, I know who Elser is."

"Apparently they'll be holding him here with his identity kept under wraps."

Dittner nodded his head. "A typical Gestapo procedure. Another way to keep everyone in the dark. They'll keep Elser out of sight until they decide where to dump him."

Christian nodded back toward solitary confinement. "What's in those rooms?"

"Humph!" Dittner snorted. "It takes this entire camp to another cesspool level. Of course, Elser may get better treatment to keep him fat and happy until they put the rope around his neck, but the rest of the prisoners in those cells pay a high price. Ever hear of the 'standing bunker'?"

Reger shook his head.

"The Gestapo lock a man in a space so narrow that he is forced to stand, even if he should fall asleep. After a while your legs cramp, but you can't sit down or stretch out. The pain goes on hour after hour. Get the picture?"

Christian nodded.

"You want to make sure you stay out of that part of the lock-up. Read me?"

"Like a book." Christian turned away and started back to the barracks by himself.

Three

That night at 8:45 the signal sounded for the men to prepare to go to sleep. By 9:00 their obligatory rest began. Every man would already be on the rack, too tired for anything but sleep. Christian edged in between his friends and closed his eyes.

"You asleep yet?" August Schmidt asked.

"No," Christian answered.

"It's been a long day," Schmidt said.

"Absolutely! I am exhausted."

"We are every night." Schmidt squirmed to gain some extra space. "What did you learn today?"

Christian stared at the boards above his head. "When I was at home in Stieglitz, I worked hard because my work as a pastor was always so joyful. Here I work even harder because I am afraid of dying. Quite an irony."

Schmidt rubbed his chin. "Interesting."

"Everywhere I turn," Christian continued, "I find prisoners frightened of dying. Who knows what will become of us? Maybe it would be easier to die rather than keep on wading through the terror that comes with each new day."

"You don't believe that," Schmidt challenged Reger. "You can't!"

"Not really, but I do know we are surrounded by men who stand close to that line. A cloud of mystery keeps us from knowing what is going on, but once anyone decides they will never be released, it becomes much easier to reach out and touch an electrified barbed wire fence to end it all."

"My, my, you have had a busy day," August said. "I think we both need to get some sleep."

"Sure."

But Christian's mind kept churning in the dark.

Like this man named Georg Elser, the camp was filled with the unexplained and unexpected, leaving Christian baffled and feeling betrayed. Of course, the Nazis could care less about what he felt, but still these experiences left him swimming in an enigma. Equally perplexing was what would follow in the morning. Who knew what could explode?

Today he had learned about some SS official called the "interrogation officer" who lived off a feast of discoveries some worthless prisoner had dredged up from the barracks. Who knew where these bottom feeders might show up?

This was one more problem for him to worry about in the morning.

In this vast multitude of prisoners, Christian kept discovering new names, new faces, important men, people who had once made a difference in German society. Now they were only pawns in an overflowing swarm of chessmen. Too many new men kept popping up! He couldn't keep up with all of their names. Names like Dr. Muhler's might stick because Christian had heard of him before being sent to the camp, but the identity of Goldschmitt and Elser could slip away. Dachau was not a place for relationships unless the individual worked next to him or had a unique place in his daily experience.

Reger expected to run across hundreds of men whose faces would only float in and out of his memory. The camp had already proved to be too big, complex, anonymous. Probably most of these people would fade away with the passing days.

The heaviness of this barren camp bore down on him with an oppressive tediousness just as the fatigue of being worked to death twisted his muscles. He heard a few men snoring. Most of the prisoners had dropped off as soon as the lights went out. Christian could no longer reflect on the day. His daily tasks had been too overwhelming. Without even being aware of slipping away, he was swept off into sleep in the dark night.

CHAPTER FIVE

TO SURVIVE—
1940-41

One

B itter, cold winds from the Bavarian Alps had dumped a large amount of snow for so early in the winter. The freezing weather only added to the burden of surviving the camp. Two men tried to leap over the small drifts to keep snow from filling their clogs.

"Why *did* you say yes?" Christian asked Dittner, quickly shutting the barracks door behind them as they entered. Each knew that any loss of heat from No. 26 would cost everyone dearly.

"Why does anyone say yes in any difficult matter?" Wilhelm Dittner stomped his feet to keep the blood circulating.

"You could have avoided any involvement against the Nazis," Christian said, rubbing his hands together as vigorously as he could. Whatever the effects of the summer heat, nothing hurt like the pain of the freezing ice. "Even in Hesse when you were organizing groups into Confessing churches, you went out of your way to attack them."

"I cannot tolerate injustice!" Dittner sneered, rubbing his hands together. "In school I also went out of my way to bully the bullies! Something within me turns into rage when people are being pushed around."

"Ah ha! You were angry!"

"Well," Dittner half-admitted as he crossed his arms and tucked his hands under his armpits, "I think of the matter as being much larger than anger. Perhaps righteous indignation is a better term."

"Hmmm." Christian studied his friend.

Steinwender burst in through the door. "Have you seen Werner Sylten? We can't locate him."

Both men shook their heads.

"Perhaps you don't like being pushed around," Christian decided aloud.

"Of course not!" Dittner snapped. "Does anybody? I hate people who make others feel small or helpless. Something wrong with that?"

"Oh, no," Christian insisted, "not at all. I'm only trying to understand your thoughts."

"Listen, Reger, evil is to be fought at all costs with all of our resources. If we don't fight it, we'll be overcome. The worst evil is the official kind, the big, all-encompassing variety that wears uniforms and can render you helpless."

"Is Sylten here?" Another prisoner interrupted the conversation. "Have you seen him?"

"I haven't seen him for two days," Dittner answered.

"The strong stands that you take," Christian continued as he began to blow on his hands, "are really prompted by resentment?"

"Absolutely." Dittner's blue eyes sparkled. "My old man used to terrorize me and my sister, stomping around just like the SS does. I can still hear him screaming and shouting to try to make us cower at his feet. His tirades turned her into a craven puppy that whined and ran from everything. But not me! I will not slink or crawl away from anyone!"

Other prisoners began pouring into the barracks, and both men eyed the opening and closing door with offense. The only good thing was that the rapid increase of bodies would eventually raise the temperature.

"Sylten?" a third prisoner questioned, tugging at Dittner's sleeve. "Have you seen Werner Sylten?"

"No," Dittner snapped. "I haven't seen the man! Shut the door!"

"You know that if they find the radios, they will probably execute you," Reger whispered.

"Kill me?" Dittner sneered. "You think that they might not just as easily kill you for nothing?

"Listen," Dittner lectured and shook his finger in Reger's face, "the trouble with you and most of the rest of Germany is that you don't think. You're like a race of robots that jump every time some official snaps his fingers. You never ask if the man in the uniform might be corrupt and worthless or if he has only come to prostitute your obedience."

"That's not fair!" Christian bristled and his eyes narrowed. "You know the Bible teaches that we are to obey all the authorities. From childhood, we have always been taught that God gives us the judges, the officials, the rulers as a defense against evil men."

"And you have no defense when they turn out to be the Devil!" Dittner poked him in the chest with his finger. "Seven years ago any half-wit should have been able to see where Hitler was going. Don't blame your blindness on the Bible!"

Feeling defensive and confronted, yet not wanting to agree, Christian wasn't sure how to answer. He acknowledged, "I did hear Hitler speak once."

"Oh, really?" Dittner raised his eyebrows in surprise. "When?"

"I was in seminary at Bethel when the National Socialists held a rally in the city hall at Erlangen. That must have been about 1928 or '29. Somewhere around then."

"And you were impressed like the rest?"

"Not in the way you think." Christian was becoming annoyed. "Sure, Hitler was compelling. Why would he have been otherwise? He screamed; he threatened; his speech was a performance in fury. Yet, I was more impressed with the effect that his uniformed troops, the swastika flags, and the frenzied salutes had on the crowd. They were on their feet screaming for Germany's freedom, *'Deutschland erwache!'*"

"What's your point?" Dittner's air of superiority was stifling.

"Simply this: The Erlangen town hall was filled with frantic men who were out of work and who saw no hope in the government. Since I was not hungry that day, Hitler didn't impress me much. But I remembered just a few years earlier when my mother cried herself to sleep because her box of inflated money would not buy one loaf of bread!"

Suddenly Christian began shouting. "So, don't sound so omnipotent and omniscient around me! Being right and prudent is not such an easy task in desperate times!"

The exchange had become so heated that it was drawing attention. When the men around them grew silent and started staring, Christian stopped and walked away. He felt like smashing Dittner in the face. Taking three steps, he halted, turned, and clenched his fists.

"I've found him! I know where he is!" A piercing voice interrupted the steady buzz of conversation throughout the barracks. Pushing and shoving his way through the crowd, Gruber kept shouting. "Help! Somebody has got to help! I know where Werner is!"

Grabbing Gruber by the arm as he passed by, Dittner demanded, "What's going on here? What are you talking about?"

"They put Sylten in the infirmary. That's why we couldn't find him."

"So what?"

"They won't let him out. That's what!"

"All right, all right," another prisoner joined in, motioning for calm. "They've got him quarantined or something. He hasn't been gone that long."

"Listen," Gruber still fairly shouted and shook his arm free from Dittner. "They are getting ready to send out another invalid transport to Linz. Don't you get it? They put Werner in there because of his Jewish background. Whether he's sick or not, they'll load him on that truck and he'll disappear just like the rest."

"Let's go!" Christian declared and darted across the room. "We have no time to waste."

The three men bolted through the door and began to race up to the bunker. The snow had started to blow again, and they suddenly realized that the barracks were much warmer than they had thought.

"Not too fast," Dittner warned. "They may think we're trying to escape. Just trot."

"We must get there and back before they turn out the lights," Heinrich puffed. "If they catch us running around after curfew, they might make us stand outside all night." Feeling the bite of the cold, he wheezed, "We don't have much time. Hurry!"

"What can we do?" Christian's words turned into steam. "We need some idea of what to say when we get there."

"Perhaps we can get some other name put on the transport list," Dittner ventured. "Maybe we can bribe a *capo* to change his roster."

"Bribe?" Gruber panted. "With what?"

"Maybe," Christian thought aloud, "just maybe we could get them to use the name of someone who has already left to fill their count. Perhaps all they need today is a quota."

As the snow cleared slightly and the light of the infirmary appeared just ahead, they realized it was dark inside. When the men stopped before the door, an eerie silence surrounded them. Sound of movement ought to be coming from the usually crowded building.

Dittner peered into a window and searched for some clue. "Every bed is empty. I can't see anything in there."

Christian jumped up the stairs and barged through the door into the darkness.

"Hey! What's going on?" a voice said from the nearest corner. "What are you doing in here?"

"Where are the patients?" Reger demanded.

"Who are you?" shot back from the blackness.

"Who are you?"

"No. 18 643. Are you a guard?"

"No, I'm a prisoner," Christian snarled. "And I want to know where they've gone!"

"Listen," the surly voice volleyed, "I'm the *capo* who works here, and if you don't get out of here I will call the guard. Don't come in here acting like you run this hellhole!"

"Please," Christian pleaded, changing his tone. "I'm not looking for trouble. I'm just trying to find a friend who disappeared. We know he came here."

"Don't stick your nose where it doesn't belong, and you might keep it on your face."

By now Christian's eyes had adjusted to the darkness, and he could see the room was empty. The voice in the corner was the only person he could see in the barracks.

"Look," he asked as kindly as he could, "just tell me if they have sent another transport to Linz."

"All I'm saying is that they cleaned house two hours ago, and everybody in here was loaded up."

"But have the trucks left?"

"Listen, if you want to get a truck ride, you just stay around here and keep asking questions. Yes, the trucks left! I saw their lights go out the gates. Now that's it! Get out of here!"

Mechanically, Christian backed out. As he shut the door, his hand stayed on the knob while he reached with the other hand as if he might push the door open again. Everything within him insisted that he ought to be able to walk in once more and this time the room would be filled with people and that somewhere Werner Sylten would be lying in a bed.

"They're all gone," he whispered.

"Oh, no!" Gruber groaned. "Werner is gone."

"Ya," Dittner concluded bitterly, "Werner is gone."

Each man stood rigid in his place, staring straight ahead. Finally, Gruber began to pray, "Out of the depths I cry unto Thee, O Lord. Lord, hear my voice. Let thy ears be attentive to the voice of my supplication that I make for Werner Sylten and each man who left today."

"Amen," Christian mumbled.

Dittner said nothing as the three men turned back to the barracks. His face was set like a rock, his jaw locked.

The biting wind no longer seemed to bother him.

Two

The loudspeaker continued to pour out its vilification and demands as each man stood erect and faced forward. The roll call assembly was no place for deviation. Still, No. 26 661 could carefully study Herman Metz in the row just in front of him.

Dittner had been able to identify Metz and another *capo* named Zimmermann as the main leaders in the infirmary. He had discovered that the hospital was being run as a separate unit from the rest of the camp. For some reason, an SS physician had independent control of the whole operation, and these two *capos* were allowed to do any sadistic thing they wished.

Once, Metz had been seen stomping a Pole in the doorway of the infirmary. Apparently, two other Poles had carried the man in, only to be confronted with Metz's accusations that they were trying to avoid work. After kicking the unconscious man in the groin, he turned on the two friends with a leather belt. That night, the sick man died in his barracks. No. 26 661 was struck by how ordinary Metz appeared. Standing at attention, he seemed to be just another prisoner. Yet he could apparently kill with ease.

With their dismissal, the work units assembled. Once more No. 26 661 and the rest of the throng began tramping through the snow. Metz turned toward the infirmary and his own "work."

Winter had not changed the nature of the tasks, and

hauling dirt was even more painful in the cold. By 1:00, Christian was completely exhausted and felt numb all over. It was then that he spotted a man lying facedown in the dirt and snow. He realized that if an SS guard saw him, a club would begin to swing.

"Quickly!" Christian half-shouted to the nearest prisoner. "Help me pick him up." Reluctantly, the prisoner walked toward the slumped form.

Though he did not know him well, he recognized it was Heindrich Van Mohl, one of the Dutch prisoners. Because Van Mohl was unconscious, it was difficult to steady his weight between them. At least the guards couldn't argue that he wasn't capable of further work. In fact, as they struggled out of the field with Van Mohl's feet dragging in the snow, no one even paid attention.

"Let's get him to the infirmary," No. 26 661 told the other prisoner.

"Look at his feet and hands," the man said.

"I'm sure the swelling means that edema has set in."

Trudging along, Christian thought about the night when Heindrich Van Mohl had first appeared in Barracks No. 26. The Dutch professor of theology had been caught hiding Jews in his house. In the overcrowded, smelly barracks, the tall, thin, and refined scholar, who appeared to have spent his life reading books, had become bewildered and disoriented. Obviously, the work of Dachau would soon devour him.

"I'm afraid his condition is serious," the other prisoner speculated as they reached the door of the infirmary.

As the two men supported Van Mohl's weight between them, No. 26 661 knocked twice. A well-fed Zimmermann opened it.

"This man is seriously ill," No. 26 661 said.

Zimmermann studied the situation for a moment, his eyes traveling across the red blotches on the Dutchman's neck and hands. His gaze shifted back and forth between the three men, narrowing as it went.

Then without a word, he swung his arm and smashed his fist into the center of Van Mohl's face. Before anyone could react, his other fist hit the right side of the professor's head. The force of the two blows sent all three men lurching backward.

"That's your medicine for today," the *capo* answered. "And if you two swine come back here again, I'll give each of you another treatment." Then he slammed the door in their faces.

"What will we do?" the other prisoner cried. "We can't leave him here, but we'll be punished for taking him to the barracks."

"What else can we do?" Christian asked. "He'll die in the fields today. We don't have any choice but to leave him inside regardless of what they do." Off they went down the bunker.

Once inside Barracks No. 26, they pushed Van Mohl as far back into the beds as possible with the hope that he would be overlooked in a corner. Christian tried to stop the bleeding from Van Mohl's nose.

"Listen, I don't want anyone to know I've been a part of this," Christian's helper warned. "I've fulfilled my responsibility, and that's it."

"There are some things bigger than responsibility!" No. 26 661 snapped back.

"Look," the other prisoner said, "I know all about you pastors who are kept in here. And I'm no heathen. I was baptized on the first day my parents brought me to church. I respect what you're about. But I've done all I can."

"We all have a responsibility for one another," No. 26 661 charged.

"Ya," the man insisted, "and the Bible also says that living dogs are better than dead lions."

"Would you dare twist what Scripture says in a place like this?" Christian felt his anger raging out of control.

"All the same, leave me out of this."

"We are not animals unless we let them turn us into that," Reger shouted.

"Whatever you say, Pastor. All the same, I don't want anyone to know I was here."

"All right, all right!" Christian agreed as the prisoner left the barracks.

Perhaps this one time they might overlook an obviously sick prisoner. Dittner had thought that the cross should be a sword with which to strike enemies.

No, Christian mused to himself, *it is a symbol of shared life, shared pain, of mutuality.*

"Well," Christian said to the unconscious man, "we did the best we could." With that, he shuffled back to the fields.

Three days later, with his face swollen and bruised, the Dutch theologian died.

Three

During the following days, the snow came down thick and heavy. During the night, one to two feet could accumulate. Soon, the prisoners recoiled at the sight of snowflakes, because the SS had a strange compulsion about removing every flake of the downfall from the camp. And the clergy were their favorite targets for work with the snow commando.

The commando of at least a thousand men would be rushed out into the streets to begin clearing them. Though the temperature was freezing and the shovels were crude, the group would be pushed at a furious pace for eight to ten hours.

"Tempo! Tempo! No delay!" crackled through the cold as teams of men scurried in every direction.

Wet, heavy snow would be carted off to the Wurmbach River. If the carts were full, snow was piled on tables that took four prisoners to carry them. Eventually, the men would become so exhausted that they would stumble and fall.

No. 26 661 worried about falling. Even in this brutal weather, sweat would pour out and soak his clothing. To fall or lie unconscious on the ground in that condition would make him an easy target for pneumonia. Of course, being on the ground would soak his clothing even more, and there were no dry ones to change into! On this particular morning, a delay in getting the path open to the river allowed an unusual period of rest. Sitting next to him was a small, dark man who leaned over to ask a question.

"You are a priest?" he inquired.

"No," No. 26 661 answered, rubbing his hands together to help the circulation. "I am a pastor of the Confessing Church."

"Oh, really!" the swarthy man said. "I have known other men like you."

"You are a priest?" No. 26 661 asked the little man in return.

"Oh, no, no," he said cynically. "I am only a gypsy. That is why I am here. The Nazis don't like gypsies any better than they like Jews."

"I am sorry," Christian said, not knowing what else to say.

"I came here from Buchenwald," the gypsy confided. "I met a great man there who also was from your Confessing Church."

"Who?" No. 26 661 asked earnestly. The fate of any comrade became personal news.

"His name was Paul Schneider. He was the bravest man I've ever met," the gypsy said, as if divulging a sacred secret.

"Paul Schneider!" Christian exclaimed, gripping the man's arm. "Yes, I knew Paul Schneider! He was, indeed, a brother. What do you know about him?" He could feel the warmth of the gypsy's breath against his ear.

"The Nazis killed him!" the gypsy said bitterly. "Then they made me make a special flower wreath to put on the casket so it would appear to his widow that they had treated him honorably!" He stopped to spit disdainfully on the ground. "But I tell you, I never made anything with flowers so good in my life. Those pigs may have used my wreath to deceive his wife, but I made it to honor one of the best men God ever created."

Up ahead, the snow commando was starting to move again, and the work was about to begin. They both stood up.

"I tell you, Pastor, sometimes I'm not sure what I believe," the gypsy said. "But I know this: whatever Paul Schneider stood for, I will believe in on the day I die."

"Move on!" the guards warned. "Stop wasting time!"

Whatever the obstacle to work had been, it was now removed. The convoy of wheelbarrows and huge wooden trays full of snow began to wind its way down to the river.

The gypsy had blended back into the stream of gray-striped uniforms and disappeared. From a short distance it was almost impossible to identify anyone, even a friend. There were so many things Christian wanted to ask the gypsy, but his attention was directed back to the work.

The snow seemed even heavier than before. Reger's mind fastened on the gypsy's story. At first, he thought of what an extraordinary witness it was. Suddenly, the words slipped away. Nothing positive remained from their conversation. All he could think of was that Paul Schneider was dead. They had killed him. They had killed Van Mohl. They had killed Werner Sylten.

They had killed . . . they had killed . . . they had killed!

The list didn't seem to end until he came to the thought, *And they will kill No. 26 661.* His mind hung there and couldn't seem to turn elsewhere. A vortex of despair sucked him down to its center. From out of the depths, other thoughts emerged. *What if I do fall? What if I do catch pneumonia? What if I do die? I no longer mean anything. I am nothing. I didn't even get the name of the gypsy. So what. What's the difference? What if I had given him my name? None of this means anything. Nothing is left.*

Though the sunlight seemed to dazzle with new brilliance as it bounced off the snow, the deepest darkness was settling over all hope. Despair wrapped its icy fingers around Christian's throat.

The Nazis have made us think that we are as worthless as dung, he accused himself. *Why should I keep trying to go on? In the end, they will win.*

As Christian bent over his shovel, staring at the ground and ready to quit, another idea ventured into his imagination. From somewhere long ago, from some forgotten catechism class, a simple sentence reappeared: "I have called you by your name." It echoed again and again. "I have called *you* by your name. I have called you *by* your name. I have called you by *your name.*"

As he searched his memory for the time when he had memorized the verse, other memories surfaced. He remembered his extraordinary seminary experience, when Christ had come to him in a blinding flash of light. When he had been unsure of his faith, that moment had confirmed that Christ was and would be with him. The warmth of that light once more pervaded his doubts.

Then the red and green matchbox that had been slipped to him in Schneidemuhl prison danced before his eyes. Just thinking about it was like a surge of hope.

When he hadn't been sure of his faith, confirmation had come. The matchbox had taught him how God is present even in the smallest things. He was not just a number! He had a name, and God still *called him by his name.*

"I may be poor, isolated, and beaten down," he thought aloud, "but I will never be annihilated!" Another Scripture came to mind. "We are saved by this hope."

"No! The Nazis have not won!" he found himself muttering under his breath. "Glory to God, I do have a *name!* I am not forgotten! I will thank Him that in this moment there is sunlight!"

Overhearing a few of Reger's words, a prisoner next to him looked up with a startled expression. Christian nodded his head and shook his fist in defiance at everything around him. The prisoner was perplexed.

"And you are not nameless either!" Christian said suddenly as he passed him, wheeling his cart toward the river. "You are called by a name. Have hope!"

CHAPTER SIX

A LIGHT IN THE DARKNESS— 1942

One

"Y ou will not believe what I heard!" Dittner whispered in Christian's ear as they leaned against the barracks wall. The intense cold caused each of them to cross their arms tightly to force body heat back inside their skins.

"What?" Christian answered, trying not to waste even the warmth of his breath.

"Our hidden radios picked up an astonishing report. Some time in December the Americans entered the war on the side of the British."

"Really?" Christian's hands dropped to his sides. "The United States is in the war! What does this mean?"

"No one seems to know, but it is clear that Nazi propaganda has changed its direction. The new party line is that now we must defend our victories."

"Maybe that's why our food has become so meager."

"I tell you," Dittner said, gripping Reger's arm, "God is not ignoring what has happened in Germany! His judgment has already been announced by those radios."

Karl Leisner and Leonard Steinwender overheard him and immediately turned to join the discussion.

"You believe judgment is coming on Germans?" Leonard probed.

"Like a beast being shot down in the entrance to its lair!" growled Dittner. "God hasten the day!" With that he moved on to share the news with other men.

"How hard it is," said Karl, "to love your country and hate its government."

A train whistle from somewhere beyond the barbed wire fence interrupted the conversation. The sound signaled the arrival of another load of human cargo and reminded them that the endless flow never seemed to satisfy the insatiable appetite of Dachau.

"How can they pack any more men in here?" Leonard wondered aloud, and shook his head. "There's no space left, and the food rations are becoming critical."

"All-consuming hate runs this place," Karl declared as his eyes blazed with emotion. "Nothing rational can explain it!"

"Nazi fanaticism is like a disease that infects your feelings and then moves on to eat at your mind, until finally it devours your heart and soul."

"Fanaticism is like that, Leonard," Christian mused. "It takes a part of life and makes it the whole. The fanatic believes his cause is the center of the world."

"And any of his actions are justified in the name of that cause," Karl said, pushing his glasses back up the bridge of his nose. "I think a conscious dishonesty is involved. Look at the great lengths that Goebels must go to in deceiving the nation."

"You know," Reger added, "it is possible even for Christians to become such fanatics. Even our zeal can become twisted."

"And is not dying for the cause a strangely seductive invitation?" Leonard asked.

"Certainly!" Karl answered. "Every one of us wants to be absolutely right. And martyrdom seems to allow us the chance to baptize our yearning and seal it with an eternal promise."

"But," Christian pondered, "how do we not shrink back and still keep from being seduced?"

"We must never forget what it means to be sinful men." Karl slowly and carefully chose his words. The deacon's natural humility forged his insights with their own mettle of truth. "Only God's mercy overrules our misinterpretations and blunders. All of us can be victimized when our pride is disguised as light."

"I think that is why real courage transcends itself," Leonard offered, sitting down on the bed. "While the fanatic is zealous because he is convinced he is absolutely right, true courage never has such certainty. All we can do is try our best to get beyond ourselves."

"The cross," said Karl, reaching for his crucifix before remembering it had been stripped away by the guards, "the cross is truly a symbol of courage as well as of sacrificial love. In this place, it is the only true power we have, but I must believe that in the end it will be enough."

"The chapel is ready for worship," someone shouted from the doorway. The trio stopped talking and turned to crowd into the place that had become the true center of warmth for Barracks No. 26. Each man found it hard to move forward as the "bedroom" had swollen to almost two hundred men in a space about seventy feet square.

Inside, several of the Catholic clerics had moved two tables together to form an altar and had covered the rough wood with a white sheet. From somewhere, two candles and a figure of Christ had appeared. In the center, an empty tin can had been cut and shaped into a shining monstrance. An Austrian Communist had secretly made the little worship symbol and smuggled it into the barracks as a token of admiration for the pastors' courage. Only one mass a month was allowed, and only one priest could be the celebrant.

As Christian entered the chapel, a Polish priest grabbed his arm with an emaciated hand. The man slumped against the doorframe and began to slide down. "I can't go on, and I am the celebrant tonight," he groaned. His coarse hair fell down into his eyes as his head rested against the wall.

"Here, let me help you," Christian said, and tried to support him.

"I'm starving," the priest confessed. "I think I'm going to faint."

"I can help you stand." Christian gripped his arm. "Don't give up. You will be able to celebrate the mass tonight if I have to hold you up."

"I'm afraid I just can't continue," he sighed. "I must eat first, or I know I will collapse at the altar."

The prisoners surrounding them spread the word through the barracks.

From somewhere a hidden crust of bread miraculously appeared. Quickly it was passed to the priest. He savored each minute bite as if it might multiply within him. Whether it was the thought of the food or the charity of the gift that energized him, within minutes he was ready to go on with the service. Relief rippled through the group.

Catholics, Protestants, and Orthodox all knelt together. Their many backgrounds blended together as surely as the uniforms and haircuts removed all visible marks of rank or distinction.

Christian watched the men around him drop to their knees. *What an amazing transformation!* he thought to himself. Clergy who have warred with each other for centuries were praying as brothers. No longer did anyone argue over dogmas or differing opinions.

"Only one thing matters," the Polish priest began. "Jesus Christ is among us tonight."

As Christian dropped to his knees, he felt the deepest personal confirmation. The priest's prayer lacked polished oratory, and yet it communicated with a conviction that lifted each man's heart and with it his sense of dignity.

"Thou art joy in all our sorrow," was started by a song leader in the midst of the group. The chorus of men poured out, "O Thou loving Jesus Christ, source thou art of all of heaven's bounty, true and only Saviour Christ!"

"No amount of starvation," Christian whispered to the man next to him, "can keep us from the nourishment of these words."

"Let us hear God's words." The priest opened a little Bible that had made its way past the SS in the Jourhaus. "In your weakness is My strength made perfect," he read slowly and loudly. "In this difficult place, one can learn fully what such words mean." The priest began his exposition haltingly. His German was not good, and he struggled to speak clearly. "Also, God is giving us special opportunity in such a place to experience His promises." He gripped the table with his bony hands to steady himself. "You must see Jesus Christ is perfect combination of power and goodness. But when He came among us, He was here in complete powerlessness. He refused to use power."

Christian thought of Dittner and wondered what he might think about this frail man whose words rang with such force. "Is the cross a symbol of power? Not to the ancient Romans!" The priest struck the altar feebly. "But in the end it conquered them with the most irresistible power in the world—the might of irresistible love! Such love that is willing to suffer for the redemption of others contains over-whelming power of goodness able to conquer even ultimate evil!"

As the priest turned to complete the mass, his words burned in Christian's mind. Warmth had begun to rise up at the center of his being, and a wave of peace swept over him. He felt comforted, consoled, reassured. Things that could not be explained seemed to matter no longer. He prepared to receive the bread and wine. When the words of the last hymn died, the men drifted slowly out of the chapel. Little was said until they were back in the larger room.

"The priest's words touched me tonight," Christian told Leonard.

"Not me!" Dittner answered from the bed. "I don't understand such talk about powerlessness overcoming the world. It is contradiction; it is nonsense."

"No, you wouldn't," Leonard replied, shaking his head without seeming condescending. "It's a paradox. Christians have always known about this secret of the crucifix. It is the mystery of how God is with us when everything else in the world seems to deny His existence."

Dittner shook his head.

"I once had an amazing experience of God's presence," Christian said, turning to Leonard, "at a time when I felt totally lost during my second year in seminary."

Suddenly the overhead lights went out, and the room was plunged into darkness. As if they were in some children's game where the loser becomes "it," men scurried for places on the racks. Christian and Leonard slid in beside Dittner.

"Well?" Dittner asked in the darkness. "What happened to you?"

"I was very confused because my faith had no certainty," Christian began. "I had never experienced any personal confirmation of what I professed to be true. Really, I doubted the very faith I was preparing to proclaim."

"Please, a little louder," some prisoner down the line requested.

"Strange as it may sound, I was studying one of Plato's essays about the problem of knowing anything with certainty. He wrote that everyone needs some anchor to hold him steady in the pursuit of reality." Christian tried to lie flat, but it was difficult being wedged between two men so tightly.

"Ya! Ya!" another voice confirmed. "I believe that too."

"I was in such despair that I began to pray fervently that God would give me such an anchor. I was heartbroken when I finally pleaded, 'Lord Jesus, please be real to me. Please come into my life and live again in what I am and what I do.'"

"What happened?" Leonard asked.

"Ya, what happened?" someone on the left implored.

"Please." Christian felt very uncomfortable not knowing who was listening. "I am very hesitant about sharing this story. I know that it is unusual and, well, I don't want anyone to get a wrong impression."

"Of course," another nameless voice answered him. "We are all sensitive to these matters. Just tell us your experience."

"Well," he said, propping himself up on his elbow, "it was like a magnificent explosion of light bursting upon my tiny room. Like a Roman candle on a summer night. Each part of my room was bathed in the warmth of a wondrous, healing radiance. Without any comprehension, I tumbled from my bed to my knees. My meager bedroom had become holy ground."

"What was the light like?" asked Dittner.

"It was not a kindly light as much as a terrible flash of brilliance. I buried my face in my hands and tried to say something, but 'O my Lord!' was all I could repeat. And then the light was gone. As quickly as the radiance had come, it disappeared. Then a passage of Scripture began to run through my mind: 'For the same God who said, "Light shall shine out of darkness," has shined in our hearts, to give the light of the knowledge of the glory of God in the face of Jesus Christ.'"

"Do you believe this really happened?" Dittner's voice was more hopeful than skeptical.

"At times I wondered whether it was all in my head. Yet afterward, I knew that I was different."

"Rationalists like me have no fondness for visions and mysteries," Dittner confessed. "Yet I don't doubt you."

"Therefore the night is never as dark as it seems," Leonard concluded, "or as long as we might wish. Thank you for sharing such an experience with us."

Two

"No. 26 661?" the SS guard screamed.

The sky was still black; it felt more like night than morning. Christian ducked his head and tried to appear inconspicuous. The only way to avoid extra abuse was to be unseen.

"Where are you, 26 661?" the guard demanded.

"They're after you for helping the Dutch theologian," Dittner whispered.

"I was afraid they'd get you sooner or later for bringing Van Mohl back here," Leonard said, stepping in front of Reger to shield him from view.

"You worthless pig! Step this way or I will strangle you with your own towel." The guard pushed his way through the men in the barracks. "Here is a lesson for every one of you to learn!" Timidly, Christian stepped out from behind his cover of fellow prisoners.

"Look at this towel!" the guard yelled to the whole barracks. "It is dry! No. 26 661 has not washed himself."

Silence fell over the whole group. Obviously, no towels had been used that early in the morning. Most of the time, the crowding was so bad no one ever saw a towel anyway.

"Are we going to tolerate such filth and unconcern? Are you going to allow your fellow prisoner to contaminate your clean barracks that the Reich has so graciously provided?"

No one made a sound, but all understood the real message.

"No. 26 661, you are to serve as an example to this group! We will teach you a little lesson about taking care of things." Grabbing the back of Reger's striped shirt, the guard jerked him toward the door. "Since you do not appreciate the services we have provided, some time by yourself will sharpen your manners."

Pushed out the front door of the barracks, Christian found himself standing with a "select group" of prisoners from other barracks. Apparently, the guards had staged an early morning round-up for a number of men marked for special punishment.

"*Schnell! Schnell!*" The guards double-timed the group down the bunker.

"Oh, God!" a prisoner next to him moaned. "I hope they don't put me up on the stake."

Christian was able to glance down at the emblem on the man's shirt and see that he was also a political prisoner. Obviously, his thin arms wouldn't take much strain. If they did put him on the stake, he could be hung for hours with his wrists chained behind his back and pulled up high enough that his heels could no longer touch the ground.

"Shut up, fools, or it will be worse!" crackled over their heads as they marched down to the detention cells.

"No. 26 661, here's a place for you to think about our rules," the guard said indifferently as he pushed him into a small room that couldn't have been more than thirty inches square.

"This is a great place for you to see the light," he chuckled as he slammed the door, leaving Reger in total darkness. "A couple of days' rest in here will be good for you."

This is the "standing bunker" where you have to stand day and night, Christian thought to himself. *Surely, this can't be too bad.*

But time soon revealed the diabolical nature of the cage. Though Christian tried to slump against the sides to rest, there was no way for his body to get any relief. His muscles began to ache and cramp. His only light was what came in when the bread-and-water meal was pushed through the door.

Some time later in the day—or perhaps night, or maybe it was the next morning, or maybe the next week—his imagination began to play strange tricks. No longer could he tell whether it was morning or evening. Time seemed scrambled together in a jumbled, hazy twilight that was neither sleep nor alertness. He thought only about eating, and imagined food as an adolescent boy dreams of women. Hunger and heaviness hung over his mind like a veil.

Once, in the strange flow of timelessness, he heard a voice coming from another cell. As he listened intently, he knew he had heard the voice before; perhaps it was an old friend. Could he be hallucinating?

Then he realized whose voice it was. Niemoller! The man in the next cell was Martin Niemoller! Although he had looked for Niemoller for days, he had never seen him in the camp.

Christian thought he would call to Niemoller, but then he realized there was no way to know who might be listening on either side. If he called out, it might endanger everyone. So he just pressed his ear closely against the wall to hear anything he could.

A few more words came through, and then everything faded away; but his mind had become crystal clear! The spell of solitary confinement was broken! The tortuous scheme had been defeated because he was reminded that he wasn't alone.

Once again he remembered the matchbox and how it had first taught him that truth. *That is the key to everything,* he decided. *I must remember that I am not alone.*

The darkness of his cubicle didn't seem different from the much larger cell at Schneidemuhl prison. His mind's eye began to recreate those final days before he was shipped to Dachau. The loneliness and solitude of being cut off from his wife and of not having any idea of what was ahead had eaten away at his self-confidence. Depression, like a shroud—worse than any he had ever experienced—closed around him. God seemed to disappear, and he lost all touch with the things he believed.

No longer did he care what he looked like. He quit washing his face and combing his hair, and he sat in the corner of the cell staring at the wall. Time started to slip past him, and he lost track of the days and weeks. Then in the midst of his utter hopelessness, a letter had been tossed through the cell-door window.

It had already been opened and read by the secret police. The postmark read June 11, 1940. Three weeks had passed since Mina had been to see him. He began to realize how badly he had lost his grip on reality.

Yet he knew immediately that the letter was from Mina, and that recognition was like a knife cutting through his mental fog. Eagerly, hungrily, he fumbled at the envelope to get the pages out.

She was all right. Her health was good. Nothing harmful had happened to her, to their house, or to the church. Life was going routinely, and the congregation was concerned for him and praying for his well-being. Just reading those words began to make Christian feel alive again.

To encourage him, Mina had written out Acts 4:25–30.

Why did the heathen rage, and the people imagine vain things? The kings of the earth stood up, and the rulers were gathered together against the Lord, and against his Christ. For of a truth against thy holy child Jesus, whom thou hast anointed, both Herod, and Pontius Pilate, with the Gentiles, and the people of Israel, were gathered together, for to do whatsoever thy hand and thy counsel determined before to be done. And now, Lord, behold their threatenings: and grant unto thy servants, that with all boldness they may speak thy word, by stretching forth thine hand to heal; and that signs and wonders may be done by the name of thy holy child Jesus.

Christian could only sit there wondering why Mina had sent this particular passage. He felt as if he would never again have confidence, much less boldness.

Before he could finish the rest of the letter, the door of his cell swung open and a guard beckoned him to follow.

"Do I need my things?" he asked, fearing this might be his final exit.

"No, leave them. You are going only for a judicial inquiry."

"What does that mean?"

"Follow me!" The guard's answer was harsh and indifferent.

As they walked down the narrow corridor, Christian could see a fellow prisoner, a clergyman, coming toward them. Even though he did not know the cleric well, he had heard of his arrest. The man had dared to hold a worship service on Ascension Day, the day Hitler was preparing to attack Russia. Hitler had forbidden any services on that holy day because they might affect the people's view of the war.

The approaching prisoner kept looking into Christian's eyes as if he were trying to tell him something. As Christian and his guard turned sideways to let him and his guard pass, the man thrust a small matchbox into Christian's hand. Quickly, Christian slipped it into his pocket as they passed.

Though Christian wondered what was in the matchbox, his mind was on the inquiry. Often Jewish and Polish prisoners were tortured during these inquiries. To his relief, the interrogation was brief, without violence, and he was quickly on his way back to the cell with the final words of the Gestapo officer ringing in his head. "You are to leave immediately for Dachau Concentration Camp. *Seig Heil!*"

Entering the cell, he began gathering his things until he knew the guard was gone and the peephole was closed. Then he sat down to look inside the matchbox.

The contents were nothing but a small piece of paper. He unfolded it and found written, "Read Acts 4:25–30."

Acts 4:25–30? He rummaged through the pile on his bunk searching for Mina's letter. He pulled it open to check, and there it was! Mina had quoted the exact same passage— Acts 4:25–30!

Two people with no possible contact had sent him exactly the same message within ten minutes. Only God could arrange such a thing! The heavenly Father had intervened to show Christian that he remained under His special care. He wasn't abandoned! He wasn't alone! The care of the heavenly Father had reached through the Gestapo's security and surveillance.

He again looked at the bottom lines of Mina's letter:

> *And now, Lord, behold their threatenings: and grant unto thy servants, that with all boldness they may speak thy word, by stretching forth thine hand to heal; and that signs and wonders may be done by the name of thy holy child Jesus.*

A wave of joy and relief swept over him, and the icy grip of despair melted away. What had been lost in that cell was found again. Before, he had not been able to remember a single word of consolation, but now they seemed to pour in upon him.

"Peace I leave with you; My peace I give unto you: not as the world gives, give I unto you." He recalled what Martin Luther had written about that passage. The world assumes that peace comes only when a burden is taken away. If a man is poor, he thinks of becoming rich. If a dying man can escape death, he believes be will have peace. But Luther taught this is not how Christ gives peace. On the contrary, Christ often allows the burden to lay on us. Rather than taking the burden from the person, he takes the person from the burden!

Christian had been left to struggle with his burden during the weeks of solitary confinement in order to discover the most important lesson he could learn. Pain and difficulties remained, but now he knew the source of a new strength that would allow him to stand under the load and to speak "with all boldness."

Placing his face in his hands, he wept. The dread he had felt at coming to the end of his confinement was gone. The days ahead at Dachau would be much harder, yet he could endure.

A splinter gouged Christian's leg, reminding him of where he was. In his standing cell, all of those memories had taken on a necessary immediacy. Over and over, he recalled the lines of Scripture Mina had sent. Shifting his weight, he once more tried to rest against the wall and this time drifted off to sleep.

Three

"How was your vacation?" August Schmidt asked with the usual twinkle in his eye.

"Most relaxing and restful," Christian answered, looking straight ahead. Reger could get away with talking during assembly roll calls if he didn't look as though he were carrying on a conversation. "I found Niemoller."

"Really! They did accommodate you well."

"He was in the cell just on the other side of the wall."

"Good! How are you feeling?"

"Starved!"

"We are all hungry." As Schmidt spoke, it was obvious he had lost another tooth. "The food rations are even less than before."

"*Achtung!*" blasted over the loudspeaker, and the men sprang to attention. "To your assignments!"

Since the snow had begun to melt and the arctic cold was gone, work was more bearable. Christian had also been given additional responsibility; he was now one of the cooks. But as the spring wore on, he began to realize that a subtle and deadly game was being played with the food. On visiting days or times of special review, the menu was made to look adequate. The next day, rations were cut back to compensate for any extra food consumed the day before. On regular working days, the food was never adequate. In fact, the soup became increasingly diluted.

At the same time, the radios told them of the great victories Germany was amassing. Each broadcast made it sound as if every German was now living in abundance. Nevertheless, the prisoners were becoming weaker and weaker.

When Reger carried buckets of food into the fields, he could sense that hunger was beginning to rule. Men were desperate and anxious at the sight of food. They would crowd and push to get near the food bucket. But once their bowls were filled with watery soup and pieces of bread were distributed, cruel disappointment remained in their eyes.

Conversations seemed always to turn to food. "How can they feed us so poorly if the war is going so well?" a prisoner would ask. "Do you think there will be more vegetables in the soup today?" another would say. "I remember the bread my wife used to bake," a third would add.

Even Christian's reflections about Mina competed with the intrusive thoughts of hunger. She had always been the dearest desire of his heart, but he found he didn't think about her as often as before. He was becoming obsessed with food.

With the coming of summer, work began at 4:00 in the morning. The early hour and the summer sun caused a drain on energy and strength that was not being replenished. Though the flow of new prisoners was endless, nothing could hide the mounting count of dead bodies. They were dying from exhaustion and lack of food.

One of the prisoners coined the phrase, "the death summer." Quickly, it spread throughout the camp. "We are in the death summer of '42," prisoners confided to one another.

By the end of July, the buckets of food had become almost more than Christian could carry. He dreaded the times he had to trudge into the fields with those heavy weights hanging from his shoulders. Yet at 5:00 in the morning, noon, and 7:00 at night he staggered into the fields.

Starvation was beginning to take its toll. Even August Schmidt had to be taken to the infirmary. Many of the prisoners were losing emotional control.

One evening as Christian entered the barracks, he noticed that one of the sleeping racks was shaking. A prisoner named Husar was rolled up in a ball and crying uncontrollably, his arms pulled up over his face.

"What is it, Husar?" Christian said, shaking him. He didn't respond, but only seemed to curl up more tightly.

Christian pleaded, "Let me help you!"

There was no reply. He knew Husar lacked nothing in courage. Because this pastor had publicly protested the Nazis' program of euthanasia, he had been sent to Dachau. Surely, only the bravest of men would accuse the Nazis in public!

Slowly, Husar began to recognize Christian. "I can't stand it any longer!" he sobbed. "I can't take it any more!"

"Yes, you can," Christian assured him. "You must! You must keep on."

Christian prayed frantically, offering words of encouragement, hope, and comfort. Finally, he rocked the man to sleep.

How hard it is to live what we believe, Christian thought. *At times, the answers seem to trickle through our fingers and we can't grasp the things we thought were most important. None of us are heroes. We just do the best we can and try to survive. Perhaps tomorrow night Husar will comfort me when I try to sleep.*

Yet the next day's rounds came without relief. At noon, Christian sat down in the field to eat with the rest of the prisoners. Glancing at the ground, he noticed some plants growing at his feet. Since they were cultivating such plants, he reasoned they would be edible. Christian put several stems into his soup. Within minutes, he knew something was wrong. Stomach cramps began to double him over.

"I'm sick!" he moaned, rolling in agony. Looking into his bowl, a prisoner quickly saw why. "For God's sake, man!

You've eaten some of the digitalis plants we're cultivating. That stuff will kill you!"

"Help! Help!" Christian called out as he staggered to his feet and down the rows. "My stomach is killing me." But no one reached out as he staggered down the road to the infirmary.

His obvious pain and weakness kept the nurses from rejecting him. Even *Capo* Metz gave him a quick look and nodded for the nurses to put him to bed. Cramps made his abdomen feel like one gigantic knot. His body pulsated with the effects of the poison. Finally, he slipped into a fitful sleep.

Several days later, Christian was able to get out of bed and walk slowly to the bathroom for the first time. On one of these trips, he saw a set of scales in the corner. He decided to check his weight.

"Oh, no!" he gasped. "These scales must be wrong."

To his left, a male nurse was scrubbing the floor. He looked up and affirmed, "They're right."

"No," Reger insisted. "When I entered this place, I weighed 198 pounds. These scales can't be right."

"What do they say?" the nurse asked.

"Ninety-five pounds!"

"Look at yourself," the nurse said in disgust. "Look what they have done to you. Just look at your legs."

"I've lost a hundred pounds!"

The male nurse cast an eye around the room to see who was listening. "You better get yourself out of here, or you'll lose the rest of it," he warned.

Christian leaned against the infirmary wall. "I had no idea I was this bad," he admitted.

The nurse went back to his scrubbing, and Christian tried to order his thoughts. He found himself going blank.

"August?" He suddenly remembered August Schmidt was here somewhere.

"Do you know where a prisoner named Schmidt might be?" he asked the nurse. "August Schmidt is his name."

The nurse didn't raise his head, but continued as if he hadn't heard him.

Christian limped a little closer to the *capo*. "August is a friend of mine. He came here maybe two weeks ago."

The nurse shook his head and kept scrubbing.

"Who could I ask about him?" Christian persisted.

"Don't!" the *capo* said abruptly. "Mind your own business and you'll live longer."

"Please," Christian said, tugging at the *capo's* shirt. "Please tell me what you know. This man is a good friend."

Once again looking around the room, the nurse dropped the brush into the bucket. "He's gone. The whole batch of them is gone."

"He went back to the barracks?"

"No, you fool! Don't you understand? The SS cleaned house and put all of them on the transports just before you came in. By now they have gassed him. Now don't ask me any more of your idiotic questions."

August's impish, toothless smile and cheerful face were all that Christian could see. The priest had always been able to find some humorous twist even in the worst moments. And now he was gone. So many prisoners had "disappeared" that Christian could no longer feel loss and pain like he had in the beginning. Yet the little priest had been very important to him. The grief that might have welled up within him was pushed aside by the realization that if August had been taken, he could be dead too.

"I've got to get out of here." Christian grabbed the end of a bed as desperation seized him. But all he remembered later was falling on a bed before he lost consciousness.

Not until the next morning did he wake up. The *capo* who cared for that section of the infirmary was shaking men and warning them not to go into the washroom.

"Wait a while before you go to the bathroom," he told Reger.

"Why?"

"Dead men are in there. They died during the night, and their bodies haven't been moved yet. Wait thirty minutes or so, and we will have them taken away."

Only then did Christian fully realize that August Schmidt was dead. The evening's conversation came back in bits and pieces that slowly blended into the horror that was all around him. His mind and emotions were so assaulted that he couldn't respond to his friend's death. The only thought that made any difference was getting out of there. *The transports are going to come for another load any time now,* he worried.

Reaching for all the strength he could muster, he walked from the bed to *Capo Metz's* desk.

"I am ready to return to work," Christian mumbled.

"Then get out!" Metz's round face was a reminder of where the food went. "Your name will go off our roll right now."

"Oh, thank you, thank you." Christian felt ingratiating, but nevertheless he was alive.

Christian wasn't sure how he was alive or, at that moment, why he was alive. As he limped back to the fields still holding his shrunken stomach, he was only aware of the fact that he had survived again. Living didn't feel very good, but he thought it must in some way be a gift.

CHAPTER SEVEN

THE END OF SUMMER—1942

One

With his worn wooden clogs and the camp's striped prison uniform hanging as if on a rack, Christian stood silently outside his barracks watching the sun set on another scorching August day. Bone-weary from working in the fields, his hands ached and his feet hurt. Thank God, the day's work was over.

Groups of prisoners shuffled past, walking toward their barracks equally exhausted. Fatigue finally forced Reger to slide down the doorframe and to sink on the porch. For a moment, he closed his eyes to blot out the sun's brilliant rays and to carve out a few moments of solitude. In the sanctuary of his mind, he wanted to talk with Mina one more time. Just a few words . . . some intimate thoughts . . . a few words of consolation.

Through his imagination Christian could see his wife sitting at the church organ, playing a hymn. Reger opened the back door of the church and quietly slipped inside to tiptoe down to the front pew where he could listen to her practice unnoticed.

With her eyes closed, Mina seemed enraptured by the Thomas John Williams tune that had put moving music to the words of James Russell Lowell's poem "Once to Every Man and Nation," transforming the lyrics into one of the great hymns of the church. With her eyes closed, Mina swayed back and forth playing the melody that almost lifted her above the organ bench.

The words leaped in Christian's heart. "Once to every man and nation comes the moment to decide." He wanted to sing, but instead listened silently while the organ offered the hymn to heaven like a prayer. "In the strife of truth with falsehood, for the good or evil side; some great cause, some new decision, offering each the bloom or blight, and the choice goes by forever 'twixt' that darkness and that light."

"What are you doing sitting there with your eyes closed!" a harsh voice demanded.

Christian jumped; the daydream evaporated instantly. "W-what?" he gasped, his eyes springing open.

"Don't you know it's dangerous to sit out here with your eyes shut?" Wilhelm Dittner lectured. "You must stay alert!"

"After a day roasting in the hot fields?" Christian snapped back. "I have a right to retreat into the solitude of my own mind now and then."

"A *right*?" Dittner sneered. "No one has any rights in this hellhole. If the camp leader heard you talking about privilege, you'd find out quickly how many rights you have left."

"Camp leader?" Christian frowned. "I know about the commandant who runs this clink, but no one told me anything about other leaders."

"The camp leader is responsible for keeping the numbers up," Dittner said. "He's in charge of stability and the execution of criminal procedures. If you bring this man's wrath down on your head, you'll get to know him well."

Christian eyed Dittner carefully. "What do you mean?" No one seemed to know so much about the ins and outs of the prison as Wilhelm did. Where Dittner picked up the information eluded Christian. At times he wanted to dispense with the man's constant cynicism, but the flow of data always proved helpful. "Tell me more."

"The current leader's name is Zelig. Rutger Zelig." Dittner bent nearer to speak more softly. "Zelig has a nasty little habit." He cupped his hand over his mouth to make sure no one heard. "SS Hauptsturmfuher Zelig enjoys brutality, pain. The man's becoming famous for his cruelty and punishment of prisoners."

Christian stiffened. He understood what it was like to be beaten for some slight violations of the camp's rules.

"Zelig's favorite form of discipline is catching some small transgression, and then stringing the prisoner up on a high stake by tying his hands behind his back and attaching the rope to a high pole. The prisoner must stand on his toes or face the excruciating pain of having his shoulders dislocated. Sooner or later the prisoner can't stand on his toes any longer. You can see what happens. Zelig seems to like that little exercise."

Christian blinked several times, trying to organize his response. Having gone from listening to his wife play "Once to Every Man and Nation" to the description of the sick quirks of this Zelig character left Reger feeling disconnected, and he didn't say anything.

"And you should know that there are also report leaders lurking around," Dittner continued. "These assistants to Zelig execute his orders. They are absolute beasts. You must watch them carefully because they enjoy playing tricks on prisoners."

"Really?"

"Beating, kicking, ill treatment of every kind is their daily fare. Get the picture?"

"Sure. How could I miss."

"There's one more type of guard you should watch out for, Christian. In this wonderful place, we also have block leaders."

Christian shook his head. "You are trying to overwhelm me with these stories and make me paranoid. If I listen long enough, I will believe everyone in this prison is watching me."

"Good. Such fear can keep you alive," Dittner snapped. "Now listen carefully. Block leaders are confidants of the SS. These worthless toads crawl to the authorities by walking over the men considered to be their inferiors, and you are one of those valueless entities they would love to step on. Want an example of what you can expect?"

Reger looked away and shook his head. He had heard enough.

"I will tell you anyway," Dittner said. "A Captain Veyssieres arrived in our cozy little camp recently. The block leaders stripped him of every belonging except a cap and his sword belt. One morning while he was taking a shower, the block leaders stole his clothing. When the captain came out of the shower, the block leaders put his cap on him along with the belt and began parading him up and down in front of his men. Ten times. Twenty times! Screaming 'hurry up, hurry up,' these camp officers ran him naked up and down until Veyssieres collapsed in rage on the ground in front of his comrades. Get the picture?"

"What's your point?" Reger asked.

"Keep your eyes open and pay attention." Dittner leaned into Christian's face. "It's the only way you'll stay alive in Dachau." Dittner stomped defiantly into the barracks.

Two

Two days had passed since Christian's conversation with Wilhelm Dittner. Despite his desire, he found himself returning again and again to Dittner's warning. While he didn't like the prisoner's warnings, the threat was real. Christian couldn't stop thinking about the implications. He found himself worrying about the authorities that he had to please. To avoid being punished for some careless mistake, he started looking over his shoulder constantly.

After returning to the barracks in the evening, Christian heard an uproar across the way. Hurrying to discover what was causing the racket, he rushed out the front door before stopping in his tracks. Block leaders had men from the barracks behind No. 26 lined up in front of the entrance. Christian retreated back inside his doorway to watch from a safe distance.

"We've had enough of your foolishness!" one of the guards screamed at the stoic prisoners in front of him. "No more!" the large man pounded his fist with a riding crop. "Turn and face each other!"

Christian watched the prisoners turn slowly toward each other. He surmised the exercise was more to create fear than anything.

"Attention!" the block leader demanded. "Now, I command you to strike the person in front of you."

No one moved.

"Did you not hear me?" the SS officer screamed. "I demand that you hit each other this moment. Hard!"

No one moved.

"You have hearing problems?" The block leader rushed toward the man in front of him, pushing him into the prisoner across from the inmate. The two men's heads smacked together, sending both of them to the ground. "You're deaf?" The block leader started kicking both men.

No one moved.

"Okay! You fools think you can defy your leaders." The block leader snapped his fingers, and guards wearing black leather gloves started walking between the rows of inmates, punching each man in the face.

The prisoners bounced back and forth, falling to the

ground with dull thuds. The guards didn't stop. Each prisoner gritted his teeth, trying to maintain his ground, but the blows to their unprotected faces were fierce. The guards didn't stop until all the men lay on the ground writhing in pain.

Pounding his riding crop on his palm, the block leader finally began walking over their bodies, kicking some of the inmates, leaving others alone until he finally came to the end of the row of broken men. Looking around at the prisoners watching from other barracks, the SS officer apparently thought it was time to share the lesson.

"If they had beaten each other as I ordered, it would have been much better for them," the block leader shouted. "Their failure to follow directions has cost them dearly. Let this be a lesson to you. Follow your leaders regardless of the cost, and you will find life in Dachau Concentration Camp much easier."

Christian slipped back inside the door. He had gotten the message. He was better off to avoid these beasts who thrived on pain.

What have we done? Christian wondered. *All these men ever did was to speak their judgment that the Third Reich was politically wrong. For being true to our consciences, we have been subjected to hideous exercises in cruelty. The Reich will exist either by compliance or abuse.*

Reger shrunk back into the Pastors' Barracks, looking for a corner to hide in lest the block leader turn on him next. Hiding behind one of the large racks the men slept on, he remembered lines from the book of Revelation: "I know your tribulation and poverty . . . be faithful unto death, and I will give you a crown of life."

Bowing his head, Christian prayed in a whisper. "Lord, crown those hurting men out there in the dirt with your crown of life. They have earned the reward."

Three

Christian figured it had to be around August 29 or 30. The relentless sun hadn't let up, and each day proved to be like a walk over hot coals. Summer had to be coming to an end, and he was ready for fall to come. With a resolution that he had practiced throughout the hot months, he trudged back into the camp from his work assignment. Sandwiched in the midst of the prison crew, Reger knew all the men were too tired to say anything to one another. The prisoners hobbled along silently.

The camp buzzed with prisoners running back and forth, attempting to appear preoccupied lest some guard start beating them to increase their motivation. Reger had just stepped inside the barbed wire confines of the Dachau camp when he realized a group of guards were walking briskly in his direction. The guards had two prisoners in plain pants and shirts held between them. Although one of the prisoners had a moustache, both men's heads had been recently shaved, and they looked as forlorn as the rest of the camp. The guards kept pushing the prisoners to keep them at a brisk walk.

"Hey," someone behind Christian half-whispered. "That's

Dr. Alois Hundhammer, the Bavarian minister of agriculture. I heard the Nazis dragged him in here."

"Why?" Christian asked without turning his head.

"Don't know," the man behind Reger said. "Must have said the wrong thing."

The guards with the two prisoners continued trotting down the street until they were directly in front of Reger's unit.

"Stop!" the block leader demanded.

Guards and prisoners halted in front of Christian's squad. The field workers screeched to a stop. The two groups stared at each other.

"We have a little exercise for you men who have not yet done a decent day's work," the block leader said, pushing his two prisoners forward. "The camp's street needs to be rolled smooth before you are ready for supper."

Christian wasn't sure what the SS guard meant, but he studied the two prisoners in front of him. The man the guard called Hundhammer was taller than the second. His eyes had a hard, resolute look as if he would do whatever was commanded even if it killed him. The second man seemed more intimidated by the situation.

The block leader pointed with his riding crop to a large, heavy steel roller at the edge of the street. A long steel bar stuck straight out of the circular drum. It had metal handles welded to the bar. One look told Christian it would take a couple of draft horses to pull that monstrous roller down the streets.

"Our fine young prisoners are eager to help improve our camp," the SS guard continued. "Of course, they will need some assistance to push the roller up and down the street." The guard pointed his riding crop at Reger's unit. "We'll need a few of you men to help them." Suddenly he pounded his palm with the leather crop. "Fourteen of you prisoners get over here to pull this roller."

The field workers froze.

"Get over here *at once!*" The guard rushed toward the prisoners and began grabbing men. "We don't have all day!" He yanked Christian by the shirt and pulled him forward. "Get hold of those handles and start pushing."

The men picked up the heavy iron bar made for harnessing the roller to horses. Christian found himself pushing a handle across from the smaller of the two men. He glanced more closely at the man's face and thought the new prisoner had a regal bearing, but he didn't know him.

"Move it!" the guard screamed. "Push!"

Christian put his weight against the metal handle, but the roller barely moved. He heaved again, sensing that the men behind him were straining with all their might. Slowly the roller turned.

"Let's go!" the block leader kept shouting. "Now!" Other guards fell in alongside the prisoners, shouting, demanding, and striking the prisoners.

The roller began to creak forward. For what seemed like an eternity the team of inmates kept pushing the monstrous steel roller up and down the streets. Christian could see other prisoners watching them go by. They had looks of apprehension in their eyes. No one slacked lest they lose the momentum created by the roller's forward motion.

"I can't stand it any longer," one of the men gasped. "I'm going to fall."

"Get out of the way of the roller," someone warned.

The prisoner stumbled and fell out of the path of the roller, tumbling to the street in exhaustion.

"Slacker!" the block leader screamed as he started beating the man with his leather crop. "Take this fool away."

Christian pushed harder, and the roller kept moving. After fifteen minutes of the excruciating exercise, a few of the guards drifted away and the roller stopped. The prisoners tumbled to the ground, huffing and puffing, sweating in exhaustion.

Christian leaned over to the new prisoner. "Who are you?"

"Heinrich," the man barely spoke. "Dr. Heinrich Held. I was an engineer."

Reger pushed himself up from the ground. "Why did they arrest you?"

Dr. Held looked around carefully, making sure none of the guards were nearby. "My father was the prime minister of Bavaria." He stopped to gulp in more air. "He went into hiding, and the SS thought I knew where he was. Because I wouldn't tell them, they sent me here."

Christian nodded his head. "I see," he said slowly. "Most unfortunate."

"No! No. It would have been more unfortunate if they had caught him," Dr. Held said. "If I can help keep my father free, I will gladly take their punishment."

Christian nodded and stared at the steel roller. "Yeah. You've got to keep this place in context."

CHAPTER EIGHT

THE ROLL CALL—1942

One

The first of September lumbered in at the crack of dawn with the 6:00 morning roll call. Even though it was Sunday morning, the shrill wake-up whistle warned prisoners to line up on the square in front of all the bunkers. The entire camp would pay a heavy price for any missing men. Roll calls had lasted as long as seven hours at times when an unaccounted-for prisoner remained at large. The rumor was that on those unending days corpses had been carried away. These were exhausted men who died standing in line. Some prisoner couldn't get out of bed or had fallen ill, and that held up the tabulation.

If a prisoner couldn't be found quickly, the rest of them would stand in the blistering sun until the numbers were rectified or the missing were identified. No one wanted to endure such harsh punishment before being marched off to the difficult work assignments.

"Hurry up!" Dittner screamed at Reger. "We're losing precious time. Get out there in line before they start swinging clubs."

"Okay. Okay." Christian mumbled, pushing his clogs on. "I'm hurrying." He grabbed his cap to keep the sun off his head.

"You're not fast enough," Dittner griped, and he dashed out the door with Christian close behind him.

From all over the camp prisoners ran to assemble. Guards and the commandant were standing in front of the ranks, eyeing them critically as they stumbled into place. The quicker the head count was done, the better. Men pushed against one another, jockeying for the right position within their units. Each inmate snapped to attention, trying to look as innocuous as possible.

"Stand in straight lines!" the camp leader ordered. "All caps off!"

Reger snatched his cap from his head, and stiffened. Immediately guards started walking down the rows counting heads. Out of the corner of his eye, Christian recognized the block leader coming their way. Reger had seen him ordering prisoners to hit one another. Dittner had later reported the man was SS officer Otto Zorin, an officer to be watched. Today the SS officer was wearing black leather boots and one of the formal uniforms seen around the camp. Zorin's Luger pistol hung at his hip from a thick leather belt fastened around his waist. To Reger's surprise, the block leader seemed to stagger.

"Zorin's been drinking," Dittner whispered.

"At this hour?" Christian mumbled under his breath. "Isn't 6:00 rather premature?"

"I heard the man's a bad alcoholic. Guess it's not too early for him."

"Not a good sign." Christian stiffened.

SS officers kept running up and down the rows, counting every man. The guards trotted up to the block leader who in turn sent the exact count on to the commandant. The process continued on and on while the glaring sun began to bear down on the men. Clearly they would be subjected to extreme heat before long, but the SS officers kept the count running. Someone seemed to be missing. Zorin didn't look happy, but he kept pacing back and forth with wobbly steps. After an hour and a half of constant checking and rechecking, the exact correct count must have been achieved because the officers started releasing the men to return to their barracks.

For reasons that weren't clear, the unit of pastors and priests was not sent back. Keeping the clergy lined up by themselves was highly unusual. Reger glanced at Dittner. For once Dittner had a worried look on his face. The smug sense of knowing everything had vanished. As the other prisoners disappeared, Otto Zorin turned his full attention to the clergy.

"Well, well," Zorin began cynically. "Here we are on Sunday morning with this assortment of renegade holier-than-thou mindless villagers." His words slurred, but the SS officer didn't seem to care. "I thought you boys would like a little sermon from *me* this morning!" Zorin thumped on his chest.

The group maintained attention as if any movement might be interpreted as disapproval. Zorin began pounding his fist with his riding crop and sneering at the prisoners.

"Thought maybe I would preach a little sermon to you boys. You know. Get your minds straightened up; your thoughts clear. How does that sound to you altar boys?"

No one moved.

"Ah, come on," Zorin taunted. "Don't be afraid. If you want to speak back to me, I invite it. After all, I'm your friend."

The group almost quit breathing.

"I mean it," Zorin continued. "It's always good to have a little heart-to-heart talk with you clergy types."

Christian fastened his eyes on a flagpole off in the distance. He didn't want to allow any distractions to cause him to make a wrong move. No one could perceive what this camp leader was about today.

"Let's see." Zorin scratched his head. "Since it's Sunday maybe I should preach on the church. How about that? The church that you boys love so well." He strutted across the front of the group, talking with garbled words. "I believe that Jesus the Jew once said, 'Thou art Paul, and upon this rock will I build my church.' Isn't that your teaching? Come on, you Catholic priests! Isn't that where the indoctrination begins?" Zorin smiled at the men.

"No sir!" a Polish priest in the back row spoke up.

"What?" Zorin looked surprised and caught off guard. "What's wrong with what I said?" He sounded sincere.

"Jesus said, 'And I tell you, you are *Peter*, and on this rock I will build my church, and the powers of death shall not prevail against it,'" the priest replied in a matter-of-fact manner without relaxing his attention stance.

"Peter?" Zorin blinked several times and then suddenly flew into a rage. "Peter . . . Paul . . . they're all the same to me! You bunch of dunderheads! Fools! Idiots! You know nothing!" Zorin abruptly started laughing. "Whether that crazy rock was called Peter or Paul or Gerhard, we're going to blow that hunk of clay to pieces. Yes sir! The Reich is today our rock, and it will remain as hard as steel, crushing your little pebble to nothing. Hitler remains at the stern of our ship." He reeled backward.

The prisoners clenched their teeth, fearing that at any moment Zorin would charge into them, but the camp leader shifted, standing in front of them giggling.

"Peter . . . Paul . . . oh, that's a good one!" He turned around and started staggering toward the Jourhaus where the SS officers worked on the upper floor. His gait became even more unstable as he walked away. "Go home," he called over his shoulder. "Get lost."

The prisoners looked at one another, uncertain of what to do, but it appeared that this drunken fool had really dismissed them. Finally they started walking back to their barracks.

"The rotten man's an idiot," Dittner declared under his breath. "No one can come out here like a drunken sot and get away with behavior like that for long."

"I'm glad he didn't turn on us," Christian answered.

Two

Sundays were like any other day. The pace of another workday unfolded in its usual repetitive pattern. Leisure time seldom existed, but occasionally a few minutes could be snatched at the end of the day. The camp leaders never left time for the prisoners to rest or relax. The constant pressure pushed many of the men over the edge. Sometimes a prisoner would be found on the ground in front of the electric fences where he had been pushed beyond his capacities and had reached out and grabbed the charged wire.

Christian Reger's crew lined up and marched out to the fields with the usual stomping of their clogs to a cadence set by one of the guards. No one knew for sure what had happened with the drunken block leader Otto Zorin or whether the whole mess might turn into a trap for the prisoners. At least Zorin had disappeared, and nothing had happened to them. A good turn of events—and that was an encouragement.

Although September had come, the days were still long, hot, and arduous. Christian had learned that he must make his mind concentrate on the work. If he let his thoughts wander, he tended to think about Mina. Once he began reflecting on his wife, his thoughts spun out of control, taking a life of their own. In addition to making him homesick, Christian was in danger of making errors, slipping up, and that could be dangerous if a guard caught him in a mistake. Even when his assignment was no more than running back and forth with buckets of water on his back, Reger knew that to slip and spill water on the ground could be treated as a serious offense. He didn't want to think about the penalty.

By late afternoon the pace had slowed somewhat, and the guards didn't seem to be as watchful. Reger stopped by a group of priests to make sure they had a drink of water.

"Good brother," Fritz Seitz spoke quietly. "God bless you for this refreshment."

"Certainly," Christian answered, "but don't forget that they call me No. 26 661 if a guard sees us talking."

"Naturally, naturally," the priest gulped the water. "I can go on now. Thank God for this water."

Christian hobbled over to the next group of men and held out the buckets to them.

"You've saved us!" Heinrich Gruber gasped, and swallowed the water like a wild man. "Thank you. Thank you."

Christian nodded and kept watching the guards.

"We are going to worship together tonight," Gruber added, wiping his mouth. "That's the best part of Sunday."

"Of the week!" Christian added.

Other men crowded around, eagerly reaching for the ladle. The clergy prisoners encouraged one another with reassurances that they would worship together in a few hours.

"Immediately after supper," Gruber added. "Leonard Steinwender is our preacher tonight. I am sure he will have something important to say to us."

"Yes. Yes." The clergy sitting in the circle echoed their approval. "Definitely."

"Hurry up!" A guard snapped. "We don't have all day. Back to work!"

Christian nodded to the men and hurried to the next group. At least he had something to look forward to. In this camp a simple sermon held the promise of a night of enchantment.

Three

Sitting in the midst of prisoners eating furiously, while he nibbled on a small piece of black bread, Christian realized again how meager his rations were. Nothing could be done about the situation, and he certainly didn't want to say a word and be beaten or thrown into isolation. But the meals were so marginal that the prisoners would eventually be depleted of energy.

Christian knew that nothing in the concentration camp happened by chance. The Nazis knew exactly what they were doing, and a lack of energy also made it more difficult for the prisoners to be resistant. Everything was moving along just as SS leader Heinrich Himmler must have ordered.

Reger tried to savor the meager flavor from the hard black bread as long as possible, chewing carefully to make sure every particle of nutrition dissolved before washing it down with watery soup. No one talked while the men devoured their last meal of the day. Only the clank of metal bowls broke the silence.

"We must hurry back to the barracks," Dittner said in Christian's ear. "Worship will start quickly to make sure we have enough time before the entire camp is shut down for the night. Get with it! Lights go out at 9:00."

Christian nodded. Of course he knew! How could he not be aware of the time schedule. Dittner remained the master of the obvious.

"I need this service tonight," Dittner stood up. "A spiritual shot in the arm keeps me going in this hellhole."

"The same is true for all of us," Christian answered. "Worship is vital to our existence."

Dittner nodded. "I will meet you in the chapel." He hurried away.

Christian watched Dittner march out of the mess hall like a man who owned the camp. If the Nazis ever noticed his defiant gait, they might grind him under their heel, but Wilhelm Dittner appeared to get away with the insolence . . . at least for the moment. Christian took his utensils back to the service window and followed Dittner back to the barracks.

By the time he arrived, pastors and priests had already packed the room. The sun hung on the horizon, providing adequate light for the small room. Men kept moving around to make sure everyone got into the small space. Christian wound his way through the group until he found a spot next to the back wall. More men appeared, and the area directly behind the chapel room filled as well.

Five minutes later the crowd divided, allowing the pastor to walk into the inner area. A tall man, Leonard Steinwender always carried himself with dignity. Even though his threadbare prison uniform appeared dirty and tattered, he walked in with such stateliness that the German preacher might have been walking down the aisle of a cathedral. Immediately a hush settled over the room.

Leonard found a place near the front corner of the room, allowing the men to stand closely around him. Bowing his head, he prayed silently for several moments.

"My brothers in Christ," Steinwender began slowly, "in our hearts we thank God for giving us this time to praise and worship Him." Leonard glanced toward the door. "Please make sure all is secure and safe as tonight we will have a Scripture reading."

A murmur of understanding ran through the group. A hidden Bible appeared out of nowhere, and a reading followed. One of the priests edged his way to the front of the group and started to read the tattered Bible. "Looking to Jesus the pioneer and perfecter of our faith, who for the joy that was set before him endured the cross, despising the shame, and is seated at the right hand of the throne of God. Consider him who endured from sinners such hostility against himself, so that you may not grow weary or fainthearted."

The priest stopped and looked slowly around the room at

the thin faces. "The Word of the Lord," he said, and faded back into the group of men. "Thanks be to God," the clergy responded collectively in a hushed murmur.

Steinwender stepped forward, stretching to his full height. "My friends," he began in a low bass voice, "when I hear this passage I behold a mystery and a model. Truly it is a mystery why innocent people are forced to endure such pain in this world. Good people are ground under the heel of oppressors because they spoke a simple word of truth. With God sitting in heaven watching over His universe in love, we must struggle to understand such a mystery. However, the Scriptures offer us a model for survival during these times. 'Consider him who endured from sinners such hostility against himself,' the writer of Hebrews declares. Jesus Christ remains our model for living through difficult days."

"Yes! Yes!" echoed around the room. Christian felt warmth rising from deep within. The word of Scripture had found a powerful affirmation with what the preacher was saying. A new sense of encouragement welled up within him.

"My brothers in Christ," Steinwender continued, "this model we find in our Lord encourages us to see a powerful truth. The cross of Christ transforms the meaning of our suffering. Experiences that are so painful can be corrected and even changed through what Jesus did on the cross. He offers us the strength we need to endure."

Again affirmations rose from the crowd. Reger glanced around. It was not the habit of the Roman Catholics to shout "amens," but obviously these priests and pastors were starving for what they were hearing.

"Each of us understands how easy it is to succumb to hate," Leonard continued. "Whether it is political or personal, everyone knows how easy it is to allow ourselves to be sucked into the vortex of evil, but the cross of Christ calls us to follow an alternative." Steinwender raised his fist straight up toward the ceiling. "Let evil be transformed!"

The clergy started clapping, confirming his statements. Someone yelled a long 's-s-s-sh!' to quiet the group, and the uproar died down.

"We must remember that the truth of Christ corrects error," Leonard said. "Veracity redeems rather than coerces, and in that sense God's truth ultimately transforms even the worst errors that humanity can commit." His voice lowered to nearly a whisper. "Love finally conquers hate."

Silence fell over the room. The men stared as if they wanted to believe what they had heard, but under the circumstances the idea seemed almost incomprehensible.

"Like the victims of war in Leo Tolstoy's *War and Peace*, our courage and loyalty only seem to deliver us into the hands of blind and destructive forces. Nevertheless, when with all the integrity of our souls, we dare to hurl ourselves into a battle that we cannot win, but is worthy of the fight, we will find in the end that the war was worth everything it cost us. We may die, but the truth will finally redeem all error!"

No one spoke. Silence gripped the men as they devoured

the message as if they were dining at an elegant banquet. Christian was deeply moved.

"How do I know this is true?" Steinwender asked. "Because I have considered Him who endured from sinners such hostility against himself." He nodded his head several times as if to underline the truth. "God created us to be in partnership with Him, to be full partners. Our suffering confirms that we have accepted this agreement. Can there be a higher calling?"

Christian felt tears welling up in his eyes. For reasons that exceeded his ability to grasp what he had heard, Reger saw his imprisonment in a different light. The struggle, the pain, the agony had a point far exceeding anything he had recognized before. Christian found himself stretching to stand taller.

"In the midst of this mystery forced upon us, the model which Christ offers will keep us from growing weary or fainthearted," Leonard said. "This passage tells us not to regard lightly the discipline of the Lord because He chastens those whom He loves. Even though the bite of the lash is severe, we must remember that we are dear to His heart because our Lord has led us to attend the graduate school of suffering."

Christian nodded. Surely these men were part of one of the most hideous abuses of power in human history. But Leonard had reached into the Scriptures and offered them a reason to endure these circumstances. He had offered something new and powerful to hang on to.

"My brothers," Leonard concluded, "light has come to dispel the darkness. We must put hate away and walk in the light."

Across the room "amens" resounded. Prayers began to break out among the prisoners. Some of the men offered names of individuals; others lifted up circumstances. Outside the chapel door the prayers rumbled down the hall. Voices blended together in a symphony of intercession, each man asking God's help in his struggles. Finally the fervor died out and the prayers stopped. The men turned to one another, hugging and blessing one another for what they had experienced.

"Let us go in peace," Leonard Steinwender finally said, and then he dismissed the prisoners.

The men shuffled out of the room back into the barracks. When Leonard walked by, Christian patted him on the back. Still lingering by the door, Reger watched the men climbing into the bunks. The first of September had been a hot day, filled with hostility, trials, and circumstances that only a believer could interpret as the discipline of God to train them to know His love more profoundly. And yet, tonight he could close his eyes and know it had been a good day. A good day in which he had experienced unexpected meaning. Tonight he could crawl into his bunk sandwiched among the prisoners, close his eyes, and remember that Jesus Christ had also endured such hostility.

Four

Two weeks later block leader SS officer Otto Zorin disappeared from the camp. The alcoholic never returned.

CHAPTER NINE

PREY FOR THE BEAST—1942

One

"Things are changing," Dittner puffed, as the group trotted down the bunker.

"Ah, but the autumn weather is such a relief from the death summer!" Christian panted.

"Not just the weather—look around you."

Christian took a quick glance at the barracks and the streets that led off the bunker. Everywhere, men were milling around or working tightly together. Many of them were wearing civilian clothes, not striped prison uniforms.

"A lot of people died last summer," Dittner explained, and he nodded in the direction of the infirmary. "But for everyone who died, two more came in. Things are not going so good with the war."

"Company halt!" The SS guard stopped the convoy of men. In the center of the assembly ground, a large pile of clothing in all shapes and sizes was strewn on the ground.

The prisoners could even see some women's and children's clothes in the pile. The guard walked here and there among the items, picking up a few pieces that caught his attention. Satisfied, he ordered, "All right, get what you want."

The prisoners leaped into the pile of clothing, grabbing anything that looked warm and durable. Even though the memory of summer heat hung in their minds, every man knew how quickly the temperature could drop.

"Where did all this stuff come from?" a new prisoner with the criminal's patch on his shirt asked.

"Where do you think?" Christian answered sarcastically.

"Auschwitz—Buchenwald—the castle at Linz," Dittner snapped.

"Humph!" the man grunted without comprehension.

Smiles broke out everywhere as the men recognized the vast improvement in their appearance. Some of the clothing was of good quality and condition, but as the men explored their new clothes, the mood slowly changed.

"What a wool coat!" exclaimed Christian, tucking his hands into the pockets and feeling the thickness of the material. At the bottom his fingers found something.

"Look at this!" Dittner pulled out ticket stubs to a theater in Prague.

Christian produced an old tram ticket from a train in Budapest.

Other men began to hold up pictures of children or letters that had been hastily scribbled on the backs of envelopes. Knowing glances were exchanged, but nothing more was said. They picked what they knew they needed and got back in line.

"My, my," Dittner remarked as he folded the coat over his arm. "What a clever way to economize on prison uniforms."

"Move on," the guard demanded. "Others need their turn here. Get on to the mess hall."

"Things are changing," Dittner insisted as they stepped into line. "Notice the food today."

Christian extended his bowl to receive his meal. Having worked in the food lines, he had a keen eye about food quality. "There seems to be a little more here."

"Ya," Dittner smiled. "Slowly but surely, they have been adding a little more to the soup."

"I'm not getting fat. What do you make of it?"

"Well, they're not giving us much more, but there is increased nourishment. It confirms my suspicions." Dittner sat down on the ground with his bowl carefully balanced so that not a drop would be lost.

"And?"

"They've given me a new job." He pointed with his thumb toward a long factory building far beyond the other side of the fence. "I'm to work on electric cables for Messerschmitt engines. This isn't any of that dirt-moving nonsense. I'm going to be doing serious production."

"So?"

"Ever since we've been here, they've obviously been trying to kill us. Now, they're changing their direction. They really want us to produce." He leaned over to whisper, "I've discovered that the SS is even going to allow us to receive food parcels."

"Really!" Christian scraped the bottom of his bowl an extra time.

"Now, here's the clincher. The radios tell us the army attacked Stalingrad and lost. Even the propaganda line isn't able to explain the trouble on the Russian front. As best we can tell, the Allies have either taken Italy or are about to."

"Are you sure of this?"

"Absolutely!" Dittner glanced around once more. "It adds up. At first, we were garbage to them; now, the able-bodied are needed for production. So they will feed us better."

Christian watched the smoke drift across the camp toward the river. "All this may be good news, and then again it may not."

"Why?" Dittner grunted.

"They may fatten us up a bit, but if the war goes badly, we may be the first to go."

"Ah ha!" Dittner laughed cynically and slapped him on the back. "You have learned to think like a prisoner and a survivor! I'm proud of you. Dachau has taught you something."

Reger stood up and said nothing.

"Mark my words," Dittner predicted as they walked along. "They'll be finding you a new job. Political prisoners have more value to them than the convicts and the Jews."

As they started across the assembly ground, a group of prisoners crossed in front of them pushing wooden carts covered with heavy cloth. Here and there a leg or arm was sticking out.

Grabbing the arm of one of the cart pushers, Dittner demanded, "What is this all about?"

"A transport train just came in from Duisburg. They didn't make it."

Refusing to let go of his sleeve, Dittner persisted. "Look at the size of this load! What happened?"

The prisoner leaned toward him and said, "They were locked in for weeks without food. Some parts of these bodies have been gnawed right down to the bone!"

Dittner dropped the sleeve and the subject. The prisoner hurried to catch up with the cart as it turned toward the crematoriums. Christian felt his body become rigid and his stomach flinch.

"Some things have not changed much," he said.

Two

"Prisoner No. 26 661 reporting for new assignment, sir."

Drawing himself to his full six feet, the young man standing in front of Christian was almost visibly flexing his muscles. Surely, he couldn't be much more than twenty-two or twenty-three, because there was still a soft boyishness about his face. He adjusted his belt and coat buttons in a calculated manner.

"I am Lieutenant Herman Boye, and I will not tolerate any inefficiency." He walked slowly around his new assignee as if he were a general inspecting a private. Obviously, he was

Aryan down to his toenails—the blond-haired, blue-eyed sort of youth that Hitler idealized.

"You are an enemy of the government, the people, our Fuhrer. In former times, people like you didn't live long. Indeed, you should consider yourself fortunate that you were not shot after your arrest."

He stopped abruptly and stared at the prisoner as if expecting confirmation. No. 26 661 nodded slightly.

"But you are even less," Boye snorted contemptuously. "You are one of the narrow-minded preachers who make people stupid. You are a teacher of nonsense." After a pause, he asked, "Don't you have anything to say?" His thin lips were tight and smirking. With his feet at parade rest, he turned sideways so that he wouldn't even have to look at Christian.

"I'm, ah, not sure what you mean." Prisoner No. 26 661 tried to sound apologetic even though his response implied a challenge.

The lieutenant seemed delighted to have further opportunity to lecture. "Take the so-called Sermon on the Mount with its teaching of turning the other cheek." When he turned back and pointed at Christian, it was obvious that his white, manicured hands had never seen physical labor. "Between you and the Jews, the whole nation has suffered the humiliation of being made poor at the hands of our enemies! Now National Socialism has risen up with power to crush any who oppose or hinder us!"

Through the office window, No. 26 661 could see about fifteen Jewish-looking prisoners harnessed together behind wooden poles and chains pulling huge rollers down the street. The first snow had already started to accumulate. Normally, it would take at least two strong horses to pull such rollers. As the exhausted men strained forward, the SS guards and *capos* yelled and cracked leather whips above the prisoners' heads.

"I will not tolerate any sloth or distractions in this office!" the guard threatened.

Reger's mind snapped back. He realized he had lost the drift of the lecture and wasn't sure what his response should be. "You will be a clerk here, and I expect you to expend the same energy you would in the fields. This office is no vacation."

Christian surveyed the door and the windows. No snow was blowing in here, and there were stoves at both ends of the room. "All of the salaries are prepared in these offices, so your work is of some value. You should be grateful to us."

His mind started to wander again. He felt guilty for thanking God for not being on the rollers or out in the fields like the other men were. On the other hand, just being in such a warm room might make all the difference in getting through another winter. He had developed a habit of praying about such things, but he wasn't sure what was right under these circumstances.

"When you come to appreciate what National Socialism has brought to our fatherland, you may be of service to your country again." The boy officer stood with his arms crossed, his starched, straight stance and leather riding boots making him look like the master of all destiny. "Your attitude in this office will be carefully observed and your repentance noted."

Once more, No. 26 661 nodded humbly. This was indeed an odd scenario, as if he were a child caught in sin being sent for penance to an unrelenting priest. Christian knew he must not provoke any confrontations.

"You are seeing a rare lesson in courage these days," Boye continued. "On all sides are men who will gladly die for their convictions. Observe us Nazis well! We can teach you about the power of faith."

No. 26 661 stared straight ahead without emotion.

"All my life I have watched men like you, men like my father. You were weaned on worry; worry about money, worry about the French, worry about the British, worry about the Communists. I grew up surrounded by doubt and fear. He used to rub his rosary beads like they were Aladdin's lamp, but nothing ever happened."

Christian shifted his weight.

"But when Hitler came, the worry and the want stopped! *Der Fuhrer* has given my generation hope. I am not like my father because I know the future. It belongs to us. It belongs to *me!*"

Leaning into Christian's face, his blue eyes narrowed. "You can't understand that, can you? Well, you will come to see that we are right because we are superior. Because we believe in ourselves, we will prevail. We are invincible."

Pleased with this beginning, the lieutenant swaggered back to his desk. "Someone will be here shortly to tell you what to do. Sit down and be quiet until we call for you."

Reger took a chair against the wall and realized again how warm the room was. No amount of verbal abuse could be compared to the work outside.

Yes, he thought to himself, *even a puffed-up toad like Herman Boye can be easily tolerated in a room with a stove.*

Three

"Did I not tell you they would give you a new assignment?" Dittner smacked his lips as he tried to use some restraint in gulping down the soup.

"I may even survive this job," Christian mused as he drank his broth slowly. "I'm a payroll clerk for the SS now."

"That's good. Your placement could be of some help to us. But don't underestimate what they will do if you make any mistakes."

"So?" Christian knew how unnecessary the question was.

"Fanaticism has no limits." Dittner set his bowl on the ground. "I saw it again today in the factory."

Reger eyed him as if he didn't really want to hear the story. "A young Russian, an excellent worker, was assigned to our detail. We all liked him because he had a good sense of humor. Well, as a little joke on one of the men, he incorrectly connected a cable to the engine."

"And they caught him?"

"There had been two cases of sabotage and they blamed

everything on him. As we left the factory, they had us watch as they hung him by the neck from one of the gables."

"My, my, but these Nazis are certainly brave men."

"Now, Reger, let me warn you about something that will help you keep your mouth shut and do your work right. Have you heard of Dr. Claus Schilling or Dr. Sigmund Rascher?"

Christian thought for a second. "No, I don't think I've ever heard of them."

"As you work in the office," Dittner instructed, "watch for their names. They are the doctors doing experiments on infirmary patients."

"What have you learned?" Reger stirred uncomfortably.

"Some of the Polish priests have learned that they are using mostly Russians and Poles for their experiments. A Pole told me that they are injecting them with a serum that causes them to become very sick; many have died. Some of the men believe the illness to be malaria, but that isn't the worst part."

"I don't want to know any more." Reger stood to leave. "Enough is enough. I don't want to hear it."

"You must!" Dittner hung on to his sleeve. "None of us may survive this place, but if anyone does, we must not forget anything that happened here. We must remember everything that these maniacs have done."

Christian started to turn away, but then shrugged his shoulders. "All right, what else are they doing?"

"They are dropping men into big basins filled with freezing salt water," Dittner whispered. "Then they try to warm them up to see what happens when people are freezing to death. Most die in convulsions immediately after the experiment."

"How did you find this out?"

"It is hard to muffle screams of pain. But what's important is word has slipped out that Schilling and Rascher are in charge of these debacles. So, watch for their names in the SS office."

Reger nodded his head mechanically.

"Oh, yes, if you ever see either of them, snap to attention and salute. Failure to treat them with respect can get you a free trip to the laboratory."

"All right, all right," Christian acknowledged. "Let's get back to the barracks."

As they walked along, Dittner observed, "Have you noticed that there are no birds at Dachau?"

"Ya. I've not seen a bird since I came."

"Years ago, this place was a veritable bird sanctuary, but when the smoke began going up, all the birds left." He stopped and pointed ahead. "Look! New prisoners are coming in!"

A new group was moving toward the Jourhaus to be processed.

"I know that man!" Christian exclaimed as he and Dittner got a closer look. "That's Dr. Hermann Hesse! He's a dear friend!"

"Don't yell, for God's sake," Dittner warned. "We'll all be in trouble."

"Dr. Hesse was one of the original signers of the Barmen Confession. He is a key leader in the Confessing Church."

"I know, I know."

"Look! That's his son Helmut coming through the gate. See how sick and weak he looks."

Dittner had already started to drop back.

"We must welcome these men," Christian said, trying to wave inconspicuously. "The first hours here are always depressing and hard to bear."

Again Christian tried to get their attention, but when he looked around, Dittner had disappeared.

That night Reger found Dr. Hesse in the back of the Pastors' Barracks. His shaved head, dejected face, and ragged prison uniform made him look like a bundle of misery.

"Dr. Hesse," Christian addressed him respectfully.

The old man looked up and blinked several times as if he were bringing a faraway object into focus.

"Brother Reger!" he exploded. "Brother Reger!" Leaping up like a spry athlete, he grabbed Christian and began hugging him. "Brother Reger! Brother Reger!" he kept saying.

"How can I possibly welcome you to such a place as this?" Christian apologized.

"Ah, it is exactly as in the words of the apostle Paul, 'My beloved friend, whom I long for, my joy, my crown, stand firm in the Lord.'"

"I want you to know that you are among many brothers here. We even have a wonderful bond with the Catholics. I want to introduce you to many of these wonderful men who are my friends."

Dr. Hesse smiled and said, "Oh, I know we are never abandoned. Indeed, even the apostles are a part of this fellowship of suffering. Such pain makes us their contemporaries and they ours."

"Oh, you will do well." Christian shook his hand. "You already know the secret of survival that many others here have found. I want you to meet Karl Leisner. He hopes to be ordained as a priest. His faith will encourage you."

They managed to laugh and shook hands once more.

"I fear most for my son, Helmut. He is very weak. Though I am an old man, my health is much better than his."

Christian immediately began the orientation ritual, warning Dr. Hesse especially about the infirmary. He also told him about the chapel and their worship services. "You held out a long time," he told Hermann. "How did you keep from being arrested?"

"Because my other two sons and their brother-in-law joined the army, they left us alone. The boys struggled very hard about this matter. None of us felt we should fight for Hitler and were all deeply troubled. Finally, Theodore and Friederich decided the Bible taught they should support the state, so they joined."

"Such decisions are very difficult."

"And now they are both gone." Hermann's voice trailed off. "Theodore died in 1941, and we received word about Friederich earlier this year."

"May God comfort you."

"There is nothing to be said," Hermann said with a quick gesture meant to end any further inquiries and at the same time reassure Christian that he had been consoled. "They were fine Christian men, and God has rewarded their faith.

"I want you to know that none of us has shrunk back," he continued. "Helmut has preached astonishing sermons. Even after his brothers' deaths, he accused National Socialism of being a modern Ahab that has turned God's vineyard into a cabbage patch."

"They sent you here because of that sermon?" Christian probed.

"No, there were two other things that finally got us arrested." Hermann stared out the window as if somewhere on the horizon he were replaying a scene from his life. As he looked at that imaginary drama, his body seemed to become more erect and strong. "We would do the same again tomorrow!" Hermann said defiantly.

"First, we declared our solidarity with the Jewish people and tried to protect them. Did you notice the big book Helmut brought into the camp?" Hermann asked. "That is a Hebrew Bible. Helmut carries a Torah to show our oneness with all Jews."

"I am amazed that the SS did not take it away from him," Christian observed. "They probably didn't understand what it was and overlooked it. Perhaps it was God's timing."

"God's timing? Ya," Hermann declared, shaking his finger. "Even in the worst circumstances, I have known God's timing. Indeed, preaching about His timing is the other reason they arrested us. Our town of Elberfeld was bombed in a terrible air raid. The next day we held worship services and told the people that the devastation was God's judgment on us for the Nazis' crimes against the Jews."

"I'm sure your arrest came swiftly after that!"

"Oh, yes. The police inspector told us that we should be put to the wall and shot, but I would not recant."

His voice fell, and the strong emotion was gone. "They put us in solitary confinement for five months with very little food. That is where Helmut became so weak.

"When they arrested us, they took away our Bibles," Dr. Hesse continued. "So Helmut and I began to write the Bible from memory on scraps of paper. We were able to smuggle these verses from cell to cell throughout the prison. Once more, God's timing was not thwarted by evil men."

"Ah, Hermann, you are indeed a faithful man," Christian said.

"After three months, they returned our Greek and Hebrew Bibles. I tell you that it made me rejoice with the psalmist: 'I am jubilant over thy promise like a man carrying off much booty.'"

"You have an amazing knowledge of the Scriptures,"

Christian complimented. "You will be of great help to the men here."

"If that is true," he said, grinning and patting Reger's knee, "then once again we have another example of God's timing!

"You know, Christian," Hermann added, "our case went to the highest authorities. Because of the deaths of my sons and my signing of the Barmen Confession, Himmler himself reviewed our files and personally ordered us to Dachau. So you see, we were able to make our witness felt at the very top."

"Nazis at every level of authority have heard the witness of the Confessing Church," Christian said thoughtfully. "God will hold every one of them accountable for all we have seen and heard."

Hermann nodded his head, once graced with magnificent white hair, and looked down at the pitiful rags he was wearing. "This hour is not important, but the day of His judgment and the time of His choosing will be. The Nazis cannot escape any more than did our village of Elberfeld. His timing cannot be defied."

Four

Had it not been for the celebration of the mass in the barracks chapel, Christmas Day at Dachau would have been only another twenty-four hours of work and exhaustion. Poignant thoughts of home, family, and congregations pressed in upon the men much like the overcrowding. Each wanted the other to be a representation of someone back home who might be praying for him that night.

Leonard Steinwender opened the worn little Bible and turned to the second chapter of Matthew's Gospel. He began to read of the escape to Egypt of Joseph, Mary, and the baby Jesus. "That it might be fulfilled which was spoken of the Lord by the prophet, saying, 'Out of Egypt have I called My Son,'" he concluded, gently closing the book. "Two things are clear here," Leonard shared in a quiet but fervent voice. "Since this first escape, the child of God has always been in danger in the world."

Immediately, heads nodded to one another. He continued talking of the ongoing battle with the evil dragon, then changed direction.

"Second, we can rejoice that the child of God is always saved! Let us never forget that Christ endured the grave; He has overcome this world. Jesus has said to us, 'My peace I give to you.'

"My friends, we shall be a part of the victory of Christ, and we must see our own exile in that light!" His words were swift, and they crackled with joyous energy. At the sermon's close, the pastors knelt on the rough floor to pray. They pleaded for their families and congregations. They prayed aloud for one another and for those in the infirmary lest they be snatched away by the transports.

As Christian's knees bore into the planks, a wonderful discovery began to unfold. He longed for the faces of the people of his parish. By praying for them, it was as though he once again could visit in their homes and hug their children. His prayers had become his ministry again, and once more he was their pastor. He prayed earnestly for their health, their steadfastness, and that the peace of Christ would be real to them.

And he prayed for Mina. She probably was by herself, and he was crammed into a room with many men. Yet they were both utterly alone. He could see her sitting at the kitchen table in their little house, her silhouette illumined by the glow of the fireplace. And his longing to be with her became almost too great to bear.

Reaching deep into the language of the Spirit, Christian asked that the promise of comfort be fulfilled for Mina. Almost audibly, he pleaded for the gifts of peace and forbearance to be given to her. Then warmth began to well up inside him as if to guarantee that the bridge of prayer had crossed the barbed wire and the miles. He knew that he had given her the best gift he could offer on this Christmas.

Slowly but with increasing intensity, emotion swept over him and he began to weep. The sadness, the heaviness, the cruelty seemed to be pouring out through his eyes. Emptiness, loneliness, bitterness seemed to be streaming down his cheeks. For reasons he could not name, he felt the tears dropping on his folded hands.

Yet it seemed that any hate and resentment inside him was being washed away. The more he cried, the more he prayed; and the more he prayed, the more he cried. At the end, he could not believe that he was actually praying for the *capos*, for the guards, and even for Emmerich Ost, the camp commandant. To his own amazement, he was praying that their evil deeds would be forgiven.

He didn't know how he could pray such a thing! It was as though the Holy Spirit had taken over his prayers and was guiding them as He directed. The whole room seemed to glow with peace and goodness.

As Christian rose from his knees, he realized that he had come into this little chapel with animosity, resentment, and hatred. The environment of evil had splashed more of its mud and filth on him than he imagined. Yet now he felt bathed, clean, and fresh inside.

They cannot make me hate, he thought as he wiped his eyes. *They cannot make me be like them! This place cannot keep me from the joy of Christ.* The words and melody of the first hymn of the evening came back once more. "O Thou loving Jesus Christ, source thou art of all heaven's bounty." He reached out spontaneously to embrace the prisoner standing next to him.

"Peace be unto you," he whispered. "God has given us His own gifts this Christmas. We are under His special care."

CHAPTER TEN

THE DRAGON ATTACKS

One

As 1942 drew to a close, the number of clergymen at Dachau kept increasing. Space became a critical problem when all the pastors interned at the Sachsenhausen-Oranienburg Concentration Camp were transferred to Dachau. Trains rolled in with hundreds of Polish priests who were sent to the Pastors' Barracks. Number 26 became so packed that men slept nearly piled on top of one another. Even though the cramped sleeping arrangements made it difficult to rest, being crammed together like sardines helped keep the inmates warm. Still, Barracks No. 26 had reached saturation where lack of space made it nearly impossible for prisoners to function.

"Watch out!" a prisoner shouted from near the front door. "Guards are coming!"

Christian had barely crawled out of the rack, but he knew nothing good happened when camp guards showed up at such an early hour.

Dittner grabbed his arm. "Pay careful attention. The SS may be searching for something."

"Like what?" Christian asked.

"Who knows? The block leader might be trying to set somebody up. You can't tell."

Christian pushed his clogs on and brushed his hair back, trying to look as anonymous as possible.

"*Achtung!*" an SS guard demanded as he rushed into the barracks.

The men stumbled into one another, attempting to line up properly, but crowding had become so intense that they couldn't form distinguishable lines. The prisoners ended up huddled together like apples in a box.

More guards poured into the unit. Finally a heavy-set man whom Christian had not seen before walked in. The guards saluted him. Obviously well-fed, the man appeared to be in control of the situation. Christian guessed he might be the new block leader who had replaced Otto Zorin. Without saying a word, he stomped down the length of the barracks before returning to the front.

"*Kommen Sie hier!*" the fat officer demanded. One of the SS guards hurried to speak with him.

Christian watched the two men whisper to each other before the new functionary disappeared out the front door.

"Okay!" the remaining guard shouted. "All non-Germans out! If you are Dutch, Polish, Belgian, whatever, I order you to move to Block 28!"

A low level of grumbling echoed across the barracks. Clearly the prisoners who had come to Dachau most recently didn't like what they were hearing.

"There's no chapel in 28," Dittner told Christian. "These men are being pushed into a barracks where all religious practice is forbidden."

"Do they know that?" Christian asked.

"I doubt it," Dittner whispered. "They would really scream if they knew."

"Hurry up!" the SS guard demanded. "We cannot tolerate any delay." He clapped his hands. "Leave breviaries, rosaries, any religious objects!"

"No!" a prisoner sounded.

Immediately a guard in the middle of the barracks rushed toward the reply and started swinging in every direction. Prisoners fell right and left.

"Anyone else want to argue with me?" the leader yelled back.

Silence settled over the barracks. No one moved.

"As I said, all religious objects are to be left here!" The guard snapped his fingers. "Move it!"

The prisoners began shuffling silently toward the door.

"I guess this will help our overcrowding problem," Dittner said cynically.

"I don't like it," Christian said. "These men have a right to be here near the chapel."

"Not now, they don't," Dittner answered. "No one has any rights in this place. We exist at the whim of the Nazis. For whatever reason, they've decided that all non-Germans are leaving this area. That's it!"

Christian watched the exiting prisoners file silently past him. They looked angry and confused, but they had learned to say nothing if they wanted to survive. Carrying virtually nothing, the Polish clergy nodded at their friends and walked out. In a few minutes the overcrowded barracks had been reduced to a more manageable level. Christian shook his head, and went back to getting ready for another day of work.

"I'm not sure what's going on," Dittner said, "but being German must still amount to something. We've lucked out because of our race."

"Racism is *racism!*" Reger snapped. "I don't want any privileges because of where I was born."

"In this hole I'll take whatever I can get," Dittner shot back, then walked off.

The next few days added another dimension to the early morning experience. Guards returned with a small detail of prisoners and demanded that they paint over the windows in the chapel. Non-Germans would not be permitted even to look into the chapel from the outside. The Gestapo intended to tighten all the screws down as far as they could twist. Non-Germans got the treatment first.

Even though all clergy were forbidden to be in the chapel except at scheduled worship times, occasionally the men slipped in if someone was watching outside to warn if a guard showed up. One evening Christian glanced around the barracks and felt secure enough to steal inside. Standing next to the door, he studied the scene.

Pushed together to make an altar, two small tables had two sheets spread over the top to serve as a parament. In the center of the makeshift altar a small crucifix stood auspiciously, a blend of pain and splendor. At each end of the altar, two cheap candles sat in tiny candle holders. A miniature chalice sparkled in the center of the table—the only symbol of beauty in the entire camp. From somewhere a missal had appeared, and it lay next to the chalice.

The small room appeared barren, sparse, anything but elegant. Even the little altar seemed to be more like what youth might have assembled in a camp or out in the trees during the summer. But the longer Christian studied the humble space, the more he saw. For whatever reasons, the commandant had allowed the Roman Catholics to build this chapel, but the Gestapo had no idea how effectively these simple symbols sustained the prisoners. Each time holy Communion was celebrated, the power of Christ filled the men, offering hope and strength for them to continue in their struggle. The existence of this chapel denied everything that the Gestapo stood for.

The longer Christian studied the little area, the more meaning he saw hidden in the cracks of the wood and the shadows. Undoubtedly the Last Supper of Jesus with His disciples had occurred in a room far more like this barracks chapel than in a huge cathedral draped in tapestry and gold ornaments. The simplicity of the setting spoke of Christians assembling through the centuries in bare, tiny rooms, seeking to be sustained by the life of Christ. He could genuinely thank God for providing this wonderful setting.

Christian turned to leave, but he looked back one more time. He wanted to burn this sight into his mind so that on the day he died, this one memory would be before his eyes. In the humiliation of this death camp, the humility of Christ had lifted believers out of the ashes and held them high so the light of heaven could shine on them.

Two

While the structure of the Roman Catholic Church gave the priests an edge on the rest of the prisoners, they also bore the worst of Nazi attacks when the SS officers were offended about something. Often no one knew what set off the explosion, but the blasts were always devastating. Most of the time the Nazis and the Roman Catholic cardinals played a game of chess with each other. Clearly the stakes were high, and the odds were uncertain.

Christian had returned to the camp at midday to pick up more water buckets for the men in the field when an uproar broke out near the train docks. When new loads of prisoners came in, they were processed from this area. Christian could hear shouts and jeers that meant something was going on.

Adjusting the buckets on his shoulders so he would appear busy, Christian hurried down the central corridor, turning left when he reached the Jourhaus where the prison administrators worked. He slowed his pace to leave the impression that the empty buckets might be filled with something.

"Get those swine in here," an SS guard kept screaming.

The arriving prisoners stumbled out of the freight cars, lining up in front of the docks. The bright sunlight stunned them. They had no idea what was happening.

"Hurry!" the guards kept screaming. "Move it." German Shepherd police dogs snapped at the men.

The new prisoners inched forward, but they looked dazed in the bright sunlight. The men pressed against one another to avoid the snarling dogs. An older man looked as if he had been wearing a clerical collar, but it had been torn away. He still had on a black suit.

Suddenly a guard jerked the man out of line and threw him to the ground. "What are you doing?" the guard demanded and kicked the man in the stomach. "Trying to sneak in here?"

The prisoner writhed in pain on the concrete. He kept holding a hand on his stomach.

"I think we've found another one of those priests!" the guard shouted. He reached down and jerked something out of the man's pocket. "We certainly have!"

The man rolled over and tried to get up on his knees, but Christian could see that the wind had been kicked out of the man, and he kept coughing and choking.

"Let's see what I can find in that black coat." The guard started rummaging through the man's pockets. "Look-ee here!" He jerked out an object.

Trying to get to his feet, the priest reached out to grab whatever it was the guard had taken from him. The SS guard punched him in the face, sending him back to the ground.

"Hey!" the SS guard shouted to the other watchmen. "Come over here, and see what I've got!"

Christian hung back, lest he get caught up in the pushing and shoving. He didn't want anybody misinterpreting what he was doing, but at the same time, he wanted to see what would happen to the priest. Several other guards hustled over to look at the man on the ground.

"What's your name?" the SS officer growled.

"Seitz," the priest puffed. "Franz Seitz."

"Where are you from, Seitz?" the guard demanded.

"Palatinate." Once more Seitz got to his feet.

The SS guard turned to the other sentinels now standing around him. "I found this little trinket in his pocket." He held up a rosary.

Christian watched the priest reach out feebly for the chain and cross. The man had already experienced so much pain that he knew to be cautious. When the guard pulled away, the priest quickly withdrew his hand.

"We have here one Father Franz Seitz," the guard continued. "A real old-fashioned country gentleman. Franz, can you run?"

The older man looked up with a bewildered stare, shaking his head.

"Oh, come on," the guard mocked him. "Let's give it a try. Take a little trot down the walk. I'll help you." He reached over and placed the rosary around Seitz's forehead. "Run!" the guard screamed and whacked him on the shoulders with his club.

Seitz stumbled forward. The rosary slipped down around his ears; the cross fell over his nose. He nearly slipped but managed to stay on his feet. Trying to keep from falling or getting hit again, he started running.

"Get 'im!" a guard yelled. "Keep him moving."

With the cross dangling in front of him, the priest stumbled past the guards who kept swinging at him. More than one guard caught Seitz with a solid punch or a club on the back.

"Send him through the camp," one of the guards shouted. "Let's see what he can do if he really runs."

Laughing and shouting, the guards sent the older man hobbling toward the barracks. Finally he fell on the ground.

"What do we have here?" A guard pulled a breviary out of the priest's coat pocket, and a picture slipped out. The guard held it up to the light. "Why look at this! It's old Pius XII." He passed the picture around. "Can you believe he tried to smuggle a picture of that worthless Italian dog in here?"

A guard laughed and added, "Who knows? We might have that head Roman toad in here after we get this war over with. That'll shut down the Catholic swindle forever."

Seitz reached out one more time to attempt to get the picture, but he couldn't quite grab it and dropped back to the ground. Another guard cracked a vulgar joke about Mary's virginity.

"Get into the Jourhaus," the SS officer said, pointing toward the administration building. "Hurry up."

Franz Seitz pulled the rosary off of his face and covered his head to avoid getting hit again. Christian watched him hobble toward the entry door. The guards kept laughing and turned back to other prisoners who were climbing out of the boxcars. Backing away from the scene, Reger turned back toward the fields.

Three

In order to make sure camp rules on religious practices were rigidly enforced, the commandant and block leaders selected SS guards who were hostile to religious practice to oversee all activities within the camp. Their antagonism made them even more rigid and suspicious than the average guard. These watchdogs bore down on even slight infringement of the rules. This made the pastors all the more careful to watch for any patrols slipping up on the Pastors' Barracks. But events of the war were moving in the opposite direction.

The Nazi defeat at Stalingrad sent more than a small ripple of fear through the administration. Guards kept their comments to themselves, but the prisoners overheard conversations. Hidden radios had picked up the BBC broadcasts from England, describing the horrendous battle to conquer the Russians. The defeat of the Germans in this crucial battle in the Soviet Union didn't send the signal the camp guards wanted to hear.

With a few minutes left before the lights went out, Dittner slipped up next to Christian while he washed his face. "I heard an interesting conversation this evening."

"Oh?" Christian said.

"Yeah. I was standing outside the mess hall when I overheard two SS guards talking around the corner. Obviously both men knew about the defeat at Stalingrad."

Christian nodded his head. "And?"

"The Nazis try to keep their defeats hidden, but the renegade broadcasts that the Allies keep pumping into Germany break through those silent barriers. The word is getting around."

"What did the guards say?"

"They were worried. After months and months of fighting over one city, a defeat sounded ominous to them."

"It is!"

"Absolutely. The guards know that the Russians have the Germans on the run."

"Do you think the defeat will change anything around here?" Christian shook the water off his hands.

"Their defeat will make the guards more edgy. And it *might* change things in the camp. We'll see." Dittner looked around to make sure no one had been listening and walked away.

In the next few days, Christian discovered the first change. The religion-hating guards started disappearing, and surveillance became more lax. Pressure on the Polish priests subsided. No one talked about what was happening, but clearly the camp seemed to be in some sort of retreat from the relentless mind-set that had haunted the pastors. Rumors started floating that the Poles even were having secret worship services in No. 28.

One morning Christian sat down in the mess hall next to Willy Bader. "What do you think is going on around here?" he asked.

Willy grinned. "I try not to think!" he said impiously. "Remember that I came into this camp in 1933. I was among the first because they arrested me for being a Communist." The small, broad-shouldered man leaned forward. "Because I was a b-b-b-ad boy!"

Christian smiled. Everyone who knew Willy Bader believed him to be one of the most thoughtful prisoners in the entire camp. The man worked endlessly to help everyone around him. Still, he had languished behind the barbed wire only because of his political convictions.

"What did you do that was so awful?"

Willy's grin faded. "I only had a different opinion. I studied the ideas of Karl Marx and believed they would work in Germany." Willy shook his head. "We've had nothing but confusion. Obviously the Kaiser didn't know what to do." His sly smile returned. "I committed the awful act of having a different opinion than Herr Hitler had."

"And you've been here all this time only because you had different ideas?"

Willy shrugged. "I have to be somewhere and suspect it will be in this place until the war is over one way or the other."

"And when do you think that will be?" Christian pressed.

"I am not like you believers," Willy said. "You believe there is a God in heaven watching these battles down here, and He will be the one settling matters." He shrugged. "Unfortunately, I have never been able to believe a God exists." Immediately Willy grabbed Christian's hand. "No offense intended."

"None taken. I don't agree with you, Willy, but I respect your right to have a different conviction."

"You are a good man." Willy patted Christian on the hand.

"And you are equally the same," Christian said. "No one in this camp would be critical of you. You are always honest. Every day you work hard to make sure only the best happens for the prisoners." Christian leaned closer. "They tell me that you even helped the priests by taking the sacrament to the dying. Such an activity could bring you severe punishment."

Willy shook his head. "I try," he said. "That's all. Every night when I close my eyes I ask myself if I did wrong to any of my companions that day." He shrugged. "I can only talk to myself, but you talk to God."

"I don't sit in judgment on you, Willy. But I will tell you this. If I am right in my convictions, the mighty hand of God will fall on this camp before it's all over."

Willy winked. "Yes, I want you to be right. My hope is that your convictions, not mine, prevail."

Christian nodded thoughtfully. "I must believe that wrong cannot endure. At the end of the day when the sun goes down, the lights will go out on all these perpetrators of evil."

"I hope so," Willy said. "With all my heart, I hope so."

CHAPTER ELEVEN

SHADOWS OF DEATH—1943

One

"Such a short time."

Christian stood silently as the old man rambled.

"I keep reminding myself that I have only been here a short time." Dr. Hesse thumbed through Helmut's large Hebrew Bible, his head bent, the stubble on top of it forming a bizarre pattern. "Yet it *feels* like a century has passed."

"Ya," Christian reflected. "Time passes like that here. First you measure events by days, then by weeks, and later by months. Now I measure things in years. The flow becomes very twisted."

"I never thought I would outlive all my sons," Hermann sighed, raising his shaggy white eyebrows slowly. "But I knew Helmut would not endure in such severe surroundings."

"At least they allowed you to be with him in the infirmary," Christian said, sitting down beside him.

"The last hours were special, and I was comforted. He only awoke twice, and his last words to me were, 'Oh, Father!' It was as if he had found a perfect release from all the misery."

They both slipped back into silence, trying to realize the meaning of the loss of a son. At last, Hermann laid the Hebrew Bible aside and reached for a German Bible hidden in the straw of the bed rack.

"A Dutch priest even gave Helmut the last rites of the Roman Catholic Church, and then we prayed together," Dr. Hesse reminisced. "I was grateful for such a brotherly gesture."

"Your son was a true martyr, Hermann. God will count him among His special army of saints."

"I thought that very thing the next morning, Christian. When they called me to come and see his body, I reached over and closed his eyelids for the last time. Even in my sadness I realized how very proud I was to have known such a fine young man. Though his life was short, he lived it well."

"In these days we have seen uncommon integrity—and you, my friend, have been one of those with the most."

"I want to thank you for the flowers that you placed in his hands," Dr. Hesse went on. "In that place of death, your kindness added a special remembrance."

"I'm sorry I could do no more. I begged the flowers from one of the prisoners who works in the greenhouse."

Hermann opened his Bible to the Gospel of Matthew. "Helmut loved Hebrew, and he knew his languages well. Now in his death, he has given new meaning to the last words of our Lord on the cross: 'My God, My God, why hast Thou forsaken Me?'" Then Hermann paused and reread the passage in the original language, "*Eli, Eli, lama sabachthani.*

"*Sabach-than-i,*" he repeated, emphasizing the "i" and resting his finger on the letter. "That dot on the final 'i' is the axis point around which this whole world turns. Because Christ did not shrink back in His hour of trial, because He endured total abandonment, none of us will ever face death as if we are abandoned. Helmut was not forsaken!"

He closed the Bible with a tone of finality. "My son is gone, but I am most comforted! Our world still turns around that axis."

"The service is about to begin!" someone shouted. "Please gather in the chapel."

As the two men stood up, Dittner appeared in the crowd, moving from man to man, informing everyone of the service and of other items of news and gossip that he seemed to have the uncanny ability to gather. As he approached Reger and Dr. Hesse, Dittner reached out to pat Hermann's shoulder in a consoling gesture, then whispered, "The radios are bringing us incredible information! Italy has indeed fallen to the Allies, and apparently we are in deeper trouble in Russia." Immediately he was off again, blending into the multitude that filled the barracks.

"There is much to pray about tonight," Christian told Hermann. "Let me find you a place where you can be close to the front." Knowing of his loss, the group stepped aside before the aging cleric.

Heinrich Gruber stood waiting to preach the evening message. All the pastors knew that when Gruber spoke, his words were filled with power. Opening his Bible to the eleventh chapter of John's Gospel, he began to read, "I am the resurrection, and the life: he that believeth in me, though he were dead, yet shall he live: and whosoever liveth and believeth in me shall never die."

Out of the corner of his eye, Christian glanced at Hermann's face. He was nodding his head as if he not only agreed with the Scripture passage but was bringing every part of his being into compliance with the words.

Karl Leisner stood next to them. He always seemed to be making mental notes; perhaps he would use the sermon ideas some day when he became a priest.

Heinrich began to talk in quiet, kind tones about Jesus arriving in Bethany to find that His dear friend Lazarus was dead. "You see," he said, tapping his Bible with his index finger, "that even in our darkness here in this camp, just as in the darkness of that tomb, the sovereign authority of Christ over death is evident. Nothing can destroy that power!"

The room was silent, though every inch of space was taken by the prisoners. Men leaned forward for fear of missing a word.

"Listen to our Lord's words of command as He seizes control of the situation," Heinrich exhorted. "'Where have you laid him? Take away the stone! Lazarus, come forth!' Jesus is the Master of the moment, and everyone must obey His call."

Then raising his voice as loud as he dared, Heinrich proclaimed: "The name of Jesus is no empty word! He has won the victory over death, and He has given us the assurance of eternal life!"

Suddenly from the front door an outsider interrupted the sermon. "Out! Out!" the voice demanded. "Everyone out of the chapel and into the washroom."

Obviously the interruption was timed to disrupt the service. The prisoners groaned as they lined up for another pointless inspection.

"I have heard marvelous words!" Hermann repeated as he hung on to Christian's arm. "I cannot say enough praise for what these few moments have given me. Please thank Heinrich for this message about victory over death."

As they shuffled into the washroom, Christian was struck by the fact that not even the planned confusion could diminish the impact of these few simple words.

Two

Dittner stomped carefully around the drift to make sure the snow didn't get inside his shoes. "Have you noticed how our numbers are increasing?"

"And have you noticed how the soup is getting watery again?" Christian remarked, pulling his cap down tightly over his ears. "I told you that would happen."

"The rumors are that Germany is in full retreat."

"Well, at least they released Dr. Hesse. What do you make of that?"

"Considering the broadcasts about Helmut's death, I believe the Gestapo feared that keeping him here would reveal the full extent of their political arrests. He certainly wasn't freed by accident."

In front of them, multitudes of shivering men were trying to find the right lines and places to stand. Each was waiting as long as possible before having to snatch off his cap and expose his head to prolonged cold.

No. 26 661 conducted an eye search through the ranks to see if any old friends had arrived at Dachau. It had become impossible to keep track of who had disappeared. His gaze fell on Karl Leisner. The deacon was shaking, and he looked drawn and thin. His face and neck were red with fever.

On this particular morning, several men could not be accounted for, so the guards screamed and shouted, threatened and harassed until the count was satisfied. Finally, the group was released to run back to shelter. At least the breakfast was hot.

Following the meal, No. 26 661 hurried to the SS office. Nothing must interfere with his performance lest he find himself back in the fields. As he opened the door, he found the other prisoners already standing at attention, awaiting Boye's instructions before beginning work. To his surprise, a new prisoner had joined their ranks.

When the man turned his head, Christian recognized him as one of the criminals who had been mixed in with the political prisoners. Knoll was widely known as a *capo* to be avoided; he had a reputation for being violent and explosive. His glance at Christian was less than congenial.

"*Seig Heil!*" Boye announced as he entered, extending his arm in a rigid salute. Each man stiffened to attention. "Unfortunately, you social deviates are not allowed to return the pledge of loyalty to our Fuhrer," Boye said with a smirk as he paced in front of his little company. "Perhaps even now you are beginning to feel some of the pain of being completely outside the circle of socially acceptable human beings. I trust you are learning how important loyalty and fidelity are."

A slight smile inched up the side of No. 26 661's face. Quickly he bit his lip.

The boy officer suddenly whirled and faced his troops. "You can redeem yourselves only with acceptable work! Today I expect maximum effort. Some of you have been making mistakes, and that will be corrected immediately! I have a report here on you before you have even started," he said, pointing to Knoll. "Any other problem, and you go out in the snow!"

The lieutenant thrust a piece of paper into No. 26 661's hand. "Tell this dumb swine how to do things right! Get him straightened up, or I'll send both of you back!"

Christian tried to stand even more erect.

"All right! Get to work!" As Boye heeled around and left the room, Knoll turned and faced Christian. He was a hulk of a man, with an enormous neck that ran from the edge of his ears down into the middle of his shoulders. From behind, he looked like a bull. Now all Reger could see was the defiance and contempt radiating from his eyes.

"Now, pighead, you are going to set me straight?" Knoll contested.

Christian pretended to be reading the paper. He remembered how Knoll had not hesitated to kill a Jewish inmate. Maybe killing a cleric would be no different.

"I'm not looking for any trouble," Reger said without lifting his eyes from the report. "All I can do is follow orders. No harm is intended."

"No harm is intended?" Knoll snarled.

"Of course not," Christian said softly, trying to avoid any further confrontation. "We are all brother prisoners here. Nothing more."

"Oh, I know about you. You are one of those pastors. A *pfaf!*" he huffed, breathing into Reger's face.

The way Knoll said *pfaf* made Christian realize that he thought the term was derisive.

"Do you know what a *pfaf* is?" Christian asked with as much casualness as he could muster.

The towering prisoner looked blank for a moment and then answered with surprising candor. "No."

"Pfaf is a Latin acrostic formed by combining the first letters of four words. The phrase is, *Pastor Fidelis Ammarim Fidelium.*"

"And what does that mean?" Knoll snapped back, waving his thick fist in the air.

"Faithful pastor of faithful souls," Christian answered. "That is all any of us wants to be. Helping others to find God's help is our business."

Again Knoll looked blank and after a moment answered, "Oh, really."

"That's all."

"What are you—some big deal priest or bishop or something?"

"Oh, no, I am a nobody. I'm just a pastor of a little church in Stieglitz, in Pomerania near Poland. I'm nobody special."

"Ya? Then why are you here?"

"I helped organize people into what we call the Confessing Church. We oppose the Nazis and their policies. After I was arrested three times, I ended up here."

"You've been arrested three times?" said Knoll with new respect in his voice. "Well, you must have been powerful in your village."

"No, no," Christian laughed. "No one would ever be afraid of me. The only strength I had was the persuasiveness of truth."

"You had guns and explosives hidden in these churches?"

"Oh, no! We didn't operate like that."

"Why would they bother with you?"

"I suppose that nobodies who won't compromise look very threatening to the people who have the guns and bombs."

Knoll just shook his head. "I've never heard anything like that before."

"Ah, my friend, truth can be a very powerful thing." Christian put his hand on the man's shoulder.

Instinctively, Knoll flinched and drew back. Taking full measure of the pastor, he pursed his lips for a moment, then grunted and turned away.

Reger watched Knoll standing in front of the window waiting for someone to tell him what to do. Suddenly he realized he had not said anything to him about what was in the report. But most of it made little difference. It seemed more prudent to let it pass for now. Later in the day might be a better time to bring it up again.

Three

At first, Reger only felt weak and his head hurt. Soon after, he became nauseated. "I am getting sick," he told Dittner as they rolled out of the bunks. "I can feel a fever starting to develop."

"Hide it!" Dittner said instantly. "Do everything you can to fight it off."

"I will, I will," Christian assured him. "You know I don't want to end up in that infirmary!"

"Ya, and your job is also on the line! Don't let them send you back outside to work."

"Of course not!"

For two days he was able to struggle and keep moving, but as the fever increased, his strength decreased. Finally, he had to face the facts. He had typhus. No matter how hard he tried, it would not go away.

It took great effort to get to the SS office with the cold winter wind blowing down the bunker. He feared the sub-freezing temperature would only aggravate his condition.

"Where have you been?" Lieutenant Boye screamed across the office. "I'll teach you to be late."

Even Knoll looked apprehensive. Christian slowly approached the officer's desk.

"Get that cap off!" Boye screeched. "What do you think we are running here?"

"I'm sorry," Christian mumbled, "but I'm sick. I am late because I keep feeling that I am going to faint."

Boye looked at him skeptically and puckered his lips mockingly.

"However, I didn't want to report to the infirmary without your approval."

"I guess you didn't," the lieutenant mimicked. "Perhaps you need a little fresh air that working in the fields would provide?"

"Oh, no, please. I think I have typhus."

"Typhus!" Boye exploded. "Get out of here at once!" he demanded, backing away. "I don't want to catch any of the vile diseases you swine bring in here. Get out!"

"But my work?" Christian feebly protested. "I realize that my work must be done."

"I am ordering you out of here! Don't come back until the fever is gone."

Slowly, No. 26 661 turned and headed toward the door. Knoll gave a subtle but sympathetic nod. Closing the door behind him, he could hear Boye lecturing the men on exposing him to any infections.

As Reger hobbled off to the infirmary, he realized that the infectious nature of his illness was an ally he hadn't counted on. Boye had given him the official dismissal that he needed to be able to return to work. "Thank God!" he said aloud.

Once a bed had been assigned, he felt an overwhelming urge to sleep. His eyes burned, and his head pounded. Within minutes he fell into a deep sleep. Even then, his body shook uncontrollably as the fever kept climbing.

"Up! Everybody up!"

Christian turned, trying to hide from the sound, but he could not ignore the hand that was roughly shaking him. Finally, he had to open his eyes.

"Out! Everyone outside!" The *capo* who yelled in his face would tolerate no delays. "Get out, right now!"

His sleep had been so coma-like that he had no idea how long he had been there or what day it was. "What is happening?" he sputtered.

"Get up, fool! Everybody is being moved outside. Now, get out of here quickly!"

"Can I dress?"

"Who cares what you have on?" the *capo* jeered, yanking Reger out of bed and on to the floor. "Outside!"

The transports? The thought was like an ice-cold slap in the face that snapped everything into focus. *Were they loading up the transports? Had he been there that long?* Panic gripped him and he considered running, only to realize he could barely walk. It took every ounce of his strength to get to the doorway.

The icy gusts bit his bare body as he searched for any sign of the large vehicles. To his relief, none were in sight. Instead, *capos* were yelling for the sick to get inside the next barracks. For some reason, they were all changing buildings. As No. 26 661 hobbled to claim a bed, he realized his glasses had been left with his clothes.

"Oh, no! My glasses are gone," he pleaded, though no one paid any attention.

Dropping on the nearest bed, he pulled the blankets around his shaking shoulders. "I must have glasses," he told the man in the bed next to him.

"Open the drawer beside your bed," the patient said, pointing to a little night table. "You will find plenty of spectacles in there. As the men die, the *capos* just drop their glasses in the drawer!"

To No. 26 661's amazement, the drawer was filled with glasses. He rummaged around until he found a pair that fit quite well.

How grotesque, he remembered thinking as he dropped back into a deep sleep.

When he awoke, light from the window was falling across his face. At first he thought he had only been asleep for a few minutes, yet his body protested. *Surely I must have slept around the clock again.* Propping himself up, he surveyed the room.

The man who had told him about the glasses was lying with his mouth ajar. His glassy stare and ghastly purple color answered any questions about his condition. Here and there across the room Christian could see hands, arms, and legs bent at strange angles. There were no nurses, no *capos*, no doctors. Perhaps the transports would not be needed—the typhus was obviously quite effective. Since prisoners apparently weren't receiving any medicine, it would be a matter of how long a man's resistance lasted.

The days passed, but no matter how badly Christian feared being swept away in the transports, he couldn't shake the fever. His skin began to slough off, and his mouth felt strange and dead. In horror, he realized he could just tug on a tooth and it would come out.

"Something is happening to my heart," he told one of the sympathetic *capos* who finally turned up. "I can feel that it is weakening."

"Be very careful not to exert yourself," the *capo* warned. "Typhus often damages the heart."

"I can tell there is an insufficiency," Christian said "It

scares me." The *capo* said nothing; both fully understood the implications.

Almost miraculously, the transports did not come. Each morning Christian prayed for just one more day to recuperate. Perhaps the epidemic had taken its toll on truck drivers. Dittner had smuggled a Bible into the infirmary, and he tried to read it as best he could. The *capos* simply looked the other way when the book appeared. Most of the time Christian slept.

On one of the empty evenings, a Polish priest beckoned to Christian. The priest's bloodshot eyes and drawn appearance indicated the end had come. He was barely able to prop himself up.

"Plea-s-s-e," he groaned in his thick accent. "Can you help me?"

"Of course!"

"You have Martin Luther Bible?" he asked. "I need Word of God before I die."

Christian crept across the room to the Pole's bedside.

"Our suffering has broken all barriers," Reger whispered to him. "Nothing stands between us. How can I help you?"

"Please read me the Word that gives strength," the priest moaned, putting his skeletal hand on top of Christian's. "Give me word that assures me."

"In the Confessing Church we have lived by this verse. 'We are not among those who shrink back, but who have kept their faith and saved their souls,'" he read. "I know you have not retreated! Believe and have faith. We are not abandoned by God, even in this place."

The priest smiled weakly and patted his hand. "Thank you for kind word. I have tried to be faithful priest."

"Remember," Christian assured him, "if we have lived through hell, then heaven must be very close at hand. Listen to this psalm: 'The LORD is my shepherd; I shall not want. He maketh me to lie down in green pastures: he leadeth me beside the still waters. He restoreth my soul.'"

Christian kept reading long after the priest had closed his eyes. The words seemed to be a soothing lotion for his soul. His hand relaxed; his face became peaceful.

The next morning they carried the man's body out of the barracks. "He was a good man," Christian said to the man in the next bed.

"They are all good men," the raspy voice wheezed. Christian looked again. The man who had come in during the night was, to his surprise, Camill, the Communist *capo* who had helped make some of the worship articles for the Pastors' Barracks chapel and had even been in charge of the barracks for a time. The Nazis had hoped his supervision would create tension. Instead, he had absorbed the brotherly spirit.

"Camill!" Christian exclaimed. "How long have you been here?"

"Not long enough," he gasped, trying to sit up. "They would not let me stop work, and now it is too late."

He suddenly collapsed on the bed and his body went limp. Christian tried to reach him. Camill's eyes slowly opened again.

"I'm sorry," he said, squeezing Christian's hand. "I cannot find it in me to believe in God. I know in this moment you would want me to do so, Reger. But I can't go back on what I believed before I came here.

"I do not believe in angels, and I am certainly no hero," he went on, breathing heavily. "But I want you to know I was glad to have been with you. I wish that all Communists would have a good word for Christians."

"Maybe if I just read a little bit, it would be easier. Would that offend you?"

"No," Camill replied. "Please do read out of your Bible."

"Yea, though I walk through the valley of the shadow of death, I will fear no evil; for Thou art with me." Reger continued, finishing the psalm. When he looked up, the man was dead.

"Only You, O Lord, can be the judge of such things," he prayed. "I commend my brother to You."

Christian managed to get back to bed before drifting off into heavy sleep again. When he awoke the next day, he realized that his condition had improved. Perhaps the fever had decreased or the hold of the disease had been broken. Whatever the case, he knew the typhus would not kill him now. He began concentrating on getting back to the SS office. As he pondered how much energy he had left, he rubbed his chin and realized how many of his teeth had fallen out.

Two days later he eased out of the infirmary and back to the office. Just walking across the assembly area seemed impossible, but somehow he mustered the strength.

His first glance at the work station told him Knoll had been promoted to a different desk. The second glance clarified everything. At least half of the former prisoners were gone.

"Get on with it," Boye ordered, indifferently. "We're very far behind. Your place is next to Knoll over there." He immediately turned back to his desk as if he had no time to spare, even for lectures.

Sliding in on the bench, Christian observed what Knoll was doing. "What's been happening here?"

"Typhus killed nearly all of them," the hardened prisoner grumbled, pushing a pile of papers in front of Christian. "That swine Boye never gets sick!"

Taking the papers, Christian looked out the window in front of them. Cutting across the gray winter sky was the black smoke of the crematoriums. The greasy vapor seemed to be particularly voluminous as it belched that morning. "Business seems to be very good these days," he said cynically to Knoll.

When Knoll noticed Reger's gaze out the window, he also watched the smoke curl up to the sky. "I imagine they're behind in processing their claims as well," he snarled. "Well, my fine *pfaf*, what do you say to all this?"

Christian searched for the right words as he put his response together. "It would seem we have made a descent into hell, wouldn't it?"

Knoll nodded his agreement.

"Then we must remember that He who first descended also ascended. In His victory He has not abandoned us. We are saved by that hope."

Knoll looked thoughtful. He pursed his lips pensively and then turned back to his papers. For the rest of the morning the two men worked silently at the task before them.

CHAPTER TWELVE

THE HOSPITAL OF DEATH

One

For some reason, the guards became more lax, allowing the prisoners extra time to eat their meager breakfast. The prisoners ended up with extra time, which allowed them a chance to talk.

Crowding around the bare tables, the men talked quietly while sipping their "coffee" made from boiled acorns. The taste was terrible, but the opportunity to relax was precious. They had already consumed their single piece of black bread with a bit of pseudo-jam thrown in for good measure. The tediousness of the diet did little to alleviate their obsession for food, but the time to talk felt like a gift.

"What's going on with you?" Christian asked Edmond Michelet.

Reger knew Michelet had once been an important government official, giving him unusual opportunities to survive Dachau. If anyone knew anything, it was Michelet. Dittner sat close, listening carefully.

"I've been working in the infirmary," Michelet said softly. "They put me in as a night nurse." He shrugged. "Certainly a better situation than what most of the men face outside, but it has extreme demands."

"Like?" Dittner gestured for Edmond to keep talking.

"I must pay careful attention to the prisoners' needs because most of the *capos* generally could care less. I listen to make sure I hear their needs when the men cry out for water. Sometimes I help men who dirty themselves or even clean their soiled straw mattresses. Not a pretty sight."

"We understand," Christian said factually. "Things can get hard over there in the infirmary."

"Hard?" Michelet laughed caustically. "I tell you that dump has become nothing more than a hospital of death. You'd better be near the grave before you come in because the staff will push you right over the edge." Edmond leaned closer. "One of my jobs is to put labels on the bodies."

Dittner nodded. "Yeah. Well, you aren't exposed to the heat and cold outside. You're lucky."

"Really?" Edmond raised his eyebrow cynically. "You have no idea how difficult this task can be. The number of deaths keeps increasing all the time." Michelet leaned forward. "Not only do I put tags on the corpses; I must find a *capo* to help me carry the bodies to some empty space where we can leave them, and that's not easy to find in this crowded camp."

"Certainly," Christian said. "If anyone understands lack of room, it's the pastors in Number 26."

"You see," Edmond began to talk more intensely. "Before we know it, a heap of bodies starts to pile up. We keep putting corpses on top of one another." He thumped the table with his index finger. "After a while the pile gets so high that the whole stack tumbles over and bodies roll on the floor. Guess who picks them up?"

Christian grimaced.

"The only man who helps me is Auboiroux the Communist. I tell you that people can say what they want, but this Auboiroux has been one of the most concerned *capos* in the entire lot."

"We get the picture," Dittner said. "You've made your point."

"Not quite yet!" Michelet insisted. "I have a few other details you might find interesting. When sick men come to the infirmary, there are other reasons why they don't last long in our beds."

"What are you implying?" Christian probed.

"The ones with gold fillings always develop the most unexpected fatal illnesses," Michelet continued. "Boom! They die! You'd be surprised how quickly some of our *capos* can spot those fillings."

Dittner's eyes narrowed. "I've heard those little exercises in pain adjustment happen every day."

"*Every day!*" Edmond glanced around quickly to make sure no one was listening. "We've got a couple of *capos* back there who have a remarkable capacity for using sadism and barbarity in creative ways."

"Give me the details," Dittner said.

"When a mouthful of gold fillings is identified, those two *capos* grab hypodermic needles and go to work. Their injections add significantly to the number of deaths around here. Those boys appear to have a little motto: 'Hit 'em fast; hit 'em hard! And leave 'em with empty mouths!' You can see where this story is going. Show up with gold in your mouth, and even a case of the sniffles can prove terminal."

"Somebody ought to do something about those *capos*," Dittner's voice turned hard and menacing.

"Really?" Michelet raised his eyebrow again. "Well, you better factor in the additional data that the SS physicians and the nurses divide the teeth among themselves. Who's going to make any trouble for the camp doctors?"

Christian pushed away from the table. He had heard of untold brutality in this camp, but Edmond Michelet's tale exceeded the other stories. Maybe the guards didn't physically abuse Michelet as badly as they did the prisoners working in the fields, but what these experiences did to Michelet's soul assaulted him at the deepest level.

Dittner leaned even closer. "They tell me that the doctors are performing illegal experiments." His eyes narrowed. "Experiments on the prisoners."

"You must never make that charge out loud," Michelet warned. "They keep their tests under lock and key."

"But the word is getting out," Dittner warned. "Men can't be killed without someone figuring out what's going on." He pointed his finger at Edmond. "I want to know what the facts are."

"I haven't seen their work," Edmond insisted, "but I've heard there's a Dr. Claus Schilling who's testing prisoners in an attempt to find a remedy for malaria. Of course, it's a tropical disease that doesn't occur around here."

"I'll bet the good doctor is using Poles for his experiments," Christian said.

"Exactly!" Michelet answered. "Polish folks always get the worst end of the stick in this place. My understanding is that this Dr. Schilling imported mosquitoes from the tropics to let them bite our men. The inmates rumor that Himmler told Schilling he could use as many prisoners as he needed. Of course, this idiot has no cure, and hasn't discovered one yet. We've got survivors wandering around the camp having fresh attacks all the time." Edmond grabbed Dittner's hand. "You must not tell anyone."

"One more question," Dittner insisted. "I've talked with men who say they saw large vats filled with ice cold water. What do you know about the tanks?"

"Only the same rumors you've heard," Michelet replied. "I'm not a part of any of this cruelty."

"I didn't say you were," Dittner assured him. "I just want to know what's being buzzed around the infirmary."

"They say that German pilots are getting shot down in Norway and Finland over the open ocean." Edmond stared down at the tabletop. "Apparently, the doctors are plunging inmates into vats of freezing water to see if the pilots can be trained to survive the abrupt change of temperature. A *capo* told me that by using ice in the water tanks, the doctors have lowered some men's body temperatures down to as low as 80 degrees before they died."

"Thanks for your candor," Dittner said. "I am keeping careful mental notes on what the Nazis do around here. Don't worry. Some day I will have the opportunity of making sure the world knows what happened at Dachau."

"I hope we live long enough," Michelet said, glancing out over the room filled with prisoners talking to one another. "I don't think so . . . but I can hope and plan." For a few moments he let silence fall between them. "This camp has an effect on everyone. The sadism, brutality, and cruelty wear on your sensitivities. After a while prisoners start looking the other way. Death becomes so constant we accept it as factually as reading a newspaper. Not that it doesn't remain horrible and frightening, but you stop seeing the bodies as human beings, people you once loved and respected. Everyone in this place turns into little more than firewood." Michelet stopped and stared straight ahead. "Our hearts may go on beating, but our eyes cease to be alive."

Christian swallowed hard. "I understand. We can't allow this tendency to devour us."

"Fight it?" Dittner snarled. "I suggest that the most important emotion we can cultivate is hate. Pure, unadulterated hate! You must make sure that the cutting edge of animosity slices across the palm of your hand every day until these terrible experiences burn in your soul with such intensity that when you wake up every morning, the pain is as real as the moment you were branded."

"Absolutely not!" Christian protested. "We must not lose this war with evil, lest we become like the enemy."

"Not me!" Dittner snapped. "If I survive this hole, I'll walk out of here hating the Nazis as the very incarnation of evil." He stood up. "I say keep hating them!" Dittner walked away.

Two

The winds took an unexpected nasty turn, sweeping down from the north in howling gales. From out of nowhere the clouds gathered and turned dark gray. By late afternoon the snow started to fall. By the time the sun went down, the snow flurries picked up, and the next morning eight inches of snow covered the ground. Coupled with the wind, the snowstorm turned into a blizzard, nearly shutting the camp down.

In Barracks No. 26 the men bundled themselves up to fight the intruding cold that poured through every crack and keyhole in the building. When they spoke, puffs of white steam poured from their mouths. Several fires were built in the barracks, but the amount of heat didn't help much.

"Where'd this cold weather come from?" Werner Schultz asked, rubbing his hands together.

"Feels like it blew in from the sea," Christian said. "The temperature must be well below freezing."

Leonard Steinwender agreed. "Yes. I don't know what they will do with us today, but we must be careful. No one would last long working outside in this blizzard."

"Perhaps the guards will allow us to have an additional worship service this morning," Christian thought out loud. "You can't tell."

"Great idea," Schultz answered. "I'd vote for it."

Steinwender laughed. "As if anyone votes around here!"

"Hey!" a priest named August Schmidt called from the front door of the barracks. "There's a man out here in the snow!"

Christian and his friends rushed out to find out what had happened. Schmidt stood over the man laying face down in the snow.

"I don't know who he is," Schmidt said, "but I don't think he's a pastor."

"I know!" Christian explained. "I was talking to him only yesterday. That's Edmond Michelet! A night nurse in the infirmary."

Steinwender turned Michelet over. "Looks like he was trying to get back to his barracks after a night of hard work. He must have stumbled and fallen."

"Is he alive?" Schultz asked.

"I think so," Schmidt said. "But he won't be for long out here in this freezing weather. I think he's got a temperature. This man is sick."

"Wait a minute!" Christian recoiled. "I know this disease. His nose has been bleeding." Christian squeezed Michelet's mouth open. "Look at those sores on his tongue and gums. Michelet's got typhoid fever!"

"We've got to get him back to the infirmary right now," Schultz declared.

"But they could kill him in that hellhole," Christian protested.

"True," Leonard agreed, "but typhoid fever is too dangerous. We've got no alternative. If nothing else, we have to get him out of the snow."

"Let's pick him up," Schmidt said. "We'll have to carry him all the way."

"Put him on our shoulders!" Christian added. "If we're going to take him in, we've got to hurry."

The men quickly hoisted Michelet up on their shoulders and trotted through the snow toward the infirmary. He groaned a few times, but remained unconscious. When they reached the door, the four men hurried inside. The *capo* at the door looked up in surprise.

"At this hour of the morning?" the *capo* asked.

"You know him," Christian said. "Edmond Michelet's your night nurse. He couldn't have left here long ago."

The *capo* stood up. "Why . . . yes! Michelet didn't look well last night, but he didn't say anything to me."

"Of course he didn't," another man snapped from further back inside the infirmary. "But if you'd paid attention you would have seen that he had a fever."

The *capo* glared at the prisoner. "Shut up, Auboiroux! We don't need your advice." He turned back to the prisoners. "Bring him back to an empty bed." The *capo* scratched his head. "Got to be one bed back there somewhere."

Following the *capo*, Christian and his friends lowered

Michelet carefully. Auboiroux walked behind them down the long row between the beds.

"Here's one," the *capo* said. "Put him in this empty bed."

The four men carefully put Michelet down on the bed. Auboiroux watched studiously.

"I knew he had a fever," the Communist said. "I saw it in his eyes last night." Auboiroux shook his head. "He looked dull, had bloodshot eyes. Michelet will need total quiet and a lot of sleep if he is to survive."

"You know him well?" Christian asked.

Auboiroux nodded his head. "Certainly. For weeks Edmond and I brushed all the door latches in the infirmary with disinfectant twice a day. I'm afraid he simply got too close to one of the areas where the infection was being spread."

"You think he'll be in here for long?" Schultz asked.

"No question about it," Auboiroux answered. "Typhoid's dangerous, very dangerous. He'll probably be unconscious for a long time . . . if he lives."

"Is there anyone to check on him?" Christian asked suspiciously.

"Of course," Auboiroux snapped. "If no one else does, I will!"

"Excellent," Steinwender said. "We will come back to visit when we can get away from our barracks."

Auboiroux nodded. "Don't worry. That incompetent at the front desk speaks only for himself. Other men in this infirmary have seen Edmond's care and concern. We'll make sure he gets good care."

"Thank you," Christian said. "We'll be back."

The four men filed out of the room.

Three

For three days the blowing snow kept the prisoners indoors. Eventually the winds died down, and the heavy snow started to melt. When the sun came out again, the temperature rose and the danger passed. During the next week the SS guards worked the clergy extra hard, so there was no time to return to the infirmary for a visit. Finally Sunday morning came, and the pastors filed into the chapel for their usual service.

"I'm glad most of the snow melted," Werner Schultz said, crowding closer to Christian. "It's still cold, but the weather certainly feels warmer."

"You bet," Christian agreed. "I don't want any more surprise blizzards. A sudden freeze is tough on everybody."

Leonard Steinwender walked in and stood by them. "I see you gentlemen are finally up for the day," he joked.

"Our choices were limited," Schultz said cynically.

Christian laughed under his breath. "It was either come to worship or be pressed into work. After a long debate we went for today's service."

Out of the corner of his eye, Christian caught an unexpected movement near the door of the chapel. He looked a second time.

"Why . . . why . . . look over there," Christian nodded with his head.

Schultz's mouth dropped. "My goodness. That's Auboiroux, the Communist who works with Michelet in the infirmary."

"What's he doing in here?" Steinwender asked. "If the guards catch him slipping in, they'll beat him severely."

"Yeah," Schultz said, "but he's also a Communist . . . the last man in this camp to believe in what we do here."

Christian watched Auboiroux carefully. The Communist didn't seem to be spying, but there was certainly no reason for him to be standing among the clergy. With an unusual white cloak, Auboiroux wasn't distinguishable from any of the other men. He stood reverently with his head bowed almost like he was a clergyman. Nothing that the man did would have alerted the other pastors to any problem.

The service moved along as always with one of the Catholic priests serving as the celebrant. Finally the Communion bread was distributed, and Auboiroux shuffled forward with the clergy to receive it. Christian watched him slip a small fragment of bread into his pocket, then return to the front door of the barracks. Bolting away from Schultz and Steinwender, Christian followed Auboiroux out the door.

"Stop!" Christian yelled to Auboiroux. "Wait a minute."

Auboiroux hesitated and looked over his shoulder.

"I want to talk to you!" Christian hurried after the man.

"Ah!" The Communist extended his hand. "I met you when your men brought Edmond Michelet in out of the snow several weeks ago. How are you?" he asked in a friendly voice.

"Fine. Okay." Christian studied the man's eyes. He seemed harmless. "I was surprised to see you in our clergy Communion service."

"Oh?" Auboiroux smiled. "I should have told someone I was coming. Yes. That was an oversight."

"But why would a Communist come to a Christian worship service?"

"Not for myself," Auboiroux said. "I came for Edmond."

"Edmond?" Christian frowned. "I don't understand."

"It's taken several weeks for our friend to recover," Auboiroux said. "At first I thought he would die, but after a week of intense sleep, Edmond started coming around."

"Yes?" Christian kept probing.

"In the last few days Edmond has been much more alert, but he still has some time to go before he'll be able to leave the infirmary."

"I'm glad to know he is making progress," Christian said. "My friends will be encouraged. Thank you for caring for him. But why have you come to our worship service?"

"Well, I noticed that Edmond was getting stronger, but he seemed depressed. I wanted to do something to encourage him so his spirits would brighten."

"Yes?" Christian said again.

"It occurred to me that he needed spiritual assistance. At that moment I remembered your Communion services. I thought if I could bring him some of this special bread, maybe Edmond would recover his emotional vitality."

Christian blinked several times, trying to grasp what he was hearing. "But . . . but you are . . . no offense intended . . . you are a Communist?"

Auboiroux shrugged. "Yes, but my friend is a Christian. So I'm doing what I thought would encourage him. If I take this bread back and put it in his mouth, maybe Edmond will be strengthened."

"Ah, yes! We trust so! Indeed!"

"I'm going back to give him this little piece of bread." Auboiroux smiled. "We shall see, but I think it will make Edmond happy to know it came from your altar."

Christian squeezed the man's hand. "Thank you, my friend. God bless you."

Auboiroux nodded and hurried away.

Christian stood watching in amazement. A Communist who didn't believe in God was taking holy Communion to a Christian who didn't believe in communism. He turned back to the barracks. How could he ever explain such a thing?

CHAPTER THIRTEEN

BENT BUT UNBROKEN—1943

One

"What did she write?"

Heinrich Gruber pressed forward with the rest of the men. His face was no longer round but oblong. Lines were etched around his eyes, and a great deal of his hair was gone.

Leonard Steinwender leaned closer. "Is she all right? Is Mina well?"

"Yes, yes," Christian assured the entire crowd. His frown betrayed his annoyance at having to share this moment of mail call with the group. Yet how well he felt their hunger for any personal word of warmth from the outside. "Her health is holding up quite well, thank you."

"Are they persecuting her?" some unknown prisoner asked.

"No, no." Reger shook his head. "That's all past now."

"How does she survive?" the worried-looking unknown man persisted, tugging at his sleeve.

"My wife manages on a stipend she receives for playing the organ in a nearby church."

Christian turned his back to the man as he tried to read the rest of the letter privately. Slowly he devoured each phrase and syllable, trying to stretch the small page as far as possible. Finishing, he looked up, only to find that the group was waiting for him to share additional details.

"Well," he began, addressing his comments mainly to Leonard and Heinrich, "there are not many of the Confessing Church members left in Stieglitz. Mina says that fear has caused most of the people to turn their red cards back to her."

"What are red cards?" the unknown man interrupted again.

"They are the membership cards of the Confessing Church. Things must be getting tougher. It sounds like most of the remaining members have long since scurried for cover."

"Amazing how courage can change with increased cost." Wilhelm Dittner had slipped to the front of the group of prisoners. He gestured with his head to let Reger know he had something to say in private.

"Possibly you might share just a few lines," the annoying prisoner implored. "I have not received any mail since I arrived."

"Please, just a word or two," another man begged.

"Come on, come on!" Dittner tapped his foot impatiently.

Reger surveyed the group and read their stares. They had hollow eyes, protruding cheekbones, and drawn faces. He wondered if he looked as bad as they did.

"She writes," and with this he turned back to the first lines on the front side of the page, "that she hopes I get this letter before Christmas. 'My dear husband, it is amazing that another summer has passed and the winter is already upon us. Yet we each have endured and been faithful. Each day I pray for your release and safety!'" He paused, not wanting to share her more personal comments.

"What a wonderful woman!" the persistent prisoner remarked, as if she were a close acquaintance.

"You have been here two, three years?" another man asked.

Christian nodded his head and jumped to the last paragraph. "Let us continue to hold to our pledge: we are not among those who shrink back and are lost; we have the faith to make life our own." He folded the paper and said solemnly, "Certainly, that is a word for all of us."

Murmurs of approval passed through the group.

"Come on!" Dittner pulled him away from the center of the circle as he nodded to Heinrich and Leonard to join them. The four men proceeded to the assembly ground where there would be plenty of space between them and the others.

"I have a number of things to tell all of you," Dittner began.

Christian studied his friend's face. He also had the same sunken look about his eyes. A hardness had settled into his features. Something mean seemed to creep often across his face.

"The radios are confirming our suspicions that the Allied invasions at Normandy were successful. Apparently, they are on the move through Europe."

"How do you know?" Leonard sounded dubious.

"We are beginning to get BBC broadcasts, and the Nazi party line has changed. The people are being urged to defend their just victories." Dittner clenched his fist. "God is going to smash them and obliterate the swastika from the face of the earth!"

"All right, all right," Heinrich said calmly. "What else have you learned?"

"For one thing, the crowding and the food supply will not improve. Things will get worse before they get better," Dittner predicted. "Oh, yes!" he added, "I have news that another friend of yours has come in, Christian."

"Who?"

"Ludwig Steil."

"Really!" Christian turned to Leonard and explained that Ludwig was one of the original signers of the Barmen Confession. He was well known throughout the Confessing Church. In fact, he had been in several jails through the years. "I'll find him immediately after supper," Christian said.

"What there will be of it!" Dittner snorted. "Watch the weather; it will be cold tonight. Warn Steil about getting sick and to get rid of any of his gold-filled teeth."

As Dittner shuffled off to join another group, the three men turned to observe the long line of new prisoners waiting to enter the Jourhaus for processing. "Few if any of them will survive this winter," Gruber concluded.

The other men nodded.

Two

For some reason, Ludwig Steil had not been placed in the Pastors' Barracks. When Christian found him, he was sitting at the back of a dormitory filled mostly with criminals and political prisoners.

"Hello, my good brother!"

"Ah, Christian, you are alive!" Ludwig jumped up to embrace him warmly.

Ludwig's once-broad shoulders felt thin, and his bones were close to the skin. Christian was shocked to see that he looked as bad as many of the men who had lived at Dachau for several years. Obviously, his treatment in the other Nazi prisons had been brutal.

"The word was slipped to me when they sent you here several years ago," Ludwig recalled. "I often worried and wondered how you had fared."

They sat down on the bed planks and talked about how each had managed to survive. Seeing the grayness in Ludwig's skin and the faded color in his eyes, Christian was impelled to ask, "Do you think you will be able to stand this place?"

"There are lice in this bed rack that make it almost impossible to sleep," Ludwig reported. "Of course, the increasing coldness makes it very hard as well. I'm not sure how much strength I have left."

"Your health is essential to your survival. I must caution you about what can happen in the infirmary."

"I understand. It is the same in all the prisons. My good brother, I no longer worry about living and dying. Somewhere along the way I released that terror. I try to live as honestly as I can in this present moment, and I seem to lose track of the rest."

"You have found courage, my brother!"

"Oh, no, certainly not that," Ludwig smiled. "Nothing is left in me but the necessity of trusting God. 'Give me this day my daily bread' is the only prayer I have left. His is the only glory that remains."

"I'm sure the days ahead are going to be even harder," Christian told him reluctantly.

"But God is good!" Ludwig said. "I couldn't sleep last night so I spent the time mentally reviewing all the Scriptures and songs I knew. What a wonderful way to fill a sleepless night!"

"Ludwig, you are truly a man of God." Christian felt a surge of emotion as he looked at the physically broken human being who radiated supernatural kindness. "It is an honor just to know a person like you."

"No, no," Ludwig half-laughed. "I am only a worn-out vessel whose time is nearly spent. God alone is good, and only He is able to make us sufficient for times like these."

"They've bent you, Ludwig, but they will never break you."

"Christian, how often have both of us thought of those words, 'In weakness is His strength made perfect.' I have discovered a secret through all of this. No one deserves the tragedies we have seen, but I know God is not defeated—and we shouldn't be either. Every blow they strike has the potential to further perfect our faith and our lives. God will use even their cruelty for our good. We must receive whatever our fortunes may be with that trust."

"You will be a walking lesson to us all," Christian declared, swallowing the emotion that boiled up in him. "I came to comfort *you*, and you have encouraged *me*."

"What is done to us, they must account for, but how we receive it is our responsibility," Ludwig answered.

"My good brother, let me pray for you."

The two men bowed their heads. In the midst of the crowded barracks, only one or two noticed or even listened as Christian began. "Gracious Father, we would not have prayed to drink of this cup. Yet as it touches our lips, may You turn the bitterness to blessing and the gall to glory. Be with Ludwig in whatever way can best bring his wonderful spirit to its fullness. Give us courage. Amen."

"And multiply Your blessings on Brother Reger," Ludwig added.

Three

"Listen, you worthless wretch!" Lieutenant Boye cursed and slammed the pile of papers in front of Reger. "I want this work done by tomorrow night, or I'll put you out there with the snow commando!" He had lost his sophisticated air and no longer seemed boyish. He appeared on the verge of hysteria.

No. 26 661 nodded his head vigorously.

"Don't give me that arrogant look that you money-grabbing holy men like to use on the ignorant and illiterate!"

Again No. 26 661 said nothing, only lowered his eyes. His face showed no emotion. Across the room, Knoll turned and leered at the back of the lieutenant.

"We should have shot you high-and-mighty religious traitors in the beginning." Boye put his mouth against the prisoner's ear and shouted, "Get it done, or out you go!" His usually fastidiously combed hair fell into his eyes.

He spun on the heels of his black boots and stomped across the room. The door slammed behind him with a thundering echo.

"They're losing," Knoll jeered, "and he's unraveled today." The burly man stole across the room to Reger's desk. "You bother him because you don't crack or show anger. He doesn't know what to do with you."

No. 26 661 only smiled. How personable and warm his hardened colleague had become!

"The rest of us always have hate or terror in our eyes. Boye knows what to do with that. But you don't have the look. That eats our little Nazi toy soldier alive."

"Let's just make sure I get this work done lest I give him some excuse to carry out his threat."

"Absolutely!" Knoll wrinkled his brow and looked concerned. "We can't let anything happen to you—that's for sure!"

The outside door at the end of the corridor opened and shut quickly. Dittner tapped his feet against the wall to get the snow off and came down the hall.

"What are you doing in here?" Reger looked at the opposite door, fearing that Boye would come back.

"Who's this?" Knoll's countenance changed, and once again viciousness was in his eyes.

"He's a friend," Christian assured him. "You'd better get to your desk, or Boye will think we're all plotting something."

Knoll snatched a handful of the papers that Boye had given Christian to complete. "I'll get these done myself. I'm not about to let that gorilla throw you out in the cold." He hobbled away.

"Thank you!" Christian called after him.

As Knoll returned to his work, Dittner bent over the table in front of Reger. "I have been sent to deliver this from the factory to the salary office," he said loudly and officially. Then he added in an almost inaudible whisper, "The papers have been smuggled in. The documents from Cardinal Faulhaber and the bishop of Munster have arrived to validate Karl's ordination. Almost no one knows of this, and it must be kept secret."

Christian acknowledged his message without making a sound. Knoll continued to work, not seeming to eavesdrop.

"What an irony!" Dittner continued to whisper. "The Gestapo arrested the one person needed to complete the ordination! When I heard that the bishop of Clermont Ferrand was here, I knew God had arranged to fulfill Karl's dreams."

"When will it happen?"

"Tonight. If Karl is well enough, the ordination will be tonight."

"Wonderful!" Reger was so loud that Knoll turned around and frowned at him.

"Even the ordination vestments have been completed and smuggled into the barracks. Now I am here because they want your help."

"Of course! Certainly!"

"Because you have access to the small kitchen in this building, the bishop hoped you might prepare a little something as a banquet supper for our new priest."

"It would be a great honor, but there certainly isn't any food around here," Christian said, motioning with his thumb toward the bare cupboards in the other room.

"We all know it would be only symbolic," Dittner assured him, "but it would fulfill the traditional expectation for the way in which a new priest is honored." Without giving Reger a clue about how to find food, he added. "One more thing—Ludwig Steil has taken a serious turn for the worse. He wants to see you."

Reger made no reply. His mind was already at work trying to find some way to provide the ordination banquet.

Since it was well past the usual time to close the office and Boye had not returned, the three men decided to leave. After all, no one had an excuse to miss the roll call.

"If there's some problem and you need help with anything," Knoll crinkled his nose and showed his teeth, "you let me know."

"Thanks, my friend, but I'm sure everything will be all right." The men nodded and went in different directions. To his surprise, Christian saw a prisoner who worked in the greenhouse coming past him on his way to the mess hall. He was carrying a basket filled with brussels sprouts.

"Hey, friend, I have something for you."

The prisoner eyed him suspiciously and barely slowed down. "And so does every other starving swine I've passed in the last five minutes. Keep away from the basket."

"All I need is two or three of the sprouts," No. 26 661 said, falling in beside the man.

"You grab any and I'll turn you and your number in to the nearest guard," the man wheezed. "If I show up with an empty basket, I'm dead! So keep away."

"All right, all right, I will pay you something."

The man stopped abruptly. "I can sell you four and no more. What have you got?"

"Well, ah, well," Christian was fighting for time, trying to think of some source of barter. "What will you take?"

"You got money, cigarettes, maybe chocolate?"

"I'm sure I can get some. Give me some time."

"Are you crazy? You either got it now or you can forget it." The prisoner started to pull away.

"No, please wait!" Christian got a firm grip on his sleeve. "Look, I'm a clergyman in the Pastors' Barracks, and something very important is about to happen."

"Ya, ya." The prisoner seemed more amiable. "I know about you and the priests over there, and I know about the good you do. But people are starving all over this place. If someone's going to chance eating stolen food, it might as well be me."

"No, no," Christian begged him. "That's not it. A special event is going to happen right under the nose of the Gestapo, and this food is needed to help make it happen."

"Really?" The man sounded skeptical, but intrigued. "Tell me what it is."

"Honestly, I can't, but I promise I will somehow get payment back to you for the sprouts. I promise it on my oath of ordination."

The prisoner eyed his basket thoughtfully. "I keep my mouth shut very well. It sounds to me like you need my help. So . . ." His stare communicated he would do nothing until he heard the secret.

"No one must know until it's done." Christian's eyes darted back and forth as he tried to make the right decision. He bit his lip, struggling with each word. "You must swear to God on the penalty of your immortal soul not to tell anyone until much later."

"I will, I will," the man agreed, grinning like a naughty boy getting in on a prank. "I promise not to talk. Now, what is it?"

"We are going to ordain a priest right under their noses! We've outwitted them in every way, and I need the sprouts for the new priest's banquet."

"Really!" The man smiled broadly. "Amazing!"

"You must not tell," Christian warned.

"Listen, I'm here because I'm a thief and a liar and I know it. But I still believe. Maybe I haven't done much that's worthwhile in my life, but I'd give anything to watch that happen!"

He reached into his basket and began putting sprouts in Christian's pocket. Here are six they'll never miss. Cook 'em slow and carefully."

"How much do I owe you?"

"Nothing. Just remember me when you are on your knees next." Quietly, the prisoner moved away and broke into a trot to compensate for his delay in getting to the mess hall.

Christian almost danced with jubilation. *How appropriate that a Dachau ordination supper be prepared from food snatched from the Nazis' garbage,* he thought. *Certainly, the prisoners don't get such delicacies.*

Later, as darkness covered the camp, a small group of clerics assembled outside the Pastors' Barracks to stand guard and watch the ordination procession enter the chapel.

"The ring and the cross are already inside!" Dittner beamed. "They were made in the Messerschmitt factory right under the guard's nose!"

His frosty breath reminded Christian of how cold it was standing in the snow. He rubbed his arms trying to keep warm.

"A Trappist monk was able to make a crosier," Dittner continued. "And the cardinal sent the ordination oil. The guards never suspected a thing."

They saw the door open in the barracks across the way, and Karl came out with two men on each side. Obviously, they were making sure he did not stumble and fall.

"Congratulations! God bless you." Christian put his arms around Karl's shoulders and hugged him. "You have made it!"

The deacon smiled kindly, returning the hug, then shaking Dittner's hand.

After the other priests had escorted Karl into the Pastors' Barracks, Christian turned to Dittner and confessed, "I fear the tuberculosis is too advanced for him to recover."

"But after tonight, it will never matter. He will die a priest, and that will be sufficient for Karl."

The snow started to fall more heavily, and the wind began to blow. They began stomping their feet to keep them from going numb.

"He will die a priest and a brave man who was faithful," Christian added. "Few have ever done more, and it will indeed be enough."

He watched the snow swirl and decided it was time to begin cooking the brussels sprouts still hidden in his pocket.

When he returned with the little covered dish, the ceremony was already completed and the men were standing around the newly robed priest, who was seated at a table.

"Ah," the bishop welcomed Christian's entry, "here is our banquet for Father Leisner."

Reger set the dish on the table and pushed it toward Karl. He stepped back, smiling with delight.

"Now let us bless what God has provided." The bishop gave the blessing and ended with the sign of the cross.

Karl kept smiling and expressing an embarrassed appreciation for all the attention he was receiving.

Handing him a fork, Christian asked, "May I see your ordination ring?"

The machine-tooled ring shone on his thin hand.

"It looks perfect!" Christian complimented, then announced so everyone could hear, "We have confirmation that the everlasting arms are still holding strong."

"Hear! Hear!" the group echoed in a simulated toast.

One of the priests held the crosier as Karl bent over the dish. His regal vestments struck a strange contrast with the other prisoners' uniforms and recycled clothes; so, too, with the starkness of the room. The garments seemed obviously alien, yet hauntingly appropriate.

"Who could ever believe that here in Dachau we would have witnessed such a triumph of the gospel?" one priest asked another. "The power of the cross is hidden but not defeated!"

The group gathered around the new priest, making congratulatory comments as he ate the little cabbages. They laughed and enjoyed the moment as if a pope were being crowned. Yet each of them could hardly keep from noticing how the fork trembled in his bony fingers.

"Please forgive me," Karl finally said. "I think I must lay down now. I feel very faint."

"Of course, of course!" several men responded. "We will celebrate your first mass tomorrow," the bishop consoled. "Then you will have your full strength back."

Everyone agreed, and two priests helped Karl to his feet and back to bed. Everyone knew it would be several days before he could carry on.

"You have been here for many Christmases, Reger?" the bishop queried as Karl left.

"Ya, this is my fourth Christmas here," Christian told him. "Although it has been barren, each year God has been good and given me a special gift."

"How interesting," the bishop answered thoughtfully. "I think this year He has already given me a very important gift."

"Oh? What is it?"

"I have never known what brothers I had among the Protestants! Karl has told me how you have cared for him and been concerned for his welfare. You have been like a shepherd to him."

"You would have done the same for us," Christian pointed out.

"I was raised solely with Catholics," the bishop continued. "Now I know how much I have missed. Truly, Christ has made us all brothers."

"If we live," said Christian, extending his hand, "we must never forget this gift."

The bishop suddenly went past the outstretched hand and hugged Christian as one does when being reunited with a long lost relative. "Tonight the body of Christ has been manifested in our midst. We have been one in Him."

Christian smiled widely. "Let us pray that Karl can consecrate the mass on Christmas Day. That would make the gift complete."

Four

Ludwig Steil's condition had worsened.

"Thank you so much for coming," he said, gripping Christian's hand. "I am not doing very well today."

"Typhus is hard to defeat," Christian acknowledged. "But by God's grace I defeated it last year. You can do the same."

"I'm afraid my time is spent. I'm just too weak."

"No! You must never say that! You must not give up. Dying is God's business. Living is our business!"

"All right," said Ludwig in a surprised tone. "All right, I will keep trying."

"Tonight is Christmas Eve, Ludwig. Wonderful things happen on this night, and they are happening here. This is not the time to give up hope."

"Christmas Eve!" Ludwig sighed. "Memories alone ought to strengthen us."

"I am going to bring the evening message tonight and lead the pastors in prayer. Do you have any message you would like me to bring them from you?"

Ludwig closed his eyes as if he were searching his mind and heart for some special word. "I think," he pondered aloud, "that I would want to bring back to mind Psalm 50:2–3. I believe that text says, 'Out of Zion, the perfection of beauty, God hath shined. Our God shall come, and shall not keep silence.'"

Christian was amazed at Ludwig's memory, even under such arduous conditions. "That is, indeed, a word from the Lord! You have confirmed what was going through my own mind. Bonhoeffer once wrote something to the effect that no person can possess God in such a way that he no longer needs to wait for Him. In fact, when we wait for God, it is only because God Himself has already been waiting for us for a long time."

"So!" Ludwig said as he waved a finger in the air. "We are waiting for the One who is already on His way!"

"Now," Christian admonished him, "you keep on thinking up sermons and quit thinking bad thoughts about your health!"

"I will be incurably a preacher to the end," Ludwig admitted with a grin.

"So it seems, so it seems," Christian laughed.

Once more they clasped hands and prayed together.

In a few minutes, Reger was back in the Pastors' Barracks. Though the electricity had already been shut off for the night, candles lit up the chapel, emitting an almost unearthly glow as they reflected in the faces of the men. The prisoners huddled together more like a pack of ragged beggars than men of the cloth. Yet there was no shoving or pushing. A courtesy prevailed that seemed foreign to a room full of hungry, tired, dispossessed victims of a maelstrom.

Opening his fraying Bible, Christian read the Scripture Ludwig had suggested, then preached: "We appear to be the prey of the beast that has pulled us, beaten and broken, to the dragon's den. But the darkness has not been able to extinguish the true light, and it has not quenched His radiance on this Christmas Eve. Let me tell you what I see as I look into this dark night."

He reflected on Karl's ordination, the bishop's insights, and his own time with Ludwig. Men nodded their heads, murmured their affirmation, and found encouragement and hope. Then they all prayed together, "Come quickly, Lord Jesus."

As the worshippers filed back to their bed racks, Christian lingered in the chapel. His last prayers were that Mina, as on other Christmases, would be comforted and would have some realization that he was alive, was surviving, and was spiritually with her. He prayed until an inner confirmation allowed him to arise and return to the dormitory. Wedged between two friends, he was quickly overcome by sleep.

It was not until the day after Christmas that Karl was finally strong enough to celebrate his first mass. So many prisoners were packed into Dachau that the guards had come to pay little attention to the frequency of the services in the Pastors' Barracks. In fact, they seemed to have their hands full just maintaining the camp.

Karl was almost overwhelmed at the attention being shown him. By the time of the service, everyone knew of the ordination and considered him a walking symbol of victory. The fact that he was so sick seemed to strengthen the resolve of the others.

To the amazement of everyone but Dittner, a camera appeared. Behind locked doors, pictures were taken of the new priest in his makeshift vestments. The camera was then carefully smuggled away to make sure Karl's family would have proof and remembrance of his ordination and first consecration of Communion.

"Please come in the chapel and stand with us," Karl told Christian. "The service would not be complete without you."

The bishop smiled and motioned his approval.

Karl carried himself with priestly bearing. While he had often seemed awkward and unable to do the work in the fields, now he slipped smoothly into the place for which he had been destined. Even the crude, handmade utensils of worship received a new dignity at his touch.

His simple homily, purified through the pain of imprisonment, demonstrated a spiritual maturity that years of study could not match. Leaning on the table for support, Karl began to speak of the holy family and the shepherds on the first Christmas.

"Did they not celebrate His nativity in a poor barn in an occupied country? Here we have been given a privilege that few can know. Like them, we have been reduced to being the poorest of creatures. Yet God's grace used their poverty as His opportunity. Even the treachery of Herod was thwarted. At that moment they could not see God's plan that would only be understood from distant years.

"Our pain and poverty will ultimately be His opportunity. Let us hold to our faith and not retreat. Let us have the faith to make life our own. Amen." Karl turned to move the little wooden chalice to the center of the table.

How much that chalice must look like the true grail, Christian thought.

The priest's eyes sparkled as he raised the cup. No longer did he look weak and sickly; his face was serene and confident. For a moment he kept the chalice aloft. And in that moment, it seemed as if all questions of power, authority, and destiny were settled.

CHAPTER FOURTEEN

THE FINAL CAULDRON OF PAIN—1944

One

Thunderous explosions shook the ground; sounds of terror rang through the night air. Somewhere off in the distance, terrible destruction was falling from the sky.

The prisoners watched the Allied bombers flying toward the ammunition factories located around Munich. Huddling in the darkness, each man wondered if the torture he had survived through the years at Dachau would be ended by a stray bomb hitting the camp.

When the newer prisoners admitted their fears, Christian told them the story of the matchbox that had been smuggled into Schneidemuhl prison and how it had been an illumination that dispelled the shadows of his despair. Again and again, he shared the lessons he had learned in the furnace of adversity.

"Don't let the unseen terrify you," he comforted. "Keep remembering the words of the psalm, 'The Lord is the light of my life.'"

With the first light of day, the SS guards as usual selected some of the prisoners as death squads to search for stray, unexploded bombs. The rest trudged off to roll call and then to their jobs.

"No. 26 661!" Lieutenant Boye snapped. "You're to see the doctor."

Christian's head jerked up from his work "I'm not sick. I have not requested any medical attention."

"Nobody asked you."

A frantic sensation surged through Reger's body. "I would respectfully decline this attention, sir."

"Get to the infirmary," the officer demanded. "And don't waste any time getting back here."

Dropping his pencil, Christian headed reluctantly out the door.

Why would a physician want to see me? he thought. No one ever received special care unless a sinister purpose was behind it. Christian worried about the few teeth he had left, then remembering he had never been able to afford gold fillings, his mind quickly leaped to the secret experiments. Perhaps he had offended someone in the pay office and his name had been turned in. Was he to be disposed of in the guise of "special care"?

"O Lord," Christian prayed softly as he waited in the corridor, "please don't let this doctor be either Schilling or Rascher."

Then an unusual thought struck him. *Today is Pentecost Sunday, 1944! This is the day when the Holy Spirit empowered the church. He will indeed be with me today!*

"Come in, come in," a kindly voice beckoned. Christian was relieved to see an unfamiliar face.

"I am Doctor Klaus," he introduced himself. "I have especially asked to see you." Smiling and extending his hand, he motioned the prisoner into the examination room. "I want to make sure you are well," he said pleasantly.

No. 26 661 watched in amazement as the doctor listened to his heart and examined his chest. "My daughter-in-law asked me to look in on you," he said. "She is a good friend of your sister, and they are all concerned about you."

The kind manner and concern almost overwhelmed Christian. "Oh, thank you, thank you," he said, gripping the doctor's hand with deepest appreciation. "Please, let my sister know I am surviving."

"Well," he said slowly, staring at Reger's protruding ribs, "you are surviving, but I'm sure you know that your health is very bad. Nonetheless, your constitution is still strong."

"I hope to be released some time soon," Christian answered, fishing for some response from the doctor.

"I hope you are no longer set on any resistance to our Fuhrer," he said sternly. "We are in a new day now. Those who recognize the glory of National Socialism can find their place in the new order."

Reger wasn't exactly sure what was being suggested, but the response the doctor wanted from him was obvious.

Perhaps the right political statement might make a difference. Maybe repentance would even win his release.

His eyes glazed over, and he had no idea how long he thought about his answer. Mina's face came to mind, and he could see the parish church almost as if he were standing before it. The years at Dachau had been so very long.

And then he began to see other faces—Werner Sylten, Heinrich Van Mohl, the dying Polish priest, and finally, Helmut Hesse lying with Reger's flowers in his hands. The gypsy's description of Paul Schneider's death also was resurrected in his memory. *No*, he thought to himself, *we have all come too far to shrink back now.*

"New?" Christian answered the doctor. "No, I do not see new things growing up around me. Let me ask you a question. Do you know what today is?"

The doctor shook his head.

"Today is Pentecost. This day was the only time when something truly new and hopeful happened. All the other comings and goings of men and governments are not new. None of them will last forever. Let us not deceive ourselves about what shall remain."

The doctor stiffened and stepped back. His eyes narrowed, and he looked at Reger with disgust. Pointing the patient toward the door, he abruptly said good-bye.

A sinking feeling swept over Christian as he watched the little oasis of hope fade back into the desert of despair. The brief interlude of promise dissolved into a mirage. "Another day, perhaps?"

The doctor said nothing.

Two

"Good Lord!" Heinrich Gruber exclaimed as he stamped his feet. "This room is crawling with lice! They are everywhere!"

"It's even worse in some of the other barracks," Dittner reported.

"What's made the lice suddenly become so much worse?" Christian asked.

"The transports from the Balkans are bringing in so many people that there is no way to disinfect them," Dittner said, slapping at his arm. "These barracks are jammed to overflowing. One barracks built for two hundred people has sixteen hundred prisoners."

"I saw the piles of clothing from these new prisoners yesterday," added Gruber. "The lice were so thick that the heap was actually moving!"

"I talked with the *capo* who is responsible for disinfection," Dittner continued, "and he said there are not enough chemicals to control the vermin. It's certain that typhus will once more rage through the camp."

"Perhaps this time none of us will survive," Christian said blankly, almost casually, about death's constant presence.

"Possibly our contact with typhus last year will have built up some immunity," Gruber suggested. They all shrugged their shoulders.

As the days passed, rest and sleep became almost impossible. The attack of the lice was unrelenting. Soon men fell ill and could not leave their beds; human waste fell down on those below, and yet nothing happened. More prisoners kept piling in.

Trying to find fresh air, Christian and his friends left the barracks and began watching new prisoners being herded into the Jourhaus. A change was evident in the long lines. These were not inmates from the north or even from Russia; these were clearly German citizens.

"These are our good fellow citizens," Dittner growled. "They would not stand with us in '33 or in '38, and now they are paying the price for their cowardice."

"None of them will speak of it for fear of their lives," Steinwender mused, "but the word is out. Because of an attempt on Hitler's life, thousands are being sent here."

"They have it coming! And I hope they taste the full, bitter cup extended to them in this place!" Dittner ground his fist into his palm.

"Is that the best we have learned here?" Christian questioned, looking Dittner squarely in the face. "Are we to be consumed by the same hate that drives this place and fuels its fires?"

"The subject is so sensitive no one dares mention the assassination attempt," Dittner went on, avoiding Christian's eyes. "But they will say that the war is going extremely badly."

"More tents will be required now that the barracks can hold no more," Leonard said. "The only place left to put them is on the streets and walkways."

"Look!" Christian pointed to a prisoner trotting across the open square. The man had his hand over his mouth and was bent forward.

"That's Father Goldschmitt!" Steinwender exclaimed. "His work is unloading the trains."

"Unbelievable, unbelievable," the priest was muttering as he approached. "It's unbelievable."

"What's happened?" Dittner wanted to know.

"I can't comprehend it." His face was ashen, and he seemed to gag on his own words. "They were unloading two trains from Compiegne—all Frenchmen."

"What? What?" Dittner interrogated in his relentless way. "What did you see?"

"Piled in those cattle cars were 370 bodies," the priest said, putting his hand to his mouth. "Scattered among the dead were the living. I cannot even describe the stench!"

"Do you know how they died?" Dittner persisted.

"I'm sure it was from hunger, thirst, and the heat," Goldschmitt answered, slapping at the lice underneath his shirt. "I saw the information sheet on the train. Twenty-five hundred men had been loaded into those cars in France. But when they arrived here, there were only 950 alive."

"Do the guards know that you read the count?" pried Dittner.

"I'm afraid so," Goldschmitt said. "But they told us that the other dead had been unloaded along the way. The Gestapo said that they fought among themselves and ended up trampling one another to death."

"Did you let them think you believed that?" Dittner urged.

"Of course!" the priest assured them. "But I know the truth. Most of those men actually suffocated to death."

For a moment, they stopped talking, and once more they slapped their clothing to kill the lice that seemed to be everywhere.

Then suddenly, Goldschmitt began to shout at the top of his voice, "Germany can never make amends for this! God will not let this stand!"

Instantly, they realized that he had lost control. If anyone heard him, the penalty would be swift and severe. They tried to silence him as best they could.

Sandwiching the sobbing priest between Dittner and Reger, the men ushered him back to the barracks. Though they knew the lice would give him no peace, they stretched Goldschmitt out on one of the bed racks.

"He has seen too much," Steinwender sighed. "There is a breaking point for all of us."

As they bent over the priest, a prisoner pushed his way through the crowded room and walked up to Dittner. Cupping his hand to Dittner's ear, he whispered something that caused Dittner to jump in excitement. He slapped the man on the back, and the other inmate disappeared from sight. Father Goldschmitt became silent and motionless.

"If we can keep healthy and out of trouble, we may yet make it!" Dittner assured the little group. Then pulling them closer together, he said quietly, "The Allies have taken Paris and are moving across France."

"Ah!" Gruber said enthusiastically, "this will put new pressure on the government. They will have to do something about Dachau now."

"Pressure?" Christian responded. "Yes, but pressure to do what?"

"They will have to release us if the Allies come close enough to our borders," Gruber insisted.

"No," Christian said flatly. "They will not have to release us at all. In fact, if the tales of what we have seen here are ever told, the SS and National Socialism will be indicted for the rest of human history. If Heinrich Himmler personally knew about Hermann Hesse's case, do you think he will let all of this cruelty come back to convict him?"

"But what else would they do?" asked a new prisoner who was eavesdropping at the edge of the circle.

Christian looked at his healthy face that had not yet tasted the full wrath of the winter wind and remembered himself as he had been four years before. Through the window he could see the smoke and fire still belching from the chimneys.

"Never forget which way the wind blows here," he told the nameless face. "That smoke is the primary fact of life here."

"Well, well," Dittner chided. "After all these months you have finally come to think like me." Turning to Gruber, he added, "Now it is your turn to learn to read correctly the signs written in the clouds."

"I don't think like you!" Christian answered harshly, attending once more to Father Goldschmitt. "Not at all!"

Three

Each day the reports from the hidden radios kept coming in increasing crescendos of excitement. In September, Brussels was liberated, and a few days later Holland was free of Hitler's control. When Christian heard that Amsterdam was freed, he remembered Heinrich Van Mohl and the day he died. *He would have been overjoyed at this news*, he thought to himself.

The arrival of new prisoners increased too. Since summer, the influx of "special action" prisoners had been especially heavy. These were men who had been suspected of having some part in the assassination attempt on Hitler. Without any background of enduring hard winters and fighting off terrible infections, this group fell very quickly to the typhus that thrived on the ever-present lice.

So many prisoners died that bodies were left to pile up between the barracks. Even the SS guards began to show a loss of morale. Perhaps Hitler had been told of the need to encourage his loyal guards. Whatever the reason, in November of 1944, it was rumored that he was coming to Dachau.

"Attention, attention!" Lieutenant Boye shouted through the SS office. "I have wonderful news for everyone!"

Both officers and *capos* stopped their work and looked up. Boye was holding a communique in his hand and waving the papers in the air.

"Our glorious Fuhrer is coming to visit us!"

The officers applauded; the prisoners weren't sure of an appropriate response.

"We must make this office a model of efficiency and show the Fuhrer the high quality of service performed here at Dachau!" Boye preached like an evangelist.

The lieutenant marched around the room, firing off orders and instructions on how special details were to be handled. Each SS official seemed to be recharged with energy and excitement. Turning his back on the office group so only Reger could see him, Knoll contorted his face in mock rage and gestured obscenely. Watching Knoll's antics while looking across his shoulder at Boye's was so comical that Christian had to bite his lip for fear he would laugh and be in serious trouble.

"Of course, none of you swine will be allowed to be part of this glorious day," Boye spouted, and flipped his hand as if to wave the prisoners away. "You will he confined to the barracks. If there is any trouble, it will be stamped out in an instant!"

As the afternoon progressed, Christian was amazed to observe how Hitler's approaching arrival seemed to fuel the Nazis' fanaticism. The whole experience felt like preparation for a high moment of religious worship.

The bleakness of the camp began to change dramatically. Red and black swastika flags were unfurled everywhere; formal uniforms appeared. By the end of the day, soldiers with rifles were goose-stepping up and down the streets. Over and over again, the guards made it clear that the slightest irregularity among the prisoners would be met with violent response. Absolute security was to prevail.

The next morning, long before Hitler's motorcade arrived, a brass band began to blare the German national anthem, then went from one furious march to another. Trumpets and bass drums echoed from every corner of Dachau.

"He is here! Hitler has arrived!" swept through the barracks. "Satan is in our midst!" one priest whispered in the subdued dormitory.

Like a strange holiday of silence, the day passed quietly for the prisoners. While the bands blasted away, they sat silently on their bed racks, listening soberly to the celebration. At least they were not being worked! As the day faded, so did the sounds. By evening, the gray shroud of agony was again drawn over the camp.

The morning after, Boye paced up and down the office corridors. Walking among the rows of desks like a man whose wife had just given birth to a son, he kept describing aspects and memories of Hitler's visit over and over again.

"The propaganda of our enemies cannot keep us from the truth," he announced smugly to Christian. "I heard the Fuhrer himself say that we are winning!"

Turning to another SS guard, he continued, "Did you notice how strong the Fuhrer was? He was more vigorous than ever before! The attack on his life had no effect on him."

The office functionary agreed emphatically.

"He told me personally," Boye continued, with an arrogance that was so obvious that even the SS men must have been repulsed, "that our work here is of the utmost importance to the Reich."

The lieutenant suddenly pointed his finger at Reger. "We are upholding the truth for all Germany. You clerics could never comprehend the liberation we are bringing to the multitudes that the churches once kept captive with their delusions and lies. We will prevail because we are right."

Christian looked straight ahead, still as a portrait.

"Hitler told us in the most vivid terms that it is now our moral duty to defend the fatherland in this hour of attack on our soil. He also shared with us how secret weapons are about to be unveiled that will sweep away the adversary in a burst of flames. This is a great hour for all courageous men!"

"We are living in a glorious hour!" one of the SS guards chimed in. "Only fools cannot recognize what is happening." Knoll and Reger began dusting the furniture, ignoring the obvious inference.

Only fools cannot recognize the hour, Christian thought to himself. *So you say!*

Four

The deafening roar shook the whole building, and the accompanying explosion turned the black night into day for a brief moment. Men rumbled out of their beds and scrambled for the windows. Pressing against the panes, they could see fires burning along the horizon, only a few kilometers away.

"What's going on? Why the fires? Are those bombs?" Questions buzzed through the barracks. Ten minutes later, everyone knew the answer.

"We are being bombed! What an irony!" Christian told a friend. "This morning Boye assured me that Germany was winning. Tonight the first bombs fall on us!"

"This is just the beginning," another prisoner added. "Surely the Messerschmitt factory and the munitions plants where we work will be prime targets for air raids."

The next morning Dittner brought radio word that the Russians were in East Prussia. "Oh, no!" Christian exclaimed. "My wife is near there!"

Karl Leisner gripped Christian's wrist, trying to buoy him, but the new priest broke into one of his coughing spells.

"No, no," Gruber warned Reger. "Do not let your mind think about such things. Just keep praying for her protection. Fasten your mind on the promises that have sustained us thus far."

"You have trusted God to save you," Dittner assured Christian in an unusually kind way. "Now trust Him to save her."

The emotional agony seemed worse than any Christian had known before. He knew he had to remember that if God was keeping him alive, He could certainly sustain Mina.

Nevertheless, the pain of helplessness cut through his soul. As friends gathered around to pray for Mina, guards broke into the room screaming. "Out of here! Everybody out of here!" The prayer circle was scattered. "We are going to clean up you pigs, once and for all."

"To the showers!" *capos* and guards bellowed.

Prisoners rumbled out of the barracks into the lanes. They were being herded toward the showers next to the crematoriums. Clubs and whips were swung through the air as the screaming continued. "Faster! Faster!"

"The showers!" Gruber gasped as he hurried to keep up.

"That's how they have been gassing people!"

"No! No!" Dittner protested. "It can't be. We have had those showers sabotaged. It isn't possible that they have been able to hook up gas to run through them."

"Then what are they doing?" asked Christian.

"Perhaps this is the end," another prisoner said stoically.

When they turned the corner, each could see that the men ahead were taking off their clothes.

"Strip! Everybody strip!" the guards yelled at each group. "What? The temperature is below freezing," one of the men yelled back.

Immediately, the guard hit him across the face with a club. The prisoner dropped to the ground with a sickening thud. After kicking him in the stomach, the guard pushed him into the ditch.

"Anyone else have hearing problems?" he barked. Instantly, clothes began dropping in piles.

The word that they were being disinfected for lice passed through the line. "This is not extermination!" spread from man to man.

Yet as Reger shivered in the cold, he wasn't sure there would be any difference. The sick were obviously going to die from extended exposure. Around him, those who didn't make it were being carted away in wheelbarrows.

For fourteen hours, the process continued without break. There was no food and nothing to drink. Those who didn't move quickly enough into the showers were thrown bodily into the tanks. Some were simply dropped into the disinfecting tanks and left there. By the end of the day, the body count had reached a new high.

About 8:00, they were sent back to the barracks. Many of the men had even walked through the snow in their bare feet.

"Be grateful that we have tried to end the typhus epidemic," the *capo* snarled as they arrived at the barracks. "You priests and preachers ought to be in that chapel of yours thanking God for such good care."

A French priest huddled next to Reger in the crowded beds. The snow was blowing in through the broken window. "They are desperate," he said. "They know the end is not far away, and they amuse themselves with such tortures. Perhaps God will use this day to save some men while hastening the end of those prisoners whose condition is hopeless."

"The end is not far away," Dittner confirmed. "The Allies are not far from the Rhine River."

"I must see to Ludwig Steil," Christian coughed. "I do not see how he could survive today."

"Be careful walking around in the dark," Dittner warned. "The guards are getting very edgy."

When Christian found Ludwig, the perspiration was beaded on the sick man's flushed forehead. His body was limp, his eyes glassy.

As Christian reached for his hand, Ludwig's vision seemed to focus. "Ah, my good brother," he sighed. "Everyone has been so good to me. Catholics, Orthodox, our own Confessing Church people have tried so hard. I would never have dreamed of such unity."

"Out of our cauldron of pain, Christ has melded us together into one people," Christian agreed, mopping Ludwig's forehead.

"I can now die in peace, knowing that I have seen the real body of Christ revealed as I have never known it before," he said, speaking haltingly. "Now I understand the promise of Jesus that we are to be like a storehouse that produces both the old and the new."

"What are you saying, Ludwig?"

"God has given me a new vision of the church, Christian! I now know that the Holy Spirit does remain as the true continuity between God's people of the past and God's church of the future." His face seemed radiant, his voice more intense.

"Our suffering is not without meaning, Christian. The old and the new are all intermingled here at Dachau." Ludwig gripped his hand tightly. "What we have experienced has stripped away the barriers of the past and made all of us one in Christ."

"Perhaps that is exactly what Paul meant, when he said we are to complete in ourselves what is lacking in the suffering of Christ, to redeem His church."

"Yes, yes, yes." Ludwig gripped him harder. "God has graciously allowed us to be part of the redemptive work that can only come through the cross. Something new will come out of these days that will purify not only us, but the whole church that comes after us."

"You did *not* shrink back, Ludwig! You never faltered, my friend."

Ludwig dropped back against the rough board bed. His last words had come as a final sigh. His energy was spent; nothing more remained. The frail fingers loosened their hold, and his momentary radiance vanished. Rest crept across his face.

As Christian watched Ludwig die peacefully, he saw all the faces of his deceased friends come together in that pale countenance. Long ago he had dealt with his bitterness and hate. Somewhere in the ensuing years, he had come to an acceptance of the inevitable. Yet Ludwig had taken him to still another plateau. Meaninglessness had turned to purpose. Out of the void had come eternal direction.

"Now you have helped me see the future of the church," Christian said to his friend's unhearing ears. "From all of these lifeless bodies will arise tomorrow's people of God as surely as our Lord walked out of the tomb! Though we have died surrounded by bitterness and evil, we are being resurrected in love and compassion. The new is coming!"

Tenderly, Christian reached over and closed Ludwig's eyelids and folded his arms across his chest. "Your courage will not go unrewarded, my friend. Out of your bravery, God will bring a new day."

CHAPTER FIFTEEN

THE UNEXPECTED MONSTER

One

Ludwig Steil's death cast a long shadow over everything Christian thought and did. Some of the prisoners kept chattering that the Allies were not far away and were moving closer to Dachau every day. But many others did not believe any finale was possible. Still others stood silently at death's door with lengthening gloom clouding their eyes.

The constant reality of death chewed at Christian Reger's vitality. Having been in the camp for such a long time, the passing years reduced his own world to the size of the barbed wire pavilion. Each morning he awoke to the reality of men stuffed in his rack, swarming around him relentlessly for more space; trying to sleep as long as possible to avoid the approaching daylight. The emotional drag pulled him to the bottom. On most days it didn't seem that his imprisonment would ever stop or that he could escape the dire circumstances that devoured human life as casually as a dog chewing on a bone. If any end seemed to be in sight, it was his own death.

The trains kept rolling in with increasing numbers of prisoners. Once again overcrowding swelled the population of the barracks. Sleeping conditions in Barracks No. 26 worsened once more. One afternoon Christian saw Dittner standing near the unloading docks, watching hundreds of prisoners tumble out of the cattle cars that had brought them in from heaven knows where.

"Where'd the train come from?" Christian asked casually. "I don't see how any more prisoners can exist in this camp."

"The best I can tell is the train arrived from West Germany," Dittner said. "Over the last several weeks they've been coming in from the east and the south as well. The Balkans keep throwing prisoners at us."

Although he had a fairly good idea of what the directions meant, Christian pushed further. "What do you think is *really* going on?"

"The Allies are stomping the Nazis!" Dittner spat on the ground. "I think the Russians are killing the Germans like swatting flies. Of course, the war is lost, but Hitler and his cronies don't have the good sense to stop resisting defeat. These prisoners are shipped in to us because the Allies have overrun their camps."

Reger nodded. "Where will we put them?"

"*We?*" Dittner laughed cynically. "Have you become part of the camp staff? My! My! They are eroding your sense of identity, Reger."

Christian said nothing, but worried that Dittner's little joke could have a grain of truth in it. God forbid that such a thing could ever be true!

"I fear these refugees are going to bring in a swarm of lice, bugs, insects of every kind," Dittner worried out loud. "Heaven knows, we've already had more crawling creatures than we can stand. They've done it before, and the movement's started up again. Who knows what this could turn into before the show's over."

Christian nodded, but said nothing. No longer did he want to comment on what might happen. Everything always turned out so badly that he didn't speculate.

In the days that followed, the overcrowding swelled to threefold, fourfold, even sixfold in some barracks. Men were forced to construct makeshift tents outside the dormitories and sleep under pieces of canvas. Even the narrow alleyways filled with prisoners, scrambling to find some form of shelter.

Three days later a prisoner named Jacob Kock came running down the main street that divided the barracks into western and eastern sections. Waving his arms wildly, Kock shouted, "Trouble! We are in trouble!"

Reger grabbed Kock by the arm. "Don't make so much noise. The guards will be all over us. What do you mean 'trouble'?"

"My job is to keep the camp disinfected," the frightened *capo* said in a shaky voice, "but everything has spun out of control. I can't do the task any longer."

"Stop it!" Reger shook him. "Get hold of yourself."

"Millions of them!" Kock shouted. "I tell you there are millions of them."

"Millions of what?" Christian demanded.

"Mites! Beetles! Bugs! Spiders!" Jacob Kock shook his fist in the air. "Lice are multiplying everywhere! Vermin are taking the camp!" He caught his breath. "I tell you that we are being swallowed by millions of crawling creatures."

Christian recoiled. Dittner's predictions had come true. The outbreak had been bad in the past, but this eruption appeared much worse.

"I can't stop them," Kock's waspy voice screeched. "The clothes these new prisoners wore into the camp have sprung to life and walk away by themselves. The infestation is so severe that no one can escape." Kock stopped and took a deep breath before running off.

Christian watched the panic-stricken man disappear into the crowd. Jacob Kock had slipped over the edge. But his story was not an illusion.

The medical superintendent of the Dachau camp put the entire prison under quarantine, but it made no difference because the barracks were already filled with lice. The truth was that the concentration camp didn't have enough disinfectant to make a dent in the problem.

In a week lice started taking their toll, with increasing numbers of men falling ill. Christian found himself scratching and slapping at his shirt constantly, but nothing stopped the invasion of the vermin.

"Why don't the doctors do something?" Heinrich Gruber complained.

"I don't think they can," Christian said. "Even if they cared, the problem is beyond their control."

"Why?" Gruber insisted.

"Look around you, man! Hundreds of us are already raging with fever. We have started losing healthy men who survived years in this camp. Old-timers have been wiped out in a few days." Christian looked Gruber squarely in the eye. "We may be next."

Gruber recoiled. "God forbid!"

"Indeed! But we are as vulnerable as the rest of the camp."

Gruber started backing away. Any suggestion that he could fall sick left him unstrung and in a panic. Waving his hand to brush Christian out of his path, he hurried away.

"You can't fight this epidemic with a flip of your wrist," Christian warned.

Three days later Heinrich Gruber broke out in a fever. Soon his entire sleeping rack was filled with prisoners equally infected. Typhus rampaged through the barracks. Gruber's infected body lay piled in the midst of sick men in the wooden racks, all struggling to survive.

That night bombs exploded close enough to the camp that many men feared they would be killed by accident, but the sick men in Barracks No. 26 didn't move a muscle. Bombing of their barracks seemed only a potential blessing to end the suffering.

"The battle can't be far away," Dittner told Christian the next morning. "Allied troops are moving toward us."

"But do they know there is a camp here?" Christian asked. "Those bombers came close last night."

"I don't think they do," Dittner said frankly. "The Nazis have tried to keep most of Germany from knowing we are here. Surely they've done the same with the enemy."

"You really think the German people don't know about us being locked up in this hellhole where human experiments are being conducted?" Christian asked cynically.

"Let me tell you a story," Dittner said. "I talked with a new prisoner about a month ago. The man had just been arrested. He told me that the German people have come up with a new cliché to discipline their children." He raised an eyebrow cynically. "Kids are warned that if they don't behave, they'll 'go up the chimney' in smoke. Guess where that saying came from?"

Christian swallowed hard.

"You got it! Sure the German people know about the crematoriums and what happens here." Dittner poked his finger at Christian. "The word's out across the whole of Germany. The citizens have heard about what we face every day of the week!"

Two

The outbreak of typhoid increased with each new day. Lice and fleas swept in through every crack in the barracks, biting the men endlessly. Finally so many prisoners were sick that virtually no one was left to care for their needs. Infected men had to be left in the dormitories uncared for. Because there were so few mattresses, most prisoners slept on the bare boards of the racks.

As the disease progressed, the prisoners couldn't get out of the wooden bed racks in time to make it to the bathrooms. Generally the men on the bottom racks were too sick to complain. If they did call for help and the SS guards heard, the dirty prisoner was dragged back to the shower and scrubbed with a coarse brush before being thrown naked back into the rack.

Heinrich Gruber had hoped that he had enough immunity from the illness the year before that he might escape the epidemic, but he was wrong. Night after night, he felt the life draining out of him. Some of the time he drifted into delirium with strange images dancing though his troubled mind. Finally he slipped away in a dark, deep sleep.

"Is this one dead too?" a hard voice from somewhere mumbled.

Gruber couldn't open his eyes, but he heard the voices as if they were drifting in from some far-off land.

"I think so," another man said.

"Then we've got no choice but to get this body out of here."

"Yeah," the man said. "We can't let 'em stack up in the racks."

Gruber felt the men's hands pulling him off the rack on to the floor where he crashed with a dull thud. He barely managed to keep from uttering a scream of pain, but once again all consciousness slipped away. Eventually Gruber realized he was being carried somewhere. One man had his feet, and the other hung on to his shoulders, swinging him along like a sack of potatoes.

"Throw him in the pile?" the hard voice asked.

"You got a better idea?" his comrade growled.

"Not me."

"Toss him over."

For a moment Gruber felt like he was flying before he landed softly on what seemed to be soft bags. His exposed body felt a cold sensation like slabs of meat were laying around him. After several minutes, Gruber started trying to force his eyes open, and finally his lids parted. To his horror, he discovered he was laying on top of a pile of corpses.

Rolling to one side, Gruber stared into the half-open eyes of a cold, empty face. Catching his breath, he forced himself not to scream or lurch. He knew that he must get off this stack of bodies and work his way back to the barracks. With all the strength he could muster, Gruber pushed himself down the side of the stack of men and rolled out on the ground. The sensation of having rubbed shoulders with so many of the dead left him on the verge of a violent reaction, but Gruber forced himself to relax. The cold winds whipped around his body, keeping him from laying on the hard ground for long.

Heinrich wasn't sure if he could even walk a step, much less hobble back to the barracks, but if he didn't get out of there the next SS guards would throw him back on the pile.

Gruber had no choice but to start the long walk back to the barracks.

Several times dizziness caused him to stumble. A lack of energy made it almost impossible to keep walking, but Heinrich sensed that his life hung in the balance. It was now or never, and he wasn't about to stop unless his heart quit beating. He kept walking.

Ten long minutes later Gruber found the front door to No. 26. He pushed the door open, but didn't hear a sound. An eerie silence had settled over the long dormitory. Inching his way up the steps, Gruber looked down the long aisle between the beds. A distasteful smell rolled out of the racks. He looked again, and for the first time heard men breathing.

With his last ounce of energy, Heinrich Gruber forced himself to take a couple of steps until he fell on to a wooden rack already filled with prisoners. No one moved. For several moments he stared at the boards above his head, and then sank into a deep sleep.

Three

Reger reasoned that he had survived the epidemic because his past illness had helped him build up an immunity. He did his best to help the sick, but the scourge was so overwhelming that he had to retreat from the barracks. Hundreds of prisoners died, and the bodies could not be disposed of fast enough. The entire camp fell into disorder.

Finally at 6:00 in the morning, guards ran up and down the streets ordering everyone out. A mass disinfection of the total population had been ordered. Even men who couldn't walk were thrown naked into wheelbarrows and pushed to the decontamination zone. The bitter cold wind made the walk almost unbearable.

"I see you are still alive," Dittner said, catching up with Christian.

"And you haven't been sick?" Reger answered.

"Only by the grace of God," Dittner answered, hugging his arms tightly around his chest, "although this trip may finish me off."

Reger nodded. "My teeth are chattering like they had a mind of their own."

"They've got more brains than these idiots running the camp," Dittner answered.

"Hurry up, you fools!" an SS guard demanded. "Get in here! The showers are running. Don't slow the process down."

The men trotted along as quickly as they could. The sound of running water meant that the disinfectant would be sprayed on them through cold shower heads.

"I don't know if I can stand it," Christian said.

"You've got a choice?" Dittner shot back. "Keep walking fast or they'll drag you across the concrete and hurl you into one of those vats of water. That'll be worse!"

The inmates shuffled forward in a steady line. Once they hit the showers the men lingered only long enough to get drenched, then hurried out to dry off in the cold wind. Christian ran through water that only increased his shivering.

On the other side of the showers, he shook violently to sling the water from his purple skin.

"Oh, God, help me!" Christian prayed out loud. "I can't stand the bitter cold."

Dittner came running out behind him. "Lord bless me!" he exclaimed. "What an awful smell. I pray I'll survive."

The two shaking men trudged back to the barracks. At least they were alive. As night fell, the prisoners began counting heads. Obviously many men had died in the cold wind. One of the inmates from Barracks No. 30 came by the Pastors' Barracks and stopped.

"How did you fare today?" Christian asked.

The prisoner shook his head. "Not well. As best I can tell, out of 350 men in our unit, we lost 74 comrades today. We will probably lose more tomorrow." The man shook his head. "They were already sick, and the cold finished them off."

Christian shook his head in disgust. The camp had become so chaotic that he could walk down the streets without fearing the guards would grab him. Trying to get away from the scene in his dormitory, he trudged back to the loading docks where the trains came in. This was not much of a diversion, but the walk took his mind off what was happening around him.

Another train had just pulled in. Christian stood on a rise where he could see the prisoners coming in. Reger noticed a group of women getting off the train. At that moment another prisoner he didn't know walked up to him.

"They're from Leipzig," the prisoner said. "I guess that's where they picked up those women."

"Oh!" Christian said. "I didn't know."

"The other men were sent in from Flossenburg and Buchenwald. There's a ton of corpses lying in those train cars."

"The situation must have become critical over there."

"Humph!" the prisoner snorted. "Can't be any worse than it is here!" He walked past Christian back into the camp.

How much longer? Christian thought. *The Nazis have to be coming to the end of their rope. Sometimes the hand of God may be slow in coming, but when He arrives no man can resist the swipe of His fist.*

CHAPTER SIXTEEN

BABYLON IS FALLEN—1945

One

The fierceness of winter had passed, but the full warmth of spring had not yet arrived. But for the second of April, the weather felt good. Most of the men were still getting ready for roll call when a tall German policeman entered the Pastors' Barracks. As the men realized who he was, the room fell silent. SS guards were always expected, but a policeman seldom came unless there was unusual trouble.

Sensing their fear, the policeman announced loudly, "I have good news. Many of you are to be released today!"

"What? Who? Today? Is it me?" A hundred inquiries resounded through the room.

"Quiet! Quiet!" the policeman demanded. "I have a list of names, and I will read them to you. Now, quiet!"

The press of the group brought Christian so close that he could read over the policeman's shoulder. As he scanned down the page, his eyes leaped ahead looking for only one thing. There on the bottom of the second page was No. 26 661 and his name!

"We are being freed! We are being freed! We are being freed!" became the ecstatic litany. Men congratulated and hugged one another, weeping unashamedly.

In his joy, one pastor with an artificial leg hopped about the room, unaware that he had dropped his wooden limb on the floor. He began to shout, "The Psalms promise, 'God, You have given to my feet an open ground!'"

"We have survived!" Christian shook Gruber. "We have endured!" he yelled to Dittner, laughing and crying at the same time. "We're going to live, to leave! We have survived!"

Fearing the news might be too good to be true, the prisoners gathered everything they had and fell in behind the policeman. Only a few Bibles, eyeglasses, and some articles of clothing were left stacked around the barracks.

Each man wanted to be as close to the front of the line as possible. Some final door might still shut before they all got out.

"Line up and stop pushing!" snapped the policeman. Instantly, the men fell into ranks and waited quietly for his instructions.

"All right, follow me!"

For one last time, the group marched up the bunker. Here and there a final wave of good-bye signaled to a friend that release had been obtained. Most of the prisoners watched the freedmen pass with little show of emotion. Many seemed dazed and unable to respond. Overhead, the black smoke of the crematoriums filled the sky. In between each barracks were corpses stacked in piles. Christian's eyes moved in a steady rhythm between the smoke and the bodies. While he couldn't keep from looking, he could no longer react to the routine side of Dachau.

Their line marched on to the assembly square, passing the SS pay office. Lieutenant Boye stood looking out the window, with Knoll behind him, peering over his shoulder. Boye made no gesture, only stared at a point on the horizon. Christian nodded his head and waved, but the SS officer appeared not to notice.

"Here I am being released," Christian remarked, turning to Dittner, "and yet I think that maybe Boye has become the prisoner now." Once more, he tried to get the lieutenant's attention. Knoll held his hands up in the air and made a victory gesture. Christian waved back, as one does in bestowing a blessing.

"I wonder what will become of Knoll?"

"What will become of any of them?" Dittner shot back.

The group halted abruptly as the policeman began exchanging papers with the SS officer.

"Why are we being released," Christian asked the men around him, "when these others are being left?" His euphoria of freedom was momentarily jolted by the realities of life with the SS.

"Perhaps someone has paid to get us out," a man on his left answered.

"Perhaps the Allies are almost here," another man ventured.

"If that were so," Dittner retorted cynically, "they would either be releasing everyone or killing us all!"

The wrought-iron gate swung open, and the column of men tramped through. On the other side were the trucks they had hoped to see. As if being swept through a dream, Christian kept pushing forward as fast as possible. His hand was deep in his pocket, clutching the little bit of money he had been able to save and hide over many months.

"You will be taken to the train station in Munich," the policeman announced again and again as the men were loaded into the convoy trucks. "Quickly. We have no time to waste."

"For the first time in five years," Reger laughed nervously, "I am glad to be in a hurry!"

When the camp trucks dumped the men in front of the bustling Munich station an hour and a half later, no one seemed to notice their arrival. Once again, Christian moved quickly in a final grab for freedom. This time there were no guards, no fences, no restraints. His mouth went dry; his heart beat fiercely; his breath came in great gulps.

The smell of smoke was still in the air from the bombing raids of the night before, and an atmosphere of gloom hovered low. People appeared interested only in getting to safety. As the rest of the prisoners poured into the station house, the two old friends were left facing each other.

"You are no longer No. 26 661," Dittner said. "You have again become Christian Reger."

"And you are free, my friend."

"I sense that we will never see each other again."

"Perhaps, perhaps . . ." Christian said hesitantly.

"Well, Christian, what have you learned through all of this?"

For a moment Christian felt the cynicism that was always latent in Dittner's questions. He studied the thin, drawn face of his fellow pastor whose eyes were as hard and bitter as ever.

"What have *you* learned, my friend?" Christian replied.

"I have learned how to remember," Dittner said. "My mind will hold every detail of Dachau until every last atrocity has been vindicated. I know you would wish that I might tell you I have learned to forgive. It's not that you are wrong, but the only force that has sustained me has been my hate. Perhaps, in the end, it will consume me." He grasped Christian's hand with both of his. Where coldness was usually etched on his face, trouble and pain suddenly infiltrated. "When I leave this train station, vengeance will be burned in my heart. If it takes my last breath, I must not cease to fight until National Socialism and Nazism are eradicated from the face of the earth and justice has been done!"

Christian looked down the long tracks that led out of Munich and to his destiny beyond. The converging rails seemed to pull his whole being far away from this gateway into hell.

"Well," Dittner asked with a heavy sigh, "what did you learn?"

Christian was pensive, then looked at Dittner with compassion. "Justice and vengeance for what we have seen is beyond comprehension. It isn't possible. These matters must be left in God's hands. But I know this—the world will not be made better by any more killing."

Dittner gripped his hand more tightly. "I cannot help myself. I must go on with this fight. I will never forget what they have done to us and our friends. I do not know how to forgive such . . ." and his words trailed off.

"Wilhelm, your soul has been shriveled. These years have made you hard. Haven't we seen enough tragedy without that?" Christian covered his friend's hands with his own. "How can we ever spread the story of love by thinking of killing people?"

"And what have these endless years done for you?" Dittner's voice had become quiet and low.

"I don't know," Christian said slowly. "Right now, I only feel broken. All I can do is continue to trust God and walk one step at a time."

He grasped his friend's lapel and pulled him closer. "But we must not hate! If we do, they will have won because they will have made us like them. Unless we are faithful to the way of love, there is no hope left for any of us!"

"And what is our hope?" Dittner asked haltingly. "Our hope is that our courage has been honest and true—that we did not shrink back."

"Are you still so sure that you know what honesty and truth are?"

"Perhaps that has always been the difference between us," Dittner replied. "You must believe that you know. But me—no, I'm not sure about these things. I don't absolutely know that I am right." Dittner's eyes filled with tears. "I guess," he said, biting his lip, "that is what has always made you a man of true courage." He hugged his friend as Jonathan might have hugged David.

"Good-bye, Christian. I will never forget you. God bless you! God bless you."

Dittner turned and ran down the platform, disappearing into the crowd. Christian wanted to say something more, but no words would come.

Christian seemed strangely rooted to the ground. He had longed for this moment, yet he felt immobilized by the choices before him. Finally, his mind began to form a plan of action: the only way to reach Stieglitz would mean going through Berlin. If any rail routes were open, they would be coming out of the capital. In the next moment he rushed into the ticket office. The few deutsche marks Mina had been able to send in her last letters had been carefully hidden. Most of the savings of many months were quickly and gladly spent.

Only after the train had pulled away from the city was he able to believe that he would not be taken back to the camp at the last minute. Settling back against the seat, he watched the scenery as it blurred before his eyes. He was almost unable to grasp that just a few hours earlier he had been starting another hellish day at Dachau.

Then another realization struck him. "I could have taken Helmut's Hebrew Bible out with us!" he moaned. "What a significance it would have had in reminding us of his courage and of what our resistance had meant!"

To his surprise, as he calmed down, he found himself giving in to irresistible drowsiness, then heavy sleep.

Suddenly, he was crashing into the seat in front of him. Not awake enough to know what was happening, he found himself thrown into the aisle the next moment. The train came to a grinding halt, sending people and luggage in every direction.

The windows began to explode, glass shattered, and the metal coach ripped open. A man in front of Christian seemed to be picked up by an invisible force and flung over the top of the seats.

"Down!" shouted someone up front. "Everybody stay down!"

Then, for the first time Christian heard the airplanes. They were circling back for another attack.

Machine-gun fire began hitting other cars just before the rear of the train rocked with a gigantic explosion. As quickly as they had come, the planes were gone.

"Now run!" a man in an army uniform screamed. "Run before they attack again. American airplanes are everywhere!"

People scrambled for the windows and the doors. In the frantic escape Christian realized just how slow and weak he had become. Falling from the coach stairs to the ground, he picked himself up and began running as best he could for a clearing rimmed by large trees. Halfway up the embankment he saw the airplanes coming back for a third strike.

The planes struck like a swarm of hornets descending on a defenseless party of picnickers. Dirt began to fly, and the field erupted. Everything disappeared into blackness.

Two

Christian tried to focus his eyes, but his surroundings kept slipping away into unending dizziness.

"Please try to wake up!" pounded at his ears. At last he began to recognize the shape of a man in a white coat standing over him.

"Try to wake up!" the man insisted.

Above him was a white sky. No, it was a white ceiling, and around him were white walls. They were all too white and sterile to be the infirmary. To his astonishment, he began to recognize that some of the nurses were women.

"Where am I?" he asked, almost fearing the answer.

"You are in the hospital. I am your doctor," the man in white answered. "You keep asking for a *capo*. What is a *capo*?"

"The train? Yes, I was on a train."

"Where have you been?" the doctor wondered in consternation. "You look terrible. I've not seen many people in such emaciated condition!"

Christian didn't answer. He couldn't. He still couldn't comprehend what was happening.

"Your leg is going to be all right," the doctor continued.

"My leg?" For the first time Christian sensed the extreme soreness on the right side of his body.

"Yes," the doctor explained. "A piece of shrapnel went through your right leg. However, we have removed the pieces of metal and put your leg in a cast. In several weeks, it will be fine."

"Exactly where am I?" Christian asked.

"You are in the town of Bamberg," the doctor said as he made notations on his chart. "Like all of Germany, we have severe limitations on our rations. However, I am assigning you a special diet. It is important that you receive proper nourishment or your malnutrition will have worse effects than the shrapnel."

Christian lay back in bed and let his hands reassure him that he was really on a mattress with fresh sheets. He could almost feel the cleanliness around him. There was no shouting, no SS guards, no stench of crematorium smoke. He drifted into a deep, restful sleep.

Several weeks passed before he realized that this detour had probably saved his life. The rest and good food had restored him. Without any money and in such poor condition, he would not have lasted long out on the street. At the end of a month, he was not only walking again, but he felt stronger and healthier than he had in years.

During those weeks in the Bamberg hospital, the news came in avalanches of significance. The Russians had taken

Berlin, and Hitler had committed suicide. An unconditional surrender had been declared by Germany, and the Third Reich had ended.

No one knew anything about the prisoners at Dachau. Often he wondered what the SS had done to the men during the final days. Had they also been released? Or had something terrible happened? Uncertain of his own security, he was afraid to ask.

Day after day, from the hospital window, he watched waves of disposed, displaced, disillusioned people wandering through the streets. A world and a way of life had come to an end, and no one knew the future. Germany was like an army with no general, no strategy, and no hope.

When he hobbled down the steps of the hospital and joined the stream of travelers with no destinations, there was one thing of which he was certain. He had to find Mina. He had to get to Berlin.

Three

"No one will ever know how many of our leaders were killed," Bishop Dibeilius said, handing Christian a cup of coffee. "The SS had many of our pastors placed in the front lines. They were used as cannon fodder to slow the advance of the Russian army. At Stalingrad, many of these faithful men simply vanished in the wave of death and destruction that swept over the German infantry."

"I understand." Christian tried to balance the cup on his stiff leg. "And here in Berlin?"

"The fanatic fools fought to the very last ditch," the bishop answered, sitting down across from him. "Of course, the city was turned into rubble and, again, many of our leaders perished."

"I would like to inquire about the fate of several friends. Would you know what happened to Dietrich Bonhoeffer?"

"I have difficult news to tell you. We have heard from Flossenburg Prison that our faithful brother was hanged shortly after you were released from Dachau."

Christian stirred his coffee without looking up or even acknowledging what he had heard.

"His release was only days away," the bishop continued. "Perhaps in his death, his witness will be magnified far more than it would have been in his survival."

Christian stirred his coffee even more vigorously.

"Also, I must tell you other bad news that I have been asked to convey. Your friend Karl Leisner has died of tuberculosis."

Head still bent, Christian asked softly, "How did you find out?"

"The Dachau camp was liberated about the time you left Bamberg. Karl was taken to a hospital, but he died soon afterward."

"I see."

"Christian, you must know that your faithfulness has not been in vain. Many people remember what you did there."

"I did nothing!" Reger shouted. His hands began to shake so violently that he could scarcely hold the cup. "I only survived.

Would to God these good men would have lived rather than me!" His tears choked out his words. "I did nothing," he mumbled again, dropping his chin against his chest. He was frightened and bewildered by his own response. Yet the thought that he had lived when these others had died was unbearable. His very existence accused him of some nameless crime.

"If it is possible, Karl Leisner's family would like us to bring you for his burial."

"Where will it be?" Christian managed to ask.

"There is an old church in Xanten containing a grave of a Christian soldier who died during the Roman persecution in 303. Karl will be buried in that exact same grave."

"How very appropriate," Reger said, regaining his composure. "Once more, the old and the new are coming together. In his death, Karl will forever be a witness to our continuity with the true faith." His voice trailed off again.

The bishop let the silence do its work. "Of course," he began again, "I know you want me to help you return home."

Christian looked up and set his coffee cup aside.

"Don't do it!" the bishop warned before he could speak. "The Russians are in control in Pomerania, and no one knows what they will do."

"I'm sorry, but I cannot rest until I find her."

"You have not heard from her in a long time," the bishop argued. "Perhaps she is no longer there. Refugees are everywhere."

"No," Christian answered firmly. "I know she would wait for me if she were . . ."

"People disappear when they get too close to the Russians," the bishop went on, ignoring the implications of the uncompleted sentence. "After all you have survived, you must not let them snuff out your light."

"Bishop, do you think that after what I have lived through, I do not trust God for each hour of the day? Can I trust Him any less for my wife's well-being?"

"They told me you would not be swayed. I have already prepared the documents for you to use in slipping behind the Russian lines. But I still fear for you."

"Thank you, thank you." Christian extended his hand. Going to his desk, the bishop finished signing a letter and several documents, then carefully folded the papers and put them in a large envelope.

"Whatever happens or whatever you find," he said, handing the papers to Christian, "promise me you will come back and talk with me before making any final decisions about the future."

Four

"You are the pastor who was in Dachau Concentration Camp?" the Polish railway conductor asked suspiciously.

"Yes," Christian answered nervously. "I am trying to get to my home in Stieglitz."

"Can you prove it?"

Christian gave him the bishop's letter and documents. After reading the letter carefully, the conductor reached out and shook Reger's hand with deep respect.

"I will be more than glad to help you," he smiled. "Follow me."

As the conductor began walking across the railroad tracks, he pulled from his pocket a dirty, worn picture. "See," he said, pointing to the photo of a group of boys with a young man. "That is me. And that was our leader and pastor. His name was Dietrich Bonhoeffer."

Christian reached for the picture.

"In 1927," the conductor continued, "Pastor Bonhoeffer came to our poor parish in North Berlin. The times were bad, but he took care of us in every way possible. Oh, yes, there was great unemployment and misery, yet he taught me how to believe and survive in a cruel world."

"I can't tell you what sharing this means to me," Christian replied.

"Now, each day I must cross the East German frontier, and the terror is always there. I keep this picture of the man who was my best friend with me, to remember what he taught."

"He and I were about the same work."

"Yes, I know. You must worry for nothing, because I will get you through. It is a small gesture on behalf of the memory of my friend." They entered the back door of the luggage car where the Polish conductor hid Christian in a corner behind a large pile of boxes.

"Do not move until I return for you. All Germans will be ordered off the train at Kustrin, but I will keep you hidden."

Later, after what seemed an interminable wait at the Kustrin station, the train started to move again, the click of the wheels against the rails getting louder and louder. Only a few hours more, and he would be with Mina.

But would she be there? Were his friends' warnings valid? Perhaps all Germans would have been driven out of the village. Question after question raced through his mind—all except one. He could not even consider whether or not she was alive. When that thought arose, he refused to let it linger in his mind.

Yet one thought would not leave him. What if *all* the Germans were gone? What if he got off the train into a village controlled by Russians? Might he disappear even as he entered his own hometown?

Finally, the uncertainty forced his decision. He would disembark at a stop about fifteen minutes before Stieglitz. If he walked into town, he would not be as easily identified.

Leaving the train unnoticed, he began the long trek home. He and Mina had come this very same route as a young couple on their way to their first church.

Five

Before Christian lay Stieglitz in late-spring green. The steeple of his church still towered over the rest of the village.

Suddenly, crashing through the trees, a herd of cattle thundered only a hundred meters in front of him. Behind them came two Russians on horseback, driving the cattle across the tracks.

Christian froze, terrified that the Russians would turn on him, but they didn't even appear to notice as they vanished into the next field.

He started to run now. He knew he could see his house from the train station. Leaping on the platform to get a clear view, his heart sank. There in the distance, all he could see were the charred remains. The stone fireplace and chimney were still standing, but the rest was rubble. Most of the surrounding houses were gone.

He stared in stunned silence.

"Can I help you?" asked a young girl standing in the shadows of the station house. A small child was cradled in her arms.

"Oh, you startled me! I didn't see you."

"You are looking for someone?" She walked forward. "You are not a Russian?"

"No, no," he assured her. "I once lived here. But I don't remember you."

"I have come from another village to take care of the children who were left."

"Left?"

"Yes," she explained, rocking the baby. "In January, the Russians came very quickly and attacked one of the passenger trains, killing all the people."

"Why?" he asked in dismay.

"That is the way of the Russians. This is one of the children who survived when her parents were killed," she said, holding up the baby. "Now we do the best we can."

From the back of the station a man appeared, pedaling a bicycle. Christian had never seen the type of uniform he was wearing.

"He is a Polish policeman," the girl answered in reply to Reger's puzzled look. "I'm sure he can help you."

The policeman put down the bicycle and came toward them.

"I am looking for my wife," Christian said defensively. "Her name is Mina Reger."

"Of course, of course!" the policeman said, bowing as though a dignitary had just arrived from Berlin. "I am delighted you have returned. I will get her at once." He leaped on the bicycle and rode straight toward the village.

"Who are you?" the girl asked apprehensively.

"I was the pastor here once."

"Pastor Reger!" she said in amazement. "You are the one who has been a prisoner of the Gestapo!"

"You know of this?"

"Oh, yes. Everyone in the village knows about you and your wife."

"My wife? You know of my wife?"

"Your wife is a wonderful woman," she said reverently. "Though others left when the Russians came, your wife stayed and kept many of us alive. Your wife is one of the bravest women I have ever known."

"Where can I find her, please?" Christian pleaded, his hands outstretched.

"When the houses were burned, she gathered the women into the mill and has been staying with them there. The Russians violated so many of our women."

"Was she, ah, was she, I mean, is she all right?"

"The Russians never hurt her. Because they knew you were an enemy of the Nazis, they have shown her respect. She has been able to intercede for us many times."

"Thank God!" he said, suddenly embracing the girl. "Thank God she is all right." Hugging the child also, he added, "Thank you, thank you so much for what you have told me!"

Reger jumped from the platform in full stride.

"Where are you going?" she called after him.

"To the mill!" he shouted back over his shoulder, running as hard as he could. "To the mill!"

Christian was almost to the edge of the houses when he saw Mina running down the lane toward him.

"Christian! Christian!" she shouted. "Here I am, here I am!"

"Mina, Mina!" he yelled. "I'm back!"

"Oh, Christian!" she sobbed. "My husband, my husband, my beloved husband. You really *are* alive!"

No words would come from his mouth. As the tears ran down his cheeks, he held her, kissed her, and clutched her as tightly as he dared.

Christian looked mistily into her eyes, realizing how deeply the years of separation had etched their wear in her face. She was much thinner, and her hair was grayer. Yet the toll of worry and care did not obscure her beauty.

Christian had no idea how long they stood there. Time stopped, and in those moments the weight of five years melted away. The agonies of cruelty and fear were lost in sheer joy.

They had each other again, and nothing else mattered.

CHAPTER SEVENTEEN

A WORLD COME TO ITS END— 1945-46

One

As they finally drifted off to sleep, the sun was rising over their little village. Each moment had been seized as if another might not follow. In their five long years of separation, a lifetime of experiences had transpired. Countless stories remained to be told. But in the end, having each other had crowded out all awareness of fatigue.

That afternoon they walked through the village. At each burned or destroyed house, Mina told of the fate of the family. Among these streets that should be as familiar as his hand, Christian felt strangely displaced. The old world of his past had been swept away, and in its place were ruin and debris.

"Of course, the schoolteachers were the worst," Mina said, standing before one devastated dwelling. "They did not cease to teach racism to the children and to harass the parents about following the Nazi line. In the end, most of the people brought back their Confessing Church membership cards."

"The teachers always fought us during the church elections," Christian remembered.

"Many of the people were very irate about your arrest, but they soon turned away when the Gestapo applied pressure. They lost the courage of their convictions when it began to cost them personally."

"I know that must have been a terrible experience for you," he said, pulling her head to his shoulder.

"Often I would almost choke on my anger! To think my husband was in a concentration camp, and they were afraid to carry a little piece of paper!"

They turned and walked to the church.

"My trumpeters?" he inquired. "What became of all those young men who played in our little band? I remember so well the excellent impression they always made on the townspeople when we performed."

"1933!" she said, walking up the steps. "Is it possible that you began that little group that long ago? Well," she continued sadly, "they are all gone. Every one of them marched off to war in their magnificent uniforms to fight the Russians. None ever came back. Most of their bodies were not even returned."

Stopping in front of the door, Christian looked down on the broad, stone stairway. "I remember how Wilhelm Kralemann attacked me on this very spot. I can still see his beet-red face as he told me I was a traitor for teaching his son that he ought to follow the Bible's teaching rather than the state's."

"He was a very powerful figure in the church. You risked a great deal by your courage."

"Oh, no!" Christian laughed. "Such stands cost little."

"More than you knew, my dear husband. After you were taken, we discovered that Kralemann was a secret agent for the Gestapo." Mina turned the key, unlocking the door. "The people came to hate him. As the Russians approached, he disappeared. I'm sure he will never be seen again."

"Ah!" Christian pointed to the stained-glass windows that had been spared from the war. "Such a magnificent sight!"

"I'm afraid the building is very cold," Mina apologized. "We have not lit a fire in here for a long time."

"Then it's time to tell the people that a fire has been kindled again," Christian said, slipping into the front pew. "I must begin by reminding them that the light cannot be extinguished and that the darkness is still being overcome."

He rose and walked to the pulpit. Slowly he let his hands run across the ornately carved wooden decorations. It was all the same; yet it was all so different.

"I never ceased to be their pastor. I learned to pray for every face in this parish, whether they were faithful or not."

Christian looked up at the radiant windows and then down at his wife who seemed so small and frail sitting in the shadows. "I prayed for you every day. Each Christmas I tried to make my best prayer a gift for you."

"I love you," she said quietly.

Losing himself in their silent exchange, he murmured, "Such words are enough."

Each continued to look silently at the other, searching for some small assurance that they would still be together tomorrow and the day after that and the day after that.

"We will start again," he finally said.

"And I will play the organ."

"Spread the word that this Sunday at 9:00 there will be a fire in this church."

Two

Following the service, a small woman in a black coat and scarf lingered at the door. It was Maria Schuster. Christian could sense that she wanted to say something to him that would be difficult and emotional. After the last person left, she moved down the aisle toward him.

"Please forgive me," she said, and quickly covered her eyes with an old handkerchief.

"Why, what in the world for?" he asked.

"My husband and I supported the SS, and we caused you problems that you do not even know about." She buried her face in her hands.

"The past is past," he consoled. "God has given us all a new day. None of us must look back."

She began crying more openly and reached for his arm. "My husband is gone; my house has been destroyed; and yet, when I remember the terrible problems we caused, I still can't forgive myself."

"We must let God's forgiveness be sufficient."

"You see," she sobbed, "we were good friends of Wilhelm Kralemann, and we let him influence us. He was the one behind the first Brownshirt attack on your house. Wilhelm caused you to be arrested."

"I always thought so," he answered, "but I have forgiven all that long ago. Do you know what has become of that family?"

"Ya," she said, dabbing at her eyes. "He was wounded in the war and lost his left arm. God's judgment was truly upon him."

Christian groaned. He remembered that Kralemann had been a violinist and pianist.

"They left Stieglitz as the Russians were coming. Probably they just hoped to hide somewhere else in Germany," she explained. "Most Nazis just want to vanish."

"I wish their family no ill will," he assured her.

"I want you to know I am trying to be a new person, and your wife has truly been my inspiration. I've done bad things, but I did not know people could do what the Russians have done to me." Her face twisted in pain. "As we huddled together in that old mill, your wife's words and deeds were my salvation. I know that she knew about the terrible things we had done to your family, and yet she was the very presence of God with me."

As Mina came back through the front door, Maria rushed over and hugged her tightly. Then she hurried down the stairs. The pastor and his wife locked the building and left for Sunday dinner at a parishioner's home. Both walked silently along the streets, each savoring every moment of the morning.

"Come in! Come in!" Mrs. Schmidt ushered Christian and Mina into her living room. "How honored we are to have our pastor and his wife for this first Sunday dinner!"

"The service was wonderful!" praised Wolfgang, vigorously pumping Christian's hand. "I must tell you that I was deeply touched by your sermon. I simply can't express my feelings."

"Now, Wolfgang, we must not get into any discussions now," his wife scolded. "The dinner will get cold. Come in and sit down."

With a festive air of celebration, the pastor and his wife were accorded the seats of honor. Wolfgang explained how the Liebfraumilch had been carefully saved for such a special occasion. After the blessing, he toasted the return of their spiritual leader, and then the meager feast began.

"Pastor," Mrs. Schmidt said as they ate, "before long you will have to conduct some very sad baptism services."

"Ya," her husband agreed. "Almost every girl in this village was raped when the Russians invaded. Next fall many babies will be born."

"Those who resisted were treated worse," Mina added. "We had a burial service for the few girls who did deny them."

"One of the worst terrors," Mr. Schmidt continued, "came from the Polish laborers who had been brought into the area as prisoners of war. When they were released, they took vengeance on many of the German farmers."

"Remember all the difficulty you had with Max Warnke?" Mina asked. "Because he was a wealthy farmer, he felt he could turn the church against you."

"Well," Mr. Schmidt interrupted before Christian could speak, "his wealth and big farm didn't keep him from retribution. The Poles took his farm and moved him right out of his own house!"

"You should know of the brave thing your wife did," Mrs. Schmidt told him.

"Please," Mina said. "I would like to forget all of those stories."

"No!" Mrs. Schmidt insisted. "We will not forget your courage. When we were all hiding in the old mill, one of the Russian laborers broke in."

"Ya," her husband added. "He was looking for the village policeman because he wanted to kill him."

"The constable?" Christian remembered how the policeman had risked his own life to warn Reger he would be arrested by the Gestapo.

"Ya," replied Mrs. Schmidt. "He was already gone, but his wife was still in the mill. So the Russian said he would kill her instead."

"Your brave wife leaped up and tried to stop him. Nevertheless, the man shot and killed her anyway."

"God has used your wife in a special way," Wolfgang concluded.

"And what became of the constable?" Christian asked.

"He died very cruelly in a Polish prison camp," Mr. Schmidt answered, lowering his eyes to his plate.

"The church has never been so full," Mrs. Schmidt finally broke the silence. "Extra chairs had to be placed in the back."

"Our people are starved for spiritual nourishment," Wolfgang went on. "Everyone is afraid that the Communists may even restrict our worship. We have not seen the end of our miseries."

"No," Christian agreed. "The future may even be worse."

"Communist domination is the new fact of life," Mina said. "Every day German families are being driven out of their homes. Regardless of the weather or time of day, a family may be put out on the street."

"Ya," Christian repeated, "the future may be even worse."

Three

A cold fall rain had begun to run down the window, and the trees were swaying in the wind as Mina peered out. The vacant house where they had taken up residence was damp and dreary, but it was more than many of their fellow villagers could claim. "Christian, I think there is a plan behind these evictions."

"Ya, I have come to the conclusion that more is afoot here than Polish refugees needing shelter."

"I suspect that the Russians and Poles are systematically pushing all Germans out of the area. But many of our people have nowhere to go. I fear what will become of them."

"Because I opposed the Nazis, they have not persecuted us. Who could have expected that our enemies would be swept away and that in the end we would be in the privileged position?"

"See," Mina said, pointing across the street. "That poor woman has been pushed out of her house."

Looking through the sheer curtains, they saw a bent and aged widow walking dejectedly toward the train station. Across her shoulder she balanced a long stick with all of her possessions tied in a bundle on the other end.

"She is the last of her family," Mina observed. "Everyone else was killed in the war. Perhaps even we will have to leave before long," she ventured after a minute.

"Pastor! Pastor! Come quickly!" Hobbling up the stairs was one of the older women of the village who had also lost her entire family. "Pastor," she cried, "you must come and help. It is horrible!"

"Calm down," Mina said. "Tell us exactly what happened."

"Oh, I can't!" she cried. "I cannot speak of this most horrible thing I have ever seen. Terrible! Terrible!" she choked.

As Mina and Christian looked out the door, they could see a crowd gathering around a house at the far end of town. The woman kept pointing in that direction. Not wasting another moment, husband and wife scurried off. The closer they came to the house, the louder the commotion. Germans and Poles were mingling together; everyone seemed agitated.

"What's happening here?" Christian asked one of the

Germans. People stepped back to allow them through the crowd. Automatically, the entire group responded as if expecting the pastor to take control.

"Tragic!" a little man wailed. "Just tragic! To believe that people can be killed like this, and nothing can he done!"

"Killed?"

"Ya," the man replied. "The old couple have both been murdered."

"Why?" Mina asked in disbelief.

"Polish robbers came to their house and wanted their sewing machine," he whispered. "When they resisted, the robbers killed them."

"O, Lord," Christian moaned. "These old people killed over a sewing machine."

"They're in the bedroom," someone directed, as he and Mina entered the house.

"Stay in the living room," he told Mina firmly. "I will see."

Hesitantly, he looked around the corner into the bedroom. The old man's body was sprawled across the lifeless form of his wife. Near the window, where the sewing machine must have stood, was a blank space on the wall. A chair was overturned, and two bullet holes shattered the plaster.

Outside, many of the new Polish tenants were staring through the windows. They were grinning and pointing, leering at the bodies. It was almost as though they had discovered a village carnival.

Christian looked around the room at the pictures of the old couple's children who were now somewhere far away.

Perhaps they would never know about their parents' senseless murders.

Anger gripped him. Forcefully, he flung the curtains together and covered the bodies with the bedspread.

We cannot stay here much longer, he thought. *These Poles and Russians don't value life any more than the Gestapo did.*

When he stepped outside, the crowd once more grew silent. The German faces seemed to beg for some word of direction; the Polish eyes were cold and suspicious.

"We will hold their funeral at the church tomorrow!" Reger said sternly. "They will be buried in the church cemetery. Let us make the necessary preparations." Taking Mina's hand, he walked through a cluster of Poles who quickly stepped aside before him.

The day after the funeral, Christian returned to the graves. As he bent down to adjust some of the decorations, a rock sailed past his head. Another bounced off the gravestone in front of him.

"What is this?" he shouted indignantly, only to have another rock hit his coat.

Fifty feet away stood at least a dozen Polish peasants, rocks in hand. Suddenly he charged at them, yelling at the top of his lungs, "How dare you throw rocks in this sacred place!"

One last rock whirred by as the group retreated over the fence. Just beyond the church wall, they stopped to regroup and began hurling jeers instead. Christian stopped at the gate and realized just how many of them there were.

"Don't ever come here again without the proper respect!"

he bellowed defiantly, at the same time feeling himself retreating in the face of what might happen.

The mob's jeers faded as they walked away. He knew that only his opposition to the Nazis had kept him from worse. As he sat in his office considering the dilemma, Ursula Hinz bolted into the room.

"Pastor! Pastor!" she begged. "The Polish police have imprisoned my mother at Schonlanke. They may kill her!"

"Ya," Christian said sadly. "I have heard that Katie was taken, but I am not sure there is anything I can do."

"Oh, yes," Ursula urged, pulling at his coat. "You can let her know that I am alive and safe. My mother has no idea what has become of me."

"Of course," he answered. "Do you know why your mother was arrested?"

"For no reason except that my father was well known and in the German army. When they arrested her, they were very brutal," she explained, and began to cry again.

"My mother knows nothing of politics—everyone knows that. All the accusations against her are untrue!"

"Of course, of course. Go and tell Mina that I am going to Schonlanke and will be home late. I will do what I can."

When Christian arrived, he discovered that Frau Hinz was already in the courtroom, waiting to be tried. Cautiously, he got as close as he could to where she was seated.

As if speaking from the pulpit, he began, "And her daughter Ursula has come home. Even now she is in quite good health."

People turned to see who was talking so loudly.

"Ya," he continued, "her daughter Ursula is home and is fine."

Katie Hinz found his eyes and smiled pleadingly. The brokenness etched on her face gave way to gratitude.

"Ya," he started again, then sensing that people were staring at him as if he were a spy or crazy, his voice dropped. "Ya, she is fine." Several men eyed him as if action should be taken. After a few minutes, Christian edged out of the room.

Two days later, he discovered that Frau Hinz had died from harsh treatment.

Four

"Christian!" Mina called. "Come quickly! Look who is here!"

As Christian stepped out of his study, a man extended his hand. "Paul Hartwig!" he exclaimed. "You are alive and well!" Reger embraced his old friend.

"Christian, how wonderful that you have survived these terrible times."

"I want you to know," said Mina, "that Paul was one of the very few who did not turn in his red card. He stayed with us through it all."

"I am so grateful to you, Paul. Mina has told me that eventually almost everyone lost their convictions. Where have you been?"

"God is truly faithful to those who keep faith with Him. Whatever small amount of courage I had, He has rewarded me in far greater abundance than I deserve." He paused to catch his breath, then added, "Only two of us escaped out of nearly thirty thousand people."

"What do you mean?" questioned Mina. "You were not drafted into the army."

"I have just come from Schneidemuhl," Paul explained. "Nearly all of the German people have been driven out of their homes and are being forced to walk to Russia."

"Thirty thousand people!" Christian exclaimed.

"Men, women, and children. God only knows what will become of them."

"Why?" Mina asked incredulously.

"Only because they are Germans," Paul said.

"How did this happen?" Mina continued to probe.

"Two days ago Russian soldiers began sweeping through the area herding all the people together. Their loudspeakers told us we were all being sent to Russia and warned that resistance would be met with death. I knew I did not have the strength to survive such a journey."

"But Paul," Mina asked, pouring him a cup of coffee, "how did you escape?"

"While everyone was being rounded up in the square, I walked behind the city hall. Kneeling down, I prayed, 'Lord, You know my weakness. I know You have worked miracles in the past and that You can work wondrous things today. Please help me in my hopeless situation!'

Then, somewhere in the distance, I heard my name. I realized I was being called by a loudspeaker. When I reached the Russian officer in charge, he told me that I and a Catholic schoolteacher would be released from the march. He sent us out of the town immediately."

"A schoolteacher?" Christian queried.

"Ya," Paul explained. "He was the only man who opposed the Nazis in the whole school system. Of the thirty thousand people, only he and I were released."

"Your integrity saved you," Christian declared. "They recognized your resistance to the Nazis."

"Perhaps," Paul smiled, "but as I came here today, I kept remembering the last words of my mother. I believe her advice is the real reason I have survived."

Paul balanced the cup and saucer on his knee as he looked out the window toward the station. "Forty years ago, I brought my sick mother to that railway station, and she never came home from the hospital. But when I put her on the train, her last words to me were from Psalm 119. 'Don't forget!' she shouted from the window, 'How shall a young man steer an honest course? By holding to Thy Word!' Ever since, I have tried to live by His Word and that is why I have survived."

"You have kept the faith, Paul," Christian assured him. "You did not shrink back."

"Now I have come to warn you," Paul said, putting down his cup and standing to leave. "You must not stay here. As long as they remember that you opposed Hitler, you are safe. However, the Communists are worse than the Nazis. You must leave."

"Thank you, Paul," Christian answered. "We will consider your advice carefully."

"God bless you." As Paul started down the steps, he paused to turn and bid a final farewell. Each sensed he would not see the other again.

Five

The Schmidts were tying up the last of their bundles. Their walls had been stripped of all the family pictures, and each memento was carefully packed with their few dishes.

"We believe that we can still be on the evening train," Mr. Schmidt told Mina. "That will allow us to arrive in West Germany tomorrow afternoon."

"Your children will be there to meet you?" Christian asked.

"Ya," Mrs. Schmidt sighed. "We are so much more fortunate than most. Our family will help us get settled again."

"Stieglitz will not be the same without the Schmidt family."

"Well," Mr. Schmidt replied with a smile, "Stieglitz will never be the same anyway. Everything we had here is changed. We are not leaving any too soon."

"How did it all happen?" Mrs. Schmidt wondered. "A few years ago everything was happy and good."

"You forget the depression," Wolfgang reminded his wife. "Times were hard, and food was scarce!"

"Then Hitler promised us that he would solve every problem," Mina added. "People believed he could do anything."

"We became a nation of little Hitlers," Mrs. Schmidt commented bitterly. "Everyone believed he had a right to land, to power, to anything he wanted."

"It was that radio!" Mr. Schmidt accused. "Hitler was constantly in our living room. None of us ever had our own radios before National Socialism came to power. Because we could hear his voice, we believed everything he said."

"No," Christian said sadly. "People believed because they wanted to believe. Fear and selfishness produced a ready-made audience for fanaticism."

"Oh, you are so right!" said Mrs. Schmidt, picking up a thick red book from the table. "See this book? I have just been reading Dostoyevski again. Here," she said, holding the page to the light. "Listen to how much this sounds like Hitler. 'The Grand Inquisitor succumbs to the dread spirit of death and destruction, and, therefore, accepts lying and deception, and leads men consciously to death and destruction, and always deceives them, so that they do not know where they are being led, and all the time these poor, blind creatures believe themselves to be happy!' Is that not a perfect description of what we have lived through?"

Christian felt the blood rushing to his face. He tried to measure his words so that his emotion would not show. Yet she had pulled from him the one question that remained unanswered. "Did you have any idea that the Nazis were torturing us at Dachau and that people were being gassed? Did you know they were killing Jews?" The room became uncomfortably silent.

"Of course not!" reacted Mrs. Schmidt. Her voice sounded both embarrassed and offended. "We knew nothing of these terrible atrocities!"

Christian said no more, but he turned slowly toward Mr. Schmidt. For reasons he couldn't quite understand, he was suddenly angry with these people who had helped him so much during the past weeks.

Wolfgang avoided Reger's eyes and began to adjust the pile of boxes. After a moment he answered, "I can honestly say I did not know of these things, Christian. But I must confess that I also did not want to know of any of those things.

"I'm sorry," he continued. "Perhaps we could have known if we had wanted to. Maybe this will be our eternal curse. We did very little to stop the spirit of death and destruction when it came."

Finally, Mrs. Schmidt added, "Is not our having to leave suffering enough?"

Mina gave Christian a look that clearly said, "No more." Realizing that they might not see these people again, she moved the conversation in other directions. Quickly, their possessions were loaded in a wagon, and they were gone.

"Schmidt was right," Christian told Mina as they walked back to the house where they were staying. "Stieglitz will never be the same again. I think it is time to go. I am not afraid of the problems, but I believe our work here is finished."

"You have changed," Mina mused as she grasped his hand. "The time at Dachau has made you different."

"How?" he asked in a troubled tone.

"It is all good," she laughed. "You were always a strong person, but often too naive and innocent. You thought everybody was good. Life was very simple for you."

"That was bad?" he asked.

"No," she replied. "But now you are different. Your sermons are so strong they make me weep. The innocence and naïveté have been replaced by an honesty and candor that can cut to the bone. You leave people confronted in a way that is startling and confounding."

"I am too blunt?"

"No. What you say is good. I just find that you have seen the truth about people and power in a way few ever do. Through it all, your faith has become complete."

"No!" he objected. "Far from complete. Perhaps confident is a better word. God gave me an experience of His light long ago. In seminary He showed me how He could dispel the darkness of my doubts. I suppose that now I know He can dissolve the darkness of my fears as well."

They walked in twilight past the burned ruins of their old parsonage. "I think it is time for us to begin to pack," he concluded as they reached the house. Resolutely, he closed the door behind them.

CHAPTER EIGHTEEN

THE PESTILENCE RETURNS— 1946

W ell, I don't want to rush you, but you have been star- ing at that door for about five minutes."

The annoyance in the bishop's voice jolted Christian's mind back to the moment at hand.

"I asked you if you would agree to serve a church in the Communist-held sector of Berlin," Bishop Dibeilius repeated.

"I'm sorry," Christian apologized, slowly pulling his gaze from the huge door in front of him, "but there are so many things in your office that bring back memories."

"Oh?" The older man raised his eyebrows.

"Yes. Perhaps simple things like matchboxes and doors help me most in thinking about what is involved in saying a simple yes."

Opening the red and green matchbox, the bishop lit his pipe. Before he could speak again, Christian asked, "I know this sounds unusual, but might I have that matchbox?"

"The matchbox? Of course," he said, handing it to Christian. "Keep it if you wish."

"Why should I go?" Christian inquired, looking at the box in his hand. "Why should I enter such a battle again?"

"Because the dragon is not dead!" The bishop blew a puff of smoke high in the air. "And the beast has been resurrected again in East Berlin. Perhaps I could say better that communism is now the 'lamb that speaks with the voice of the dragon.' The battle goes on and is not finished. So why should you enter again? I will tell you simply, my friend. Because you are a man of courage. As a soldier of the cross, you have no choice. You cannot turn aside from this decision and still be who you are!"

The bishop smiled slightly. He knew he had finally found the right argument. He had won, and the matter was settled.

Christian pursed his lips and exhaled deeply. He began nodding his head slowly up and down, even before he uttered a final affirmation. "If this is the call of Christ," he said very slowly, "I must say yes." Resolutely, he placed the matchbox in his pocket. "We will accept the appointment. We will go."

"Wonderful!" the bishop exclaimed as he returned to his desk and reached for his pen. "I will sign the letter and complete the instructions in order that you may go at once. You need not delay; the church will be expecting you. Even now, you can prepare for the move to the parsonage."

"We have virtually nothing to take with us," Christian admitted. "The few items we have are in boxes here in Berlin."

"Good! Good!" the bishop murmured without awareness of what he was affirming. "Then you could leave for the Eastern Sector this afternoon."

"I suppose so."

"Well then, let us go and tell your wife."

"Perhaps it would be better if I talked to her alone."

"Of course, of course," the bishop conceded, shaking Reger's hand heartily. "We will be praying for you. Go in God's strength!"

Christian shut the door quietly behind him. Mina looked up expectantly. The large waiting room with its high ceiling seemed to encase them in a solitude and privacy that felt like a momentary shelter in the midst of a continuing storm.

"Doors," he said to his wife. "Isn't it strange how the opening and closing of doors can change everything. The simple act of turning a handle can make all the difference."

"Then you said yes," Mina said, standing to greet him. He looked down at the worn carpet and tried to avoid her eyes as he adjusted his glasses and fixed his tie.

"Are we going back into the danger?" Her voice betrayed no emotion.

"I do not want you to feel that your thoughts and feelings have no bearing on this decision. Certainly, I would not accept this appointment unless you were in agreement."

"What did you tell the bishop?"

"I am still not sure that such a treacherous environment would be right for you. After all you have suffered, I could not bear you having to live through a reign of terror once again."

"Of course," she said. "I need no reassurances. Did you say we would go?"

"Yes." He reluctantly raised his eyes to meet hers.

"Good!" she beamed. "You have made the right decision. Let us get our things together."

"But . . ." He fumbled for more explanation. "But we will face certain persecution from the Russians. No one knows what will happen to Christians under a hostile, atheistic government."

"No one ever knows what is going to happen anywhere," Mina countered, reaching down for her handbag. "Since we can't choose such things, we must make our lives our own, wherever we are. Haven't we always done that?"

"Well, yes," he agreed, gesturing futilely. "But I felt that you might want to have an easier life, a more comfortable home."

"Comfort is a poor excuse for anything." Mina shook her finger in his face in mock admonition. "When were we ever called to comfort? Is not life more than what we eat and drink?"

"My, my," Christian smiled sheepishly. "Look who has become the preacher now! I simply needed to know that you wanted to go."

"Oh, we have suffered." Her face instantly became serious. "God knows we have suffered! Yet even in the worst days of our separation, we were still completely alive. No, I would not want to relive the past years, but I would not have missed them for anything. I know in whom I have believed, and now I know that He is able. Never did we retreat from the conflict, and I know that our souls have been stretched and our characters refined by it."

"I am very proud that I have known you." Christian looked deeply into those marvelous, misty eyes that seemed so young again. "I thank God that He has made it possible for me to look just a little into your soul." Taking her face in his hands, he tilted it upward. "I was sustained by your love when everything else was dying. I drew life from you."

"Now, now." She seemed embarrassed. "You know that there is no place in the world that I would not go if I were going with you." She hugged him tightly, and they let the silence work what was beyond words.

"Remember what happened when you held the first service after your return?" Mina said. "I can still see the packed sanctuary. Those desperate, frightened people clutched their Bibles like a drowning man hangs on to a rope, the cares and woes of the centuries etched into their faces. I can still see all of those children who had seen too much and whose innocence was forever banished. They strained forward to hear as if you were their only hope. We can never forget them. Surely, their tribe must wait for us in East Berlin."

He took his hat from the stand. "Our work is certainly cut out for us."

"Did the bishop say anything about the Confessing Church?"

"No, he carefully avoided the subject. I know the Confessing Church will always be a judgment on those who cooperated with the Nazis. Undoubtedly, many of those who followed National Socialism will be very uncomfortable with our witness."

"Maybe it would be best if our movement were absorbed back into the established church."

"Remember how the Danube begins in the Black Forest?" he asked, suddenly finding a perfect illustration. "Only a little stream bubbles up, and then it disappears back into the ground. Yet it finally erupts into a great river that runs through many countries. Perhaps we Confessors will be like that."

"Arising in a great crisis," she smiled back, "only to disappear after the war; yet in other times and places when the cost is great, the work of the Confessors will go on."

"I think so. At Dachau I was part of a brotherhood of all Christians. There were no barriers between us. I hope others will remember that great lesson if ever an evil political power threatens the life of the church again."

"And like the Danube," she said, squeezing his hand, "we will be swept along together—one mighty army, beginning with the apostles, then enlisting the faithful of all generations, until we come as one people to that final day."

"Oh, I like that!" He squeezed her hand in return. "When I left Stieglitz, I felt like Lot leaving the burning city of Sodom. Perhaps the smell of burning will be upon us for many years. But like Lot, I know we have been saved and that angels have accompanied us. Rather than remembering the smoke, we must recall that great flood of witnesses and remember the communion of the saints. These are the things we must tell people."

"Perhaps it would have been nice to return to a simple, quiet parish like Stieglitz was when we first went there," Mina said wistfully. "But then, life never really was routine. I suspect that God has some interesting plans ahead for us."

"Well, I guess you know that we enter a battle that we cannot win," Christian concluded.

"To gain a victory we cannot lose," she responded. He extended his arm, and they walked across the waiting room to the door leading down to the street. Slowly he opened it, and the brisk, mid-April air rushed in to meet them.

She paused on the threshold. "Just going through a door can change everything."

"Indeed," he smiled. "But then again, we have never been numbered among those who shrunk back!"

They walked down the broad, stone steps and on to the sidewalk. Ahead, a little boy was playing by the curb, and somewhere in the apartments above, a child was crying. The spring weather felt especially fresh and invigorating. They kept walking.

... AND THEY DID NOT TURN BACK

Only in later years did Christian Reger and the world learn the full truth of what happened at Dachau Concentration Camp.

It is estimated that nearly 200,000 inmates from thirty-seven countries went through the iron gates from 1933 to 1945. Three days before the camp was liberated, the Nazi index cards listed 30,442 men living in an area built to accommodate 5,000. While this statistic is grossly inaccurate, it reveals that even according to the records of the Third Reich, Dachau was crowded beyond any ability to provide minimal humane care.

Because so many Jews were shipped on to Buchenwald, Auschwitz, and other death camps, Dachau's population figures will always be obscure. After the Crystal Night in 1938, more than ten thousand Jews were sent to Dachau. While many of them were later able to leave the country, the fate of the rest will always be a mystery. Eighty children ranging in age from eight to fifteen arrived at the camp, yet all disappeared without explanation.

The inmate count of clergymen sent to Dachau is also unclear. At least 2,720 pastors from nineteen nations were incarcerated. Ninety-five percent of those were Roman Catholic priests; five percent were Protestant. One-third of all the priests of Poland died in the barbed wire city.

The captured Nazi records verified that 360 to 400 inmates were used for the diabolical medical experiments of the camp doctors. Documentation proves that at least 3,166 men were gassed at Hartheim Castle in the Austrian city of Linz. At least 30,500 men died in the camp itself the final four months before freedom came.

Georg Elser, the prisoner accused of attempting to assassinate Hitler on November 9, 1939, stayed in the expanded facilities in Dachau's inner prison until April 5, 1945. During the years of imprisonment, the guards constantly called him Eller in an attempt to conceal his identity. However, on April 5, the commandant of the Dachau camp received the following letter from the chief of the security police.

> On the occasion of one of the next air raids on Munich or in the vicinity of Dachau, "Eller" is to be presumed fatally injured. For this reason I ask you to liquidate "Eller" in an absolutely secret manner after such an occurrence in the camp. I ask you to see to it carefully that only very few persons who are to be bound to secrecy know of it. The notice of the execution to me would then read:

> *"On _____, as a result of the terror*
> *attack on _____, the prisoner 'Eller' was*
> *among the fatally injured."*
> *Having taken notice of this letter and carried out the*
> *instructions mentioned therein, I ask you to destroy it.*

As ordered, Georg Elser disappeared.

On Sunday, April 29, 1945, while Christian was recovering in the Bamberg hospital, Dachau was liberated by American soldiers. National flags of many nations, made in secret, were unfurled, and the camp was jubilant. For the first time, religious services were held openly and men rejoiced that the long night of terror was finally over.

Emmerich Ost, the Dachau camp commandant, was killed in a Polish labor camp. A special trial was held in Dachau, charging Dr. Schilling with numerous medical crimes, and he too was executed. As did many Nazis, Lieutenant Herman Boye disappeared "underground." Ironically, he later surfaced as a policeman.

The Confessors returned to the mainstream of German church life, and the Confessing Church movement came to an end. Because they chose to forgive those who had persecuted them and to forget the indiscretions of those who had compromised with the Nazis, a reunion was achieved in the German church.

Christian and Mina accepted the challenge of Bishop Dibeilius and went into the Russian sector of East Berlin where no one else wanted to serve. They lived through the turmoil and treachery of the Communist takeover and the domination of the city and its government.

Ten years after the liberation, the prisoners of Dachau returned for a commemorative service and decided to turn the camp into a permanent memorial. Catholic, Protestant, and Jewish centers of worship were planned. On April 30, 1967, the Protestant Church of the Reconciliation was dedicated as a symbol of the healing of hostilities.

Mina continued steadfast in her devotion to her husband and their call until her death on March 25, 1970. Using a quotation from the early church, Christian had carved on her small monument:

> TO YOUR BELIEVERS, O LORD,
> LIFE IS BEING CHANGED,
> NOT TAKEN AWAY.

The summer after her death, Christian returned to Dachau to become pastor of The Church of the Reconciliation. For the next nine years, he told thousands of visitors about his experiences as a prisoner. In three different languages, he recounted the story of the matchbox, the Pastors' Barracks, and of the light that darkness could not extinguish.

Through the years, visitors were inspired and moved by his witness. Countless letters of appreciation were received, including one from President and Mrs. Gerald Ford. Christian received a citation from the U.S. Army and was awarded the Order of Merit from the German government.

Failing health brought his retirement in 1979. Even in his final years, he remained among those who kept the faith and did not shrink back.

In April 1985, a month after his eightieth birthday, his heart problems worsened. For the next twenty-two weeks, Christian's deteriorating condition caused continual hospitalization. During much of this time his memory faded. But on Friday, October 11, 1985, he suddenly became alert and learned with deep satisfaction that this book would be published. The next day Christian died quietly in his sleep. His obituary contained this poem:

> The beginning, the end,
> O Lord, are Thine.
> The span between,
> The Life is mine.
> When in the night
> I lose my way,
> I seek Thy Light,
> Thy House, Thy Day.

SOLA GLORIA DEI

```
        16.0
19 | 304
     19
    ─────
     114
     114
```

```
       15.625
16 | 250
     16
    ─────
     90
     80
    ─────
     10
```